"Katie is a charm... in-
triguing plot and ... aracters, *Brown-
ies and Broomsticks* is an attention-grabbing read that
I couldn't put down."
—*New York Times* bestselling author Jenn McKinlay

"Cates is a smooth, accomplished writer who combines
a compelling plot with a cast of interesting characters."
—*Kirkus Reviews*

"Fun and exciting reading."   —*USA Today*

"[The] sixth of the Magical Bakery Mystery series remains as entertaining as the first, with a mythology that
is as developed as Katie's newfound talent and life
within the Savannah magical community."
—Kings River Life Magazine

"If you enjoy . . . Ellery Adams's Charmed Pie Shoppe
Mystery series and Heather Blake's Wishcraft Mystery
series, you are destined to enjoy the Magical Bakery
Mystery series."   —MyShelf.com

"With a top-notch whodunit, a dark magic investigator
working undercover, and a simmering romance in the
early stages, fans will relish this tale."   —Gumshoe

"As a fan of magic and witches in my cozies, Cates's
series remains a favorite."   —Fresh Fiction

"Ms. Cates has most assuredly found the right ingredients . . . a series that is a finely sifted blend of drama,
suspense, romance, and otherworldly elements."
—Once Upon a Romance

ALSO AVAILABLE BY BAILEY CATES

THE MAGICAL BAKERY MYSTERIES

Cookies *and* Clairvoyance

A Magical Bakery Mystery

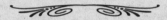

Bailey Cates

BERKLEY PRIME CRIME
New York

BERKLEY PRIME CRIME
Published by Berkley
An imprint of Penguin Random House LLC
1745 Broadway, New York, NY 10019

ISBN: 9780399587016

First Edition: August 2019

Printed in the United States of America
1   3   5   7   9   10   8   6   4   2

Cover art by Monika Roe
Cover design by Katie Anderson

Acknowledgments

I am so very grateful to work with such a terrific team at Berkley Prime Crime: Jessica Wade, Miranda Hill, Megan Elmore, Randie Lipkin, Brittanie Black, Elisha Katz, Natalie Sellars, and everyone else whose talents and hard work brought this book into being. Thanks also to Kimberly Lionetti at BookEnds Literary Agency for all she does. Laura Pritchett and Laura Resau of the Old Town Writers Group provided valuable feedback and kept me on track. Mindy Ireland, Jody Ivy, Amy Lockwood, JoAnn Manzanares, Natasha Wing, and Teresa Funke provided plenty of encouragement, sanity, and wisdom. And, as always, thank you to Kevin for . . . everything.

Chapter 1

Uncle Ben gave one last twist of the screwdriver, removed the electronic bell that had been attached to the front door of the Honeybee Bakery for over two years, and, with a smile of satisfaction, climbed down from the stepladder. He strode to where Aunt Lucy stood behind the register and kissed her on the cheek. After handing her the small black box, he turned back to retrieve his tools and take them out to his truck in the alley.

My aunt turned to me. The skin around her eyes crinkled gently as she held up the box. "I sure won't miss hearing this every time someone comes in."

I was restocking the display case with pecan rolls and gingersnaps. "Me, too, but you have to admit it's a good problem to have," I said, carefully arranging a row of cookies at the back of a tray. "Being so busy that the bell above the door was always ringing, I mean."

"A good problem indeed." She slid the contraption that had chimed thousands of times into the pocket of her hemp apron. "But it was getting to be down-right distracting."

My aunt was originally from the tiny town of Fill-more, Ohio, just like me, but she'd lived in Savannah for decades. Though they were sisters, Lucy was quite different from my perfectly coifed and buttoned-down mother. She looked like the gracefully aging hippie that she was—gray-blond hair stuffed into a messy bun, a brightly embroidered smock from Oax-aca worn over a long cotton skirt, Birkenstocks on her feet, and not a speck of makeup on her cheerful face.

Oh, and she was also a witch.

Then again, so was I. Not that I'd had any idea of my hereditary powers until I'd moved to Savannah from Akron over two years ago to open the Honey-bee with Ben and Lucy, but she'd soon filled me in.

That had been interesting.

You come from a long line of witches, Katie. Our family specialty is called hedgewitchery. It's one of the gentler branches of magic. An affinity for herbal lore, herb craft, and a heck of a green thumb. All of which you possess. Pure magic in the kitchen.

I'd spluttered and denied the very possibility, of course, but after a while I realized my gifts were why I'd always felt a bit different, like an outsider, and I warmed to the idea. Soon I delved into learning more about the Craft and began working with my aunt to add a sprinkle of benevolent magic to our baked goods.

Lucy and I were old-school herbal witches like the women who used to cross the literal hedges that sur-rounded villages in the old days to gather healing

plants for teas and other cures. *Hedge* was also met-
aphorical and could refer to the veil between this
plane and the next. My aunt had introduced me to a
group of women who practiced various kinds of
witchcraft, a loose coven of sorts that we called the
spellbook club, and they'd graced my life with wisdom, friendship, and support. We actually did meet
to talk about spellbooks each month—and occasionally practice a little magic together, of course. For the
first time in my life, I felt like I truly fit in.

Once the display trays were filled for the next wave
of treat-seeking patrons, I paused to take a sip of
sweet tea from the sweating glass by my elbow and
surveyed the bakery. It was the typical lull between
the lunch rush and people's need for an afternoon in-
flux of caffeine and sugar. Only a few customers were
avoiding the sticky July heat in the air-conditioned
atmosphere.

Arthur, our resident author, stared moodily at his
laptop screen and sipped minty green tea over in the
corner. Two firefighters in uniform traded sections of
the *Savannah Morning News* back and forth over
cups of coffee and plates that now held only crumbs.
In the reading area, three women perched on the
poufy brocade sofa and chairs, hunched over an array
of papers spread on the coffee table and murmuring
about budget numbers and fund-raising needs. In the
window beyond them sat Lucy's orange tabby—and
witch's familiar. Honeybee the cat had inspired the
name of the bakery, and now she lazily watched the
pedestrians going by on Broughton Street outside.
My own familiar, a Cairn terrier named Mungo, was

snoozing in the office off the kitchen, as he did most every day I worked at the bakery.

I went over to the firefighters' table and gathered up their empty plates. Both men worked at firehouse five, known as Five House, with my fiancé, Declan McCarthy. Randy was the younger of the two men, as well as stockier. He was handsome in a chiseled way, with dark eyes and dark hair. He'd been dating one of the spellbook club members for a few months now. Scott, a tall man with salt-and-pepper hair, a deep mahogany complexion, and a calm demeanor, was his superior officer as well as his close friend and mentor.

"How were your scones?" I asked.

Randy leaned back and grinned at me. "Awesome, like always."

Scott nodded. "Good stuff."

"Can I bring you anything else? More coffee?"

The older man shook his head and stood. "Thanks, but I've got to get going. Better load up a box with a dozen assorted pastries. We just finished our forty-eight, but I'll drop it back by the station for the new shift."

I grinned. "Deal."

"I've got it," Lucy said from behind the counter, and began to fill a box with an assortment of baked goods.

Scott went to pay, and I asked Randy, "How was your shift?"

"Boring. A minor wreck, a kitchen fire, an elevator rescue, and a bunch of building inspections." Then he brightened. "But there was that dumb guy who set his siding on fire when he was barbequing hot dogs."

"Glad you got in a little excitement."

He didn't seem to notice my wry tone. A boring shift was what I hoped for every time Declan went to work.

The two men left, and I cleared their table, wiped it down, then went to retrieve my sweet tea.

Standing beneath the tall blackboard where we listed our menu selections for the day, I inhaled the scents of sugar and spice, hints of rosemary and cheese, fresh sourdough bread, and beneath it all the undercurrent of coffee beans. Fans hung from the high ceiling, lazily moving the cooled air around a bit more. Ben had chosen the music for the day, and Ella Fitzgerald quietly drifted down from the speakers up in the corners. Behind me, our part-time employee, Iris Grant, hummed to herself over the bowl of muffins she was mixing.

Well, she wasn't exactly humming. She was murmuring a gentle incantation to invoke the benefits of the spices in the recipe. Fresh out of the oven, those muffins would join the other pastries in the case for the afternoon surge of customers, and, like the other pastries, would offer a little extra *oomph*—in this case physical and mental energy from the burst of fresh ginger they contained. Just the ticket for making it through until five o'clock.

Iris wasn't exactly a witch, per se, but she was learning. In training, you might say. Her feet shuffled in a subtle two-step, which told me she was in a good

5

mood. She was eighteen and a student at the Savannah College of Art and Design. Her chin-length hair boasted mermaid purple and yellow streaks, and a series of piercings ran along the outer edges of her ears. The moment I'd met her, I'd recognized her innate power.

Almost everyone has the power to work magic. Spell work is simply a way to harness one's intuition and intention in a focused way. But Iris was an old soul, and I felt she had more of a gift than most. The other members of the spellbook club had agreed. When she'd asked for a job at the Honeybee, taking her on as an apprentice was a no-brainer.

I took another swallow of sweet tea and allowed my eyes to close in contentment as the syrupy liquid spread coolness down my throat and into my chest. A sense of peace settled over me and—

"Katie Lightfoot!"

My heart stuttered as my eyes popped open.

"Wake up, honey! I need my daily sugar fix! And I want to hear all about how your wedding plans are coming along. Is your mother still in town?"

"Hello, Mrs. Standish," I managed with a glance at the now-silent front door. Maybe getting rid of the bell hadn't been such a good idea after all. She had been one of our first customers and was still possibly our best, but with her huge personality, swirling caftans, and loudly printed turbans, Edna Standish took a little getting used to.

"No, Mama left last week." I stopped there and tried to keep my smile from looking too tight.

My mother and I had clashed repeatedly over

6

details of my wedding in another month. She'd tried to convince me to have the same color scheme, flowers, and even bridesmaid dress design as the last wedding she'd insisted on planning for me—the one that fell through at the last minute when Andrew-the-jerk came down with an incurable case of cold feet. Thank goodness he had, of course, because Declan and I were far better together than Andrew and I ever could have been. But no way did I want anything about my actual wedding to reflect my almost wedding.

This time around, I was ditching tradition whenever it didn't fit with what I wanted for my big day. A few of my attendants were married, and a local judge would marry us instead of Pastor Freeman, who, believe it or not, Mama had actually offered to fly to Savannah. As for my attendants' dresses, they were all free to wear the colors and design they wanted, with the caveat that those colors be on the pastel side. Since the ladies I'd chosen ran the gamut from a pregnant twentysomething to an octogenarian, one design for all would have been folly.

If I hadn't converted my unused, fluffy white wedding dress into a zombie bride Halloween costume a couple of years earlier, I wouldn't have put it past Mama to suggest that I wear that. As it was, I'd chosen a simple formfitting design made of pale plum–colored lace and opted out of having a veil. The shade suited my auburn hair as well as subtly tapping into the notion of royalty. After all, what woman doesn't want to feel royal on her wedding day?

Gossip extraordinaire, Mrs. Standish didn't need to know all of that, however. And she didn't need to know my father was flying into Savannah the next day, either.

The Honeybee typically had two kinds of customers. There were the hit-and-runs who came in for a goodie and a drink in a to-go cup, and there were the loungers who stayed awhile. Edna Standish was a bit of both. A prodigious eater, she came in nearly every day for a bag of something sweet to take home, but she typically stayed to chat for anywhere from a few minutes to an hour. I personally thought she tried to time her visits for when we were slow, so she and Ben, both extroverts to the max, could gossip and chat without interruption.

Now Mrs. Standish stood with her hands on her hips surveying what we had on offer. Slightly behind her and to her left, her companion, Skipper Dean, hovered in the shadow of his considerably taller paramour. He sketched me a smile as she boomed, "We'll take a half dozen of the daily special to start. I wish you had those red velvet whoopie pies on the menu all the time."

I raised an eyebrow at Lucy, who nodded. We'd been talking about adding them to the daily roster just that morning.

Ben had returned from stowing the ladder and now stepped forward with a waxed bakery bag in hand. Our logo of an orange tabby cat was printed on the side. He smoothly put her order in the bag and held it out. "Here you go, Edna. What's new?"

Lucy and I exchanged another glance. How much could be new since their half-hour-long conversation the day before?

"Well, I tell you, Ben," she said in her voice that was designed more for outdoors than indoors. "I'm feeling a little down. This is the anniversary of my poor husband's death."

My uncle nodded, sympathy all over his face. "Oh, my dear. I'm sure it's a very difficult day. Will you be visiting his grave?"

"He's in the family tomb over at Bonaventure Cemetery. And yes, the skipper and I stopped by this morning to leave flowers." She sighed. "So sad that he was taken so early."

Skipper Dean patted Mrs. Standish's arm, and she leaned into him. He subtly braced himself with one leg to keep from being knocked over as she smiled down at him. "Thank goodness I found love with this sweet man."

I stifled a smile. Some vanilla scones from the Honeybee had paved the way for their meeting. Not a love potion—we didn't do that kind of thing. Our spell casting had been more in the way of opening a door for love and companionship to enter Mrs. Standish's life when she had been feeling particularly lonely.

Lucy cleared her throat, which had its intended effect of bringing me back to the problem at hand. Or rather, Mrs. Standish's current problem and our ability to mitigate it.

"We have some chocolate mint cookies right out of the oven," I said. "Would you like to try one?" The cocoa nibs in the cookies would help ground her, while the crunchy bits of peppermint candy and a healthy dose of peppermint extract would help lift her spirits.

"Would I!" She eagerly took the proffered treat and took a big bite. Her eyes grew round. "Oh my. You ladies have outdone yourself with that recipe. Fresh, light, and not too sweet."

"Perhaps you'd like a glass of jasmine sweet tea," Lucy suggested. "I can whip some up in a jiffy." Jasmine was a good antidote to stress of all kinds.

However, Mrs. Standish shook her head. "No, thank you, dear. We really must be going. But I'll take half a dozen of these delectable specimens as well." She crunched into the cookie again with vigor.

"That good? Perhaps I should try one, then." A man I hadn't seen—or heard—stepped out from behind her. Kensington Bosworth wore a light linen suit, a pale yellow shirt open at the collar, and huarache sandals. An oversized gold ring flashed as he removed the pair of round wire-framed sunglasses that perched on his button nose to reveal small, pale eyes peering at us all with interest.

"By all means, Mr. Bosworth." I handed him a mint chocolate cookie with a quick glance at the door. Not having the bell ring every time someone came into the bakery was going to take some getting used to. "Skipper Dean?" I asked, offering Mrs. Standish's companion one as well.

He shook his head and patted his middle with a smile. "Thank you so much, darlin', but I have to watch my girlish figure, you know."

Mrs. Standish hee-hawed a laugh at that and gave him a squeeze.

Kensington Bosworth took a bite of cookie and

gave her a sideways look that didn't hide his disapproval. She grinned at him, and I realized she was aware of her effect on his more delicate sensibilities and found it amusing.

"So good to see you, Kensington," she said with a twinkle in her eye. "Did you ever follow up with Randy Post? For your security system, I mean."

He nodded gravely. "Indeed. He has already completed the work. Most satisfactory."

"Hmm. Good to hear that." She gazed at him serenely.

After several seconds, he cleared his throat. "Well, then. Yes. Thank you for the recommendation, Edna." He turned to Lucy. "I came in for a loaf of your most excellent sourdough. I've asked my housekeeper to make a grilled cheese sandwich and tomato soup for my supper this evening."

"Of course," my aunt said. "Let me just wrap one up." She bustled into the kitchen.

Iris passed her and came out to stand by Ben at the register. "Hi, Mr. Bosworth."

He blinked at her, then he allowed a smile. "Good afternoon, Iris. You've changed your hair again."

Her hand crept to the pastel streaks. "Do you like it?"

"Indeed. Very festive."

"Thanks." Blushing, she fled to the kitchen.

Ben asked, "Will the sourdough be all, or can we interest you in a bit of lemon cake or fruit tart for your dessert this evening?"

"I don't eat dessert. That one cookie was an aberration." Bosworth drew out a leather wallet and carefully extracted the amount of his bill. "Though I must admit it was tasty enough."

Ben took the money, chatting along in his charming way. That was why he was the customer service guy, while I generally stayed in the kitchen. Right then, though, I was observing how Mrs. Standish looked at Mr. Bosworth with a mix of mild dislike and speculation.

"Thank you very much, Mrs. Eagel," he said to Lucy. "This bread will no doubt elevate my simple evening meal to something sublime."

A movement over his shoulder drew my attention. A helium balloon in the shape of a dragonfly bobbed by the front window, its string presumably attached to a child too short to be seen. My stomach gave a little twist.

A dragonfly? Now?

Surely it was a coincidence.

Please, please, please let it be a coincidence.

Lucy said, "Well, Katie is really the one responsible for the sourdough—"

"Mr. Eagel." He cut Lucy off and nodded to Ben.

Ben nodded back, then put his arm around my aunt as we all watched Kensington Bosworth march to the door and go out to the street without a backward glance.

"Well!" Mrs. Standish said in a whoosh of air. "That man. I swear. One of these days."

Before she could throw out any more cryptic non-sentences, I asked. "What was that about a security system? Did you recommend Randy to him? He was just in here for a scone after his shift."

Nodding her head vehemently, she reached inside her bulging bag of baked goods, drew out another whoopie pie, took a bite, then nodded her head some more. "Oh my, yes," she said after an audible swallow. "Mr. Post did such a nice job at our humble abode, I just had to pass his name along to Kensington when he mentioned he was worried someone might break into his house."

Edna Standish and Skipper Dean shared a home a few blocks away in Savannah's historic district that was anything but "humble."

"Never mind that he's not a real security expert," she added.

Ben laughed. "I wouldn't say that. He just happens to also be a real fireman."

"Oh, gosh, Ben, I didn't mean . . . well, you know what I mean."

Oddly, we all did. Randy and all of Savannah's other firefighters worked one forty-eight-hour shift each week, living and sleeping at the station during that time, but the rest of their time was their own. Some, like Declan, picked up extra hours here and there in the department doing routine inspections, fire safety classes, and school visits, but many firefighters worked second jobs. Randy's was installing security systems for a local company.

Though ever since he'd started dating my coven mate Bianca Devereaux, he'd spent a lot more time squiring her to art openings and the symphony than filling his hours away from the fire station with other work.

"It was nice of you to recommend him," Lucy told Mrs. Standish.

"Nice, heck! A man needed something done, and I knew another man who could do it. Though I do hope . . ." Mrs. Standish trailed off.

We all waited expectantly. She looked around at us, then said, "I do hope Kensington was pleasant. And that he paid Mr. Post whatever they agreed upon up front." She licked her lips then leaned forward. Suddenly her voice was lower than I'd known it could go. "That man has always been a bit odd. Old money, you know. A staple of Savannah society, as was his father and his grandfather before him. Wonderful philanthropists, all. Or at least until lately." She scanned the almost-empty bakery, and her voice dropped still further. "All I know is that he doesn't contribute to the animal welfare charity that I head, not like he used to. It all started a couple of years ago. I've heard rumors, of course."

"Of course," I murmured. Rumors were her bread and butter.

Then I remembered the dragonfly balloon that had bobbed by the window. "Like what?" I asked.

Lucy frowned. My aunt disapproved of gossip—most of the time, at least.

"About how he's been—" She seemed to catch herself. She straightened and flashed a big smile at Skipper Dean. "Listen to me go on and on. You'd think I had nothing better to do than talk out of school. Shame on me."

I bit off a comment about her sudden reluctance to engage in what I'd thought was her favorite activity.

"You all have a lovely afternoon, now. Thanks to you, I feel much better on this sad, sad day."

Our good-byes and good wishes followed the pair to the door. When they'd left, Ben went behind the coffee counter and started setting things up for the customers who were beginning to trickle into the Honeybee. The ladies in the reading area put away their paperwork and rose with empty cups and plates in their hands. They deposited their dishware in the tub by the door, and I thanked them. Then I grabbed the half-full tub and took it into the kitchen for Iris to load into the dishwasher.

As I was walking back out front, Lucy reached out and touched my arm. I stopped, knowing what was coming.

"Did you see the dragonfly?" she asked.

"It probably didn't mean anything," I said in a deliberately light tone.

"You should know better than that by now," she said. "Dragonflies always mean something with you."

She was right. Dragonflies were my totem. It was a witchy thing. Whenever I saw one, I knew to pay extra attention. Lucy described it as a kind of metaphysical tap on the shoulder.

And seven times, that metaphysical tap had warned of death.

I gnawed on my lower lip, then caught myself and stopped. "Okay, so maybe it's a sign. But of what? There have been false alarms before."

"Name one."

I sighed. "There's just too much going on now to have to deal with some magical emergency." I couldn't keep the frustration out of my voice.

Ignoring it, Lucy said, "More than regular magic." She was referring to my being a catalyst and light-witch. The first meant things tended to, er, *happen* around me. The latter referred to what a former mentor, now deceased, had decided was a calling for righting magical wrongs. Fighting dark magic with light magic, if you will. He'd told me I had no choice, but of course, it turned out I did. We always do, more than we realize. Yet sometimes having a choice makes it harder rather than easier to do what's right.

I tried again. "Exactly. Things are too crazy for more than my regular spell casting right now. There's the wedding coming up, dealing with my mother, my dad coming tomorrow, the renovations of the carriage house are way behind schedule, not to mention—"

"I know, honey," she interrupted with real concern. "Believe me. I'm hoping it's nothing, too." Then she stepped forward and gave me a hug as the door opened and the first two customers of the afternoon rush entered the Honeybee, chatting animatedly as they approached the counter.

Quickly, I went back to the kitchen to grab more coffee mugs for Ben. Lucy and I'd had this conversation more than once before.

All I could do was wait and see what happened.

Chapter 2

"Come on, big guy." I opened my tote bag on the office floor and moved to switch off the computer monitor on the desk.

Mungo jumped down from the club chair where he'd spent most of the day snoozing. He'd taken a break to go out to the reading area of the bakery, beg a few bites from regular customers, and then curl into his bed on the bottom shelf of the romance section.

It was a hard life for a witch's familiar.

When I turned back, he'd nestled deep into the bag for the trip home. His dark brown eyes gleamed up at me, almost lost in the black fur of his face.

"The bakery's closed. You don't have to hide," I said.

When my dog had first started coming to work with me, I'd been worried that the health department wouldn't approve. Over time, I'd realized that as long as he wasn't actually hanging out in the kitchen, it was fine.

He blinked but didn't budge.

I shrugged, picked up the tote that was part purse and part dog carrier, and hefted the strap over my shoulder. "Suit yourself."

Out front, Ben and Lucy were turning off the lights, music, and fans. I took one last look at the kitchen for the day and saw that Iris had left it sparkling and ready for the next morning's baking.

"Will you be picking up Skylar in the morning?" Ben asked me as he locked the door behind us.

I shook my head. "Declan is on days off. He'll pick up Dad and bring him by the bakery before they head to the carriage house. Dad's itching to take stock of the situation there."

"I bet he can get the workers back on schedule," Lucy said.

"There's only so much we can do on that front," I said. "It's not even the workers' fault. There were just some unforeseen difficulties, you know? Permits from the city taking longer than we thought, the wrong tile came for the bathroom, and we had to wait for the right kind, the drywaller had a family emergency . . ." I trailed off, feeling discouraged.

"In other words, the usual sort of stuff," Ben said with a smile. "Don't worry. Sky will be able to help."

I nodded. "You're right. Turns out owning the only hardware store in Fillmore has made him a bit of an expert on everything."

"Yup. Your dad's a jack-of-all-trades all right," Ben said, then, "He and Declan get along well." It wasn't a question.

I smiled. "They do." My mother had met Declan before we'd even thought about marriage, but Dad had met him only after we'd gotten engaged the previous Thanksgiving. They'd hit it off immediately.

Lucy and Ben veered off toward their vehicle, and I carried Mungo to the parking structure where my Volkswagen Beetle was parked. Once we were both belted into the Bug, I steered to Abercorn Street, around a few of the historic squares in Savannah's historic district, and continued toward Midtown.

Traffic was lighter than usual, and soon I was pulling to the curb in front of the compact house I'd bought when I moved to Savannah. Declan's big king-cab pickup was parked just ahead, and a paneled work truck with LINCOLN BARD CONSTRUCTION on the side took up most of the small driveway.

The carriage house was the last remnant of a large estate, the rest of which had long been obliterated by my pleasant suburban neighborhood. The house had been converted to a one-bedroom, one-loft, one-bathroom home with a charming, postage-stamp living room and a kitchen so tiny only two people could eat at the table.

I adored it more than was remotely reasonable, but it was awfully small for two people. After we were engaged, Declan and I had looked all over Savannah for a new place where we wouldn't be bumping into each other whenever we turned around. Nothing had felt right. The solution had come to us in an unexpected way, and now I was about to have the best of both worlds. My old home was being updated and expanded to be our new home.

The problem was, if our luck didn't turn, the updates wouldn't be done in time for the wedding, which was supposed to take place in the backyard with a combination reception and housewarming to follow afterward. The invitations had already gone out, and it was way too late to book a different venue in Savannah.

Somehow, we had to make it work.

Mungo tumbled out of the car and trotted to the middle of the lawn before lying down and rolling over three times. He sat up and gave me one of his best doggy grins, then did it again. I laughed at his antics. He was tired of being cooped up in Declan's apartment without easy access to the outdoors. He hated having to wear a leash for our walks, too. Mungo would be as glad as I would be when we could finally move back home.

Even though it was nearly six o'clock, the sound of a nail gun reached my ears, followed closely by the roar of an air compressor. I glanced over at the house next door, hoping the commotion wasn't bothering my friend and neighbor, Margie Coopersmith, and her family too much. Then I remembered they were on summer vacation in Myrtle Beach with her mother-in-law.

Declan came out to the front porch and waved to me. He wore cargo shorts and a light blue T-shirt with the fire department logo on the sleeve. I paused for a moment to appreciate how the thin cotton skimmed his muscular torso and echoed the color of his eyes, then started across the grass.

As I strode toward him, I tried to ignore the bare frame of the new garage that loomed at the end of the drive. It had been abandoned in favor of finishing the interior work of the house first. I stepped up to the porch and melted into the arms of my fiancé.

I sighed. Suddenly it all felt doable.

Sort of.

"Come on," he murmured into my hair. "I want you to see the new sink."

"Who says romance is dead?" I asked with a grin.

His eyes flashed. "Not me, darlin'. You should know that by now."

"Mmm-hmm," I said, and followed him inside. For a second, I'd thought I'd heard the lilt of an Irish brogue.

Just my imagination. Connell hasn't surfaced for months now. He's keeping his word to stay in the background.

I brought my hereditary gift of magic to the relationship mix, but my fiancé came with a little extra complication, too. A certain spirit had been attached to members of his family for over a century. His name was Connell, and each generation he chose one of the male McCarthys to shadow. This time around he'd chosen Declan. The fact that the spirit seemed to be a, well . . . okay, I'll just say it . . . a *leprechaun* only made things weirder. And it really had been my fault that Connell had suddenly started taking over Declan's body now and then. Well, sort of my fault. I'd arranged the séance that had brought Connell to the forefront. But how was I to know? I'd been trying to contact a murder victim on the other side in order to find out who killed him.

Not surprisingly, being taken over by the spirit of a leprechaun had really upset Declan, especially at first. It did me, too, even if I was a little more at ease with the paranormal. Connell was a terrible flirt, and I was afraid he'd show up sometime when Declan and I were being intimate.

However, they'd worked it out. Connell agreed to leave Declan alone except to help him when he needed it and to serve as a kind of intuition when called upon. It had been working for several months now, so I'd finally been willing to set the wedding date.

Because I didn't have to worry about Connell anymore.

Right? Then stop worrying about Connell.

I gave myself a little mental shake and brought my attention back to the sweet, handsome man standing next to me.

Declan was six inches taller than my own five feet seven. He wore his dark wavy hair just long enough to push regulations, had a day's worth of stubble shading his square jaw, and guided me with a hand that spanned most of my lower back. When I looked up at his face, I saw dark smudges under his eyes. That was rare for him, and I was glad all over again that my dad was coming to help on the home front.

The nail gun sounded again from the direction of the master bedroom. We could call it that now that it opened into the expanded bathroom, which also retained the original entrance from the hallway. As we crossed the newly laid wooden floor in the living room, I imagined I could still smell the charred odor of the original wooden planks that had been burned to ash, the singed remains of the Civil War–era trunk that had functioned as the coffee table, and the charred upholstery from the purple fainting couch I'd found on Craigslist.

I really missed that couch.

That unexpected solution to our housing problem

that I mentioned? A Molotov cocktail thrown through the front window.

Talk about lemons to lemonade.

Of course, the scents from the burned living room were long gone. The floor was hand-scraped teak now, and the ruined furnishings had been hauled to the dump. All that remained was the lamp with the tasseled shade in the corner over by the French doors that led to the backyard and gardens.

In the kitchen, Declan pointed to the sink. It wasn't particularly fancy, simply a standard-sized white porcelain unit snugged into the gray granite countertop, but both of those were more than we'd had before. The previous sink had been almost too small to wash a dinner plate in, and the counter hadn't been long enough for two people to stand side by side. Since Declan loved to cook, and I loved to cook with him, that had been a problem. In fact, the entire kitchen had been expanded to twice its original size. Unfortunately, the new back wall was still open to the studs.

"I love it," I said, and kissed his cheek. "But shouldn't the walls be finished before the fixtures go in?"

"It'll be fine," he said, tugging on my hand and moving toward the bedroom. "Come on. They're almost done framing the closet."

Closet.

It was about time. Declan had been keeping his clothes in a bag under the bed for months before we had to make the temporary move to his apartment. Still, I felt a pang at the idea of giving up the twin armoires that had housed my wardrobe for two years.

It was a small pang, though. Especially when I saw

the big ol' walk-in closet with the opening for the sky-light in the slanted ceiling above.

I followed Declan's pickup to his apartment building and parked on the street. Mungo walked me around the block, then we headed up the stairs to join my fi-ancé. The smells of warm tomatoes, basil, and lemon greeted our entrance, and my mouth immediately began to water. Declan was in the kitchen chopping zucchini, peppers, and eggplant to make what we'd come to call pasta ratatouille—a summer version of the classic primavera.

After changing into yoga pants and a tank top, I put on some low music and opened a bottle of dry rosé. Tendrils of steam began to rise from the water that was heating for pasta as I set the table and re-trieved ingredients for a simple salad from the refrig-erator. Mungo sat in front of his food bowl, watching our activities with avid eyes. Pasta ratatouille was one of his favorite dishes.

Declan and I moved through our supper prepara-tions in a comfortable dance. He handed me the knife he'd been using just as I needed it for the scal-lions. I automatically moved my hips to the side so he could get out the pasta strainer. The olive oil was in my hand the moment he reached out to receive it. I took over grating a fluffy mound of fresh Parmesan as he began to lightly sauté the vegetables.

As we worked, we talked more about what was left to do at the carriage house before the wedding. After we'd finally received the right tile for the shower, the man who was installing it had flaked out on us in the middle of the job. Declan had tracked down a woman with good references. The problem was, she was booked for three weeks before she'd be able to start, which would be cutting it awfully close. The floor and paint could be done in the meantime, but of course, the fixtures we wanted had been back-ordered. That meant we had to find other ones if we wanted the guests at our wedding to have use of facilities other than the portable toilets that the construction folks had been using.

Which, of course, was not an option at *all*.

"I have a forty-eight starting day after tomorrow," Declan said. "By then we'll have talked with your dad about priorities." He made a face. "I can handle pretty much any emergency scenario you throw at me, you know? I mean, I'm trained for it."

I nodded, knowing where he was going. "But dealing with contractors is a whole different thing," I said.

"Right. I wish I was better at it." He fished out a tube of penne from the boiling pot and bit it to test for doneness. Shaking his head, he tossed it in the garbage. "Needs a couple more minutes."

Reaching over and squeezing his arm, I said, "I'm glad Dad will be here, too. And not only because of how that kind of thing is completely in his wheelhouse, but because I miss him."

He glanced over at me and smiled. "I know. Watching you with your dad is so different than the way you are with your mother."

I retrieved our plates from the table. "No kidding. But you know how mothers and daughters are."

Rolling his eyes, he gave the vegetables he'd added to the tomatoes a stir and tossed in lemon zest and basil. "Do I ever." Since he had two older sisters and two younger ones, no brothers, and his father had died when he was quite young, he was more than familiar with the mother-daughter dynamic.

We plated up in the kitchen and sat down to supper at the small table we'd moved in front of the sliding door leading to the balcony. It was too hot and muggy to sit outside, but it was nice to have a bit of a view, even if it was just the courtyard. Mungo snarfed up his portion of pasta in seconds, then lay down to gnaw at his carrot sticks at leisure. I could hear him crunching, but he was hidden by the counter that separated the kitchen from the living room.

As I ate, I looked around the apartment. Declan didn't seem upset about moving from his place to mine. Heck, he'd practically been living at the carriage house for months before the fire.

Not my place. Ours.

But did that mean he'd want to hang the unframed Guinness poster on his wall in *our* living room? And even though the purple fainting couch was gone, no way were we going to move the old brown sofa he'd rescued from the firehouse into the new place.

That red rocking chair, though. That might work with the furniture I have my eye on.

"You're quiet." Declan speared a bite of eggplant. "Don't worry. It'll all work out."

"Mmm," I murmured, and took a sip of wine. "I just hope I can get everything else done in time for the wedding. Mimsey is handling the flowers, of course."

Mimsey Carmichael was the charming octogenarian who was the de facto leader of the spellbook club.

Our high priestess, if we'd been formal enough to have such a thing. She was also the owner of Vase Value, the best flower shop in Savannah. She'd handled the flowers for countless weddings, from antebellum reenactments to goth ceremonies with vampire themes.

I groaned. "But I still can't decide on the cake." As a baker, I wanted my wedding cake to be something extra special. "I don't know what's wrong with me."

Declan, wise man that he was, responded with only a gentle smile.

"There's just over a month before we get hitched," I said.

"Believe me, I'm well aware." He started to say something else but stopped.

"I know, I know. I made things difficult by choosing August seventeenth. But—"

"It's okay," he broke in. "I get it. And I think it's nice you want to get married on your nonna's birthday."

Never mind that she'd been gone since I was nine years old. Well, sort of gone. She still showed up every now and then to help me out when things got dicey.

I smiled and put down my fork, stuffed to the gills. I was a lucky woman to have a man who liked to cook as much as Declan did. Better yet, with so many daughters, his mother had no more than a polite interest in our wedding plans. She would come early to help with the wedding itself, but other than that had left us to our own devices.

Unlike my own mother. Sometimes being an only child came with a price.

I rose and carried our dishes to the sink. "At least I don't have to worry about planning Cookie's baby shower." Cookie Rios' first child was due in October, and the way everyone was acting, we were all having a baby.

Declan followed me and began putting away leftovers.

"It'll be the week after the wedding, and Lucy and the other spellbook club members are handling it. It'll be at the Honeybee, of course. And Lucy has some cute games for us to play." I saw the look on his face and grinned. "Why, honey. You look a little bored. I thought you wanted babies."

His eyes widened. "Eventually, sure. But that has nothing to do with girly parties."

"But you're invited," I teased. "Baby showers aren't just for the women anymore. Don't you want to play the games? See all the cool gifts she'll get? Diaper bags and onesies and bibs, oh my? There might even be a breast pump."

He looked alarmed. "Do I have to go?"

I was about to let him off the hook when Mungo let out a *yip!*, ran to the coffee table, and looked up at where my phone sat. A split second later, it rang. Side-eyeing my familiar, I snagged the phone off the table and checked the screen.

When I saw who the caller was, my stomach did a slow turn around my lovely supper.

"Katie?" Declan asked. "Who is it?"

I took a deep breath and tapped the ANSWER button. "Hello, Detective Quinn."

Chapter 3

"Hello, Katie," Detective Peter Quinn said.

The memory of the dragonfly balloon bobbing past the bakery window flared in my mind. A feeling of dread spread across my shoulders.

No. No, no, no.

"I hope you're well," he said. "I'm calling because . . ." He cleared his throat.

"Did someone die?" I asked in a low voice.

There was a moment of surprised hesitation on the other end of the line. Mungo let out a small canine groan. Declan stared at me from across the room.

I plunged ahead. "Tell me it wasn't Edna Standish or Skipper Dean." After all, that was who Lucy, Ben, and I had been talking with when I'd seen the dragonfly, and Peter Quinn was a homicide detective.

"No. . . ." He drew the word out slowly.

Then I remembered who else had been nearby when I'd seen my totem. "Is it Kensington Bosworth?"

Another slight pause, then he let out a loud expletive that made me jump. "So, you *do* know something about this." Another expletive. More of a vulgarity, actually. "Get over here." He hung up.

My hand was shaking as I stared down at the phone.

"What's going on?" Declan asked as he came to stand beside me. Next to my ankle, Mungo peered up and whined low in his throat.

I closed my eyes. *Dang it.* "I don't know, but it's not good." I opened my eyes again and dialed Quinn back.

"I mean it, Katie," he said without benefit of greeting. "I want you to drop what you're doing and—"

"Where?" I asked.

"What?" he answered.

"Where are you?"

"At Bosworth's . . . so you've never been here?"

I shook my head, realized he couldn't see me, and said, "No."

He reeled off an address in the Victorian District. Battling everything that told me not to get involved this time, I agreed to come over right away. After we hung up, I turned to Declan.

"Apparently Kensington Bosworth is dead."

Declan frowned, then his face cleared. "Didn't Randy do some work for him?"

"Yep. That's the guy."

"What happened?"

"Quinn wasn't exactly overflowing with details." I headed into the bedroom to exchange my tank for a T-shirt. "Mr. Bosworth is a regular at the Honeybee."

Declan came to stand in the doorway. "And that's enough for Quinn to call you?"

I paused, one trail runner on and its mate dangling from my hand. "Of course not."

30

He looked up at the ceiling. "Let me guess. Bosworth was murdered."

Sitting on the edge of the bed, I bent to put on the other shoe. "As I said, Quinn didn't give me any details, but that would be my guess. After all, homicide is his bread and butter."

"And there's magic involved."

I stood and met his eyes. Ran my fingers through my auburn pixie cut, dropped my hand, and sighed. "That would also be my guess."

"Well, I'm going with you."

A little of my tension seeped away. "I was hoping you'd say that."

Mungo waited by the front door.

I grabbed my tote. "Sorry, buddy, but you should stay here. I don't know what we're going to find, and I don't want to worry about you."

He whined.

"Mungo, honey, please."

He glared at me and sat down smack in front of the door.

Declan gave a little laugh. "I don't think you're going to win this one, Katie." He tipped his head to one side and regarded the dog. "Maybe it would be better if he did come with us."

He meant because the terrier was my familiar. And Quinn had probably called me because I was a witch. A lightwitch. Even if he didn't exactly know what that meant.

I sighed. "Yeah, okay. Come on." I waved Mungo out the door, and we all trooped down to Declan's truck.

As he drove, Declan glanced over at me. "Are you and Detective Quinn okay these days?"

I didn't answer right away, and when I did it was noncommittal. "We'll see."

He looked like he wanted to say something more, but let it drop.

It was true that I was a bit nervous. Peter Quinn and I had had a tortured relationship since before the Honeybee had even opened. It had started off when Uncle Ben had been Quinn's primary suspect in the murder of Mavis Templeton, and I'd stepped in and cleared his name. Since then, I'd been involved in several of the detective's other murder cases—but only the ones that had a magical element. In fact, I'd learned that I was a lightwitch from none other than Quinn's erstwhile partner, Franklin Taite, who happened to investigate black magic on the side, unbeknownst to Quinn. Taite was dead now, a murder victim himself, and Quinn worked alone.

He'd always pooh-poohed the idea that some of his cases might involve real magic until he'd seen me deflect a weapon right in front of him. Not that I made a habit of that or anything. It had been an emergency, and when I'm under sudden stress like that, my lightwitch powers seem to kick into overdrive.

Oh, and I also sort of *glow* when that happens. Quinn had witnessed that, too. He'd steered clear of me for a while after that. However, he'd approached me after I'd solved a murder that had looked like an accident the previous April, and I'd come clean with him about at least some of what I was. He'd been nonplussed, to say the least, but his own eyes didn't lie. Also, he had to admit I'd helped bring several killers to justice. We'd reached a kind of truce, but his visits to the Honeybee for the occasional pastry over the last few months had been strained nonetheless.

The Victorian District was south of Savannah's famous historic squares and considered to be the city's first suburb. Some areas of the neighborhood were nicer than others. Kensington Bosworth's home was definitely in a nicer bit. The street in front was full of flashing lights and a gathering crowd. Uniformed officers were stringing police tape around the yard. Declan drove slowly past, then pulled to the curb a block away, and we got out. Mungo agreed to stay in the truck, for which I was grateful. I suspected the police wouldn't appreciate a small dog at their crime scene. Not that he would have disturbed anything if I'd asked him to sit-stay, but they wouldn't know that.

As we walked toward the melee, Declan gestured toward a wine-colored convertible across the street. The top was up, the windows were dark, and the engine was running.

"Someone you know?" I asked.

"Nah. But it's a Thunderbird, like Lucy's. A 2005. Last year they made them. Hers is a '64. You'd never know they were the same model."

I rolled my eyes. This was totally not the time for his car obsession to kick in. But because I was looking at it when it slowly pulled away, I did notice the custom license plate on the BMW parked behind it.

DANTE.

Welcome to the Divine Comedy, I thought as an

33

official-looking van double-parked next to a police cruiser in front of the house and a white-haired gentleman got out and headed toward the house.

As we passed it, I saw the car behind the BMW was a familiar-looking Audi. I scanned the crowd but didn't see its owner.

Good.

Still, I had no doubt its owner was nearby—Steve Dawes, reporter for the *Savannah Morning News.*

Mr. Bosworth's home was close to Forsyth Park and larger than the houses around it, with three stories, an impressive turret, and more layers of decorative scrollwork, curlicues, and gingerbread trim than the most elaborate wedding cake I'd ever seen. Somewhat atypical of that style of architecture but very typical of the South, columns supported a sprawling veranda in front, and smaller Juliet balconies were bordered by wrought-iron railings on each of the two floors above. Unlike the elaborate, multicolored schemes often found on Victorian homes, Bosworth's was painted Savannah haint blue with the trim pieces soft white and smoky red. It wasn't a combination I would have chosen, but for some reason it worked. Usually, that shade of blue was reserved for ceilings and porches in the South, the idea being that it fooled spirits, or *haints*, into thinking it was water and they'd move along. I'd never seen an entire house painted so . . . defensively.

The house was set back from the street, and a meticulously maintained lawn spanned the area between the porch and the public sidewalk. As we approached it, my stomach slowly clenched like a fist. What had happened to the dapper little man I'd given a mint chocolate cookie to just that afternoon? Taking a deep breath, I tried to relax, soften my gaze, and allow my intuition free rein. I felt a twinge of darkness, muddy and unfocused, but not much more. In fact, there was so little for my senses to pick up that I immediately wondered if there was some kind of shielding spell in place.

If so, that didn't bode well at all.

Quinn came out on the porch and saw Declan and me on the sidewalk. He must have been watching for us. On one hand, that was gratifying. On the other, it was a bit alarming. There should have been a gazillion other things more important to him than little ol' me showing up.

He strode toward us, flashing an irritated glance at Declan before his face transformed into a passive mask. His thick hair seemed to gain a bit more silver every time I saw him. Like the rest of Quinn, it was precise. He wore beige slacks, perfectly polished loafers, and a white shirt that was still brilliant and crisply pressed despite the stifling summer heat. Or perhaps he'd recently changed into one of the many similar shirts he kept in his bottom desk drawer. Either way, he looked cool, smooth, and perfectly tanned, though for once he wore no sports coat and was even sans tie.

Then I saw the dark smudges under his sharp gray eyes. And wait—was his right sideburn just a bit longer than the left? Such a minor thing, yet I found it thoroughly disturbing. I'd seen Quinn slightly ruffled in the past, but only after days on end with little to no sleep while he was in the midst of a murder investigation.

I reminded myself that he might be in the middle of or just off a difficult case. After all, there was an awful lot about Peter Quinn that I didn't know.

"Katie," he said when he reached us. "Declan."

"Detective," I said with a nod.

Yep. Perfectly awkward already.

Declan smiled and stepped forward with his hand out. Surprised, Quinn shook it.

"I'd like you to come inside," Quinn said to me. "Declan, I'm sorry, but I'm going to ask you to wait outside. You can come up to the porch, though."

Declan looked at me, and I tipped my head a fraction forward. "Sure thing," he said.

Quinn raised the tape and ducked beneath it. I sent a grateful glance toward Declan, and we followed the detective.

"Quinn?" I said as we climbed the porch steps.

He stopped by the front door and turned, his posture radiating impatience.

Too bad. I set my jaw. "What am I walking into?"

"I thought you knew," he said.

Quickly, I shook my head. "Nope. Not a clue. Other than something seems to have happened to Kensington Bosworth. Since you're a homicide detective, I assume it was murder or at least there were some suspicious circumstances."

"Oh, it's murder, all right."

Beside me, Declan made a noise, and I felt the blood drain from my face. It was one thing to guess, another entirely to hear the word from an official source.

"Why did you call me?"

"Bakery bag," Quinn said.

36

I blinked. "What?"

"There's a bag from the Honeybee on his kitchen counter. Knowing how you end up involved with my cases anyway, I figured I might as well find out what you know." He quirked an eyebrow. "And then lo and behold, when I call you, you already know the poor guy is dead."

"But—" I began.

He flicked a glance around the yard. "Inside, if you don't mind."

Baffled, I followed him inside the house, leaving Declan to lean against a porch column.

As I crossed the threshold, it felt like I was passing through thicker air. Suddenly stuffy, cloying, like cotton or gauze. My breath seemed trapped in my chest. Color faded, and my vision grayed, and for a flash I saw the furnishings in the front hall as if I were looking at an old-fashioned photographic negative. Then there was an inaudible *pop*, like on a plane when you yawn to clear the pressure from your ears.

It lasted only a moment, and then everything was normal again. Slightly dazed and a little unsure of what had just happened, indeed unsure if anything *had* happened, I looked around.

Ah. Everything wasn't normal again, after all.

My intuition flared, and my witchy senses reached out as I realized I had just passed through a protection spell. I'd been practicing the Craft for only a little over two years, but I was pretty sure that thick veil I'd passed through had been cast by an expert. If it was anything like what Lucy and the spellbook club had taught me, it encompassed the entire house.

Quinn was staring at me. "What are you doing?"

I took a few more steps inside and tried a smile. "Getting the lay of the land."

He frowned but didn't say anything. It was the first time I'd been at a crime scene where he knew I was a witch. It was a relief, but it was also weird.

We were in a large entryway. Black-and-white tiles covered the floor. An imposing flower arrangement stood on the nearby console table, filling the air with the scent of lilies. A curved staircase led up to a hallway lined with dark mahogany doors. A doorway to the left of where we stood opened to a richly furnished formal dining room with a massive table that could have easily seated a dozen people. In one of the chairs, a woman who looked a bit like Meryl Streep on a bad-hair day sat staring straight ahead with a stunned expression. Her fist lay on the table, so tightly clenched around a tissue that I could see it trembling.

Opposite the entrance were three more doors, beyond which I guessed would be the kitchen and service areas. A house this big and old would have had live-in servants at one time. The third floor likely held their quarters, accessed by a back stair. To our right, another door stood partially open. The sound of voices echoed from inside.

Sure enough, Quinn strode in that direction, beckoning to me over his shoulder. Feeling a combination of curiosity and reluctance, I walked to where he'd stopped in the doorway. As I approached, I could feel the power subtly emanating from the room. He moved aside and indicated I should go in first.

Peering around him, I saw a crime scene tech with

a camera on the far side of the room and hesitated. "Is he in there?"

"Bosworth? Do you really think I'd invite you in to examine a dead body, Katie? You hardly have that kind of expertise."

I flinched at his sharp tone as well as the bluntness of his words. Then I met his eye and said too low for anyone else to hear, "Honestly, Quinn, I don't know what you'd do these days. Ever since I told you what I am and about Franklin Taite, you've been standoffish. Now you call me up and demand I come over here, but you won't tell me what happened or why you want me here."

His attention slid away for a moment, and when he looked back at me, his gaze had softened. "You're right. I'm sorry. I've been working another case for the last twenty-four hours and getting nowhere, and then the lieutenant called me in on this one, too. You know why? Because I have a great track record with cases that involve things like voodoo and strange potions. And that, of course, is in large part due to you."

"So, I'm not a suspect?"

His lips parted in surprise for a moment, and then a ghost of a smile crossed his face. "No. You're not a suspect. However, I'd sure like to know how you knew I was calling about Bosworth before I had a chance to fill you in."

A few beats passed as I considered what to say. Probably best not to go into details about dragonfly totems and the like. He was still getting used to the other things I'd told him.

I smiled. "Oh, I just had a feeling. Since I'd seen him today and all."

Quinn gave me a wry look. "Right. Well, I'll file that under *things to ask you about later* and move along. Because right now I want you to look at the murder weapon."

I blanched. "Well, I guess that's better than having to look at a dead body, but not much. Just tell me it's not a knife. I hate knives."

His eyebrow rose a fraction. "I remember. Must be a problem for someone who spends so much time in a kitchen, but okay. No, it's not a knife. In fact, I don't know what it is, but given all the other weird stuff the guy had lying around, I was hoping you could tell me."

At that, my curiosity trumped my apprehension. I stepped past him and looked around. It was an office, richly appointed in dark wood. A bank of glassed-in bookshelves marched along the wall to my right. Straight ahead, a multipaned window reached from the floor to the ten-foot ceiling. What I thought was a Hepplewhite desk and chair sat to my left. There was, of all things, a typewriter on the desk, along with an open datebook, fountain pen, and on the corner, a well-thumbed dictionary. Beyond the desk was a doorway to another room. The only other furnishings were two chairs similar to the desk chair and four long, low tables with a variety of items on display.

I glimpsed the corner of another desk in the room beyond, and the white-haired man who had arrived in the van outside moved through my limited field of vision. Again, the muted murmur of voices reached my ears. That room was where all the action was, it seemed. As it should be. I could sense death in there.

My gaze swept the room I was in again. This was

the outer office, and that was the inner sanctum. I stepped toward the tables and examined the items arranged on the surfaces and displayed under glass.

And bit my lip. No wonder Quinn had called me. And no wonder this room—and the one beyond, I realized—throbbed with potential power.

There were items from several magical disciplines. A collection of pentacles was arranged on black velvet. There were two clear crystal balls, one the size of a bowling ball and the other the size of a clementine. Three athames, which were ceremonial knives that gave me the heebie-jeebies, lay neatly within one of the cases. I shied away from them and went to the next table. There I found a good, old-fashioned voodoo doll, some ceremonial masks, a small skull, and several strands of metal beads. There were decks of tarot cards, some brand-new and still in their boxes, but also one loose deck frayed at the edges from frequent use.

Moving along, I discovered a ceremonial ankh and a scarab amulet, along with a crook, an Eye of Horus, a peacock feather, and a few pots of dried plant matter. I didn't know much about *heka*, or the power that Egyptians believed lay behind their magic, but the items were from that practice. The plants in particular piqued my interest, as Lucy had told me the use of herbs was a large part of *heka*. It was the hedgewitchery of the Middle East, so to speak. The final display reminded me of my father. It contained a turtle-shell rattle, a tomahawk decorated with leather and feathers, several examples of small medicine bags, and a chest plate with an intricate beaded pattern.

I turned to Quinn, who had been watching me.

"See?" he asked.

"Yeah. This guy was into a lot of stuff I'm familiar with. Also, a lot of stuff I'm not so familiar with." I pointed to the ankh. "That's Egyptian, but that's all I can tell you. And that"—I pointed to the tomahawk—"is obviously Native American, but I couldn't tell you what tribe it's from." I frowned and wondered out loud, "Why so many items from different disciplines? Did he practice?" He sure hadn't struck me as the type.

"Mr. Bosworth was a collector," a voice behind me drawled.

I turned to see a tall, thin, African American man with a pencil mustache and wire-framed glasses had entered the room. He wore a black suit with a white shirt and a narrow black tie. Behind him, a uniformed officer hovered in the foyer.

"A collector of all things paranormal," he continued. "Books on sorcery and alchemy, and items used in all manner of magical ceremonies across cultures and time." The almost lackadaisical tones of a deep Georgia accent rounded the edges of his words.

"And who might you be?" Quinn asked.

The newcomer gave a little bow. "Malcolm Cardwell, at your service. I am . . . was . . . Mr. Bosworth's personal secretary. I understand he's dead?" He sounded calm, but I could see the clenched muscles in his jaw and neck.

Quinn approached Cardwell and stopped in front of him. "He is. How did you find out?"

The man's lips pressed together in a thin smile. "I received a phone call from Mrs. Gleason, the housekeeper. She told me she found Mr. Bosworth and called the police."

Mrs. Gleason. The woman sitting in the dining room? She must have been the one who was supposed to use my sourdough bread to make the grilled cheese sandwich Bosworth had mentioned. I wondered whether he'd had a chance to eat his soup-and-sandwich supper before he'd been killed.

"She did," the detective confirmed. "Thank you for coming. Perhaps you can answer some questions I have about your employer. Tell me, how did you get into the house? It's cordoned off."

"When I arrived, I encountered a reporter, a very personable young man, works for the *News*, I believe. He directed me to an officer and told him I might be of some use to your investigation. The officer brought me inside."

Quinn glanced out at the uniformed man and gave him a dismissive nod. The officer inclined his head and moved away. I heard the front door open and close.

I rubbed my temple, hoping the reporter wasn't who I knew darn well it was. Steve Dawes had stopped working for his father and gone back to his old job at the *Savannah Morning News* a few months before. Not the job as a business columnist, but the one before that: crime-beat reporter.

Of course, he'd hie straight to the murder of a collector of all things paranormal, as Cardwell had put it. Heck, he might have even known about Bosworth's death in a way similar to the way I had. After all, Steve was a member of the oldest druid clan in Georgia.

And he was out front where Declan was waiting for me on the porch. Steve and Declan had hated each other long before I'd entered the picture. Steve's brother and Declan had been roommates and trained in the fire department together, but the younger Dawes had been a bit of a hot dog and had broken protocol when fighting a fire with Declan. He'd died in that fire, and Steve had blamed Declan ever since.

However, it didn't help their relationship that I'd met Steve around the same time I'd met Declan, and for a time I'd kind of, sort of, been seeing them both.

I forced my attention back to what Cardwell was saying.

"Well, Mr. Bosworth didn't have any enemies in the sense I believe you mean, Detective. He was certainly a wealthy man, though, and money always seems to make enemies, doesn't it? Then there was his collection here."

Quinn shot me a glance, then said, "Tell me about this collection. It's certainly unique."

Cardwell looked wry. "Isn't it? He inherited most of it and occasionally worked with a dealer here in town to add new items. It's quite valuable, not to mention the other contents of the house." His gaze fell on the antique desk. "It was such an invitation to burglars. I was relieved when he had a security system installed two weeks ago."

"He must not have been in the habit of arming it, yet," Quinn said. "Unfortunately for him. Mr. Cardwell, would you mind waiting for me outside? I want to talk with you more. I'll be with you as soon as I'm finished here."

Cardwell eyed me. "Certainly, Detective. But what did you mean about Mr. Bosworth not arming the security system? Because I assure you, he was quite religious about it from the very first day it was installed."

"Well, there was no report of an alarm. We thought perhaps Mrs. Gleason disarmed it when she arrived, but she said it was already turned off."

Cardwell looked thoughtful, then said, "Detective, I believe you might want to talk to the gentleman who installed the system."

I felt my breath catch.

Quinn nodded. "Do you happen to know his name?"

"Mr. Post. His given name is Randy, I believe."

"I see." The detective knew most of the firefighters in town, and I could almost feel how hard he was trying not to look at me. He jotted something in his little notebook.

"I should be very interested in hearing what he has to say," the secretary said. "You see, he had a master code that he used when he was working on the system." He looked around the room. "And he showed a great deal of interest in some of Mr. Bosworth's Native American artifacts. The statue of Ginegosh in particular. Half fox and half snake. I believe the gentleman is Native American himself."

Something tickled the back of my mind. Then it was gone.

But he was right. Randy was part Chippewa. I didn't like the turn the conversation was taking.

Cardwell frowned. "You might check to see if it's still in Mr. Bosworth's office. Also, there was a bit of an altercation between the two."

"What kind of an altercation?" I demanded.

Quinn gave me a look.

Bosworth's secretary turned his gaze on me. "And who might you be?"

"Consultant," I said shortly.

"Ah." He looked at Quinn, who hesitated then nodded.

With a tight smile, Cardwell said, "Mr. Bosworth and the security system installer had a disagreement about the amount of the bill." He pursed his lips. "A rather loud disagreement, if you understand what I mean."

Great.

I smiled at him through gritted teeth. "Thank you."

He responded with a sharp nod, turned on his heel, and went out to the foyer to wait for Quinn.

The detective was jotting something in his notebook again.

I, on the other hand, was striving to keep a poker face, because Kensington Bosworth's secretary had, more or less, accused my friend Randy Post of murder.

Chapter 4

Quinn looked up when he was finished with his note-taking. "Well, that was interesting."

"How so?" I asked brightly. Too brightly.

His eyes narrowed.

"What?" I tried a smile and failed. "Now, come on. You can't seriously think Randy had anything to do with this murder. He's a respected firefighter who happened to install a security system a couple of weeks ago. There was a disagreement about the bill, but so what?"

Lips pressed together, Quinn went into the other room. The sound of voices rose as he opened the door farther, and when he came back he was carrying a plastic bag. He brought it to me, and I saw the word EVIDENCE on the outside, as well as a form that documented the chain of custody of the contents. Inside was an object about a foot long and six inches wide. It was a figure of a doglike animal. A fox, perhaps, only instead of a fluffy tail, it had what looked like a long whip of a tail wrapped twice around itself.

A whip . . . or a snake.

The statue appeared to be carved of stone or, perhaps, a dark wood. However, I was pretty sure the red blotch at the base was Kensington Bosworth's blood.

Quinn confirmed my suspicion. "This was used to bludgeon the victim. It was found beside the body." He looked at it for several seconds, sighed, then turned his full attention back to me. "There's a stand behind the desk, empty except for a plaque that says 'Ginegosh.'"

"The statue the secretary described," I said, glancing toward the foyer where Cardwell was waiting.

Quinn took the hint and went over and closed the door.

Returning to my side, he said, "So not only did Randy Post argue with the victim and install the security system that had been turned off, he also coveted the statue that was used to kill Bosworth." He tried to keep his expression thoughtful, but I could tell he was relieved to think the case might be that simple. "Post felt he was owed more money, so he used his security code to sneak in and take the statue in lieu of payment. The victim unexpectedly walks in on him, and he strikes out with the very item he's stealing. All the magical paraphernalia aside, this doesn't look too complica—"

I interrupted. "Let me see it."

He pressed his lips together, then held the evidence bag out toward me.

I shuddered and covered my mouth when I saw there was even more blood than I'd thought, but I didn't look away. Instead, I forced myself to peer more closely, feeling a complicated energy coming from the figurine. It felt familiar, or perhaps it was more that I felt it *should* be familiar.

"My dad has a picture of something like this in a book of his." I paused, then reached out and touched the corner of the bag with my fingertip. "This is different, though. There's something . . . I don't know." I met Quinn's eyes. "But I bet my dad would."

Puzzlement creased his brow. "Your father's an expert in Native American artifacts?"

I shook my head. "He's a shaman."

Quinn just stared at me.

"Shawnee," I said.

The spellbook club seemed to think that it had been Dad's gifts combined with Mama being a hereditary hedgewitch that had made me a lightwitch.

"*Lightfoot*," he breathed.

I nodded. "Yep. Skylar Lightfoot. His given name was really Skylark, but his teachers kept dropping the K when he was in school, and it stuck. Anyway, he's coming to Savannah tomorrow, but I'd like to text him a picture of this now, if I may."

He licked his lips and looked down at the bag. "I don't know if that's such a great idea."

I shrugged. "Your call, of course. But just because my father isn't a professor at some university doesn't mean he doesn't know his stuff. I would think that in the course of your investigations you contact outside people for information all the time."

He frowned. "Of course we do. But this would be different. . . ."

"Well, you called me because you thought I might be able to help. And maybe I can. I don't know what the deal is with all this other magical stuff." I took in the room with a sweep of my arm. "But I might actually be able to get information about your murder weapon after all. Just not in the way you expected."

"I had no idea what to expect from you," he grumbled. "I never do." A deep breath, and he nodded. "Okay, take a couple of pictures and send them to your dad. But I want you to promise me something." He set the evidence bag down on an empty corner of the desk.

Taking out my phone, I turned on the camera feature and asked, "What's that?"

He gently put his hand over my wrist, and I looked up at him. "I mean it. Will you promise?" he asked.

"Well, how can I answer until you tell me what I'm going to promise?"

"Do promises mean anything special to people like, you know, witch types?"

"As special as to anyone else," I said, feeling a little insulted. Then I reconsidered. "Actually, that's not a bad question. Witches, at least those in the Wiccan tradition, try to live by the Rule of Three."

He looked uncomfortable.

"It's nothing weird," I assured him. "Think of it as karma on steroids. The idea is that anything you do comes back to you threefold—good or bad. The keeping and breaking of promises falls under the Rule."

He considered. "I want you to promise to show only your father the pictures you take of the murder weapon."

I thought about it, then, "Okay. I can promise that."

"Not Declan McCarthy," he said. "And most definitely not Randy Post."

Sighing, I said, "I won't show anyone besides my dad the pictures I take of the murder weapon. I promise." It wasn't like I really had a choice, after all.

Quinn turned the evidence bag over so the figurine wasn't obstructed by the writing on the front and stepped back. I snapped a photo, looked at it, and saw the light was reflecting off the plastic bag, which made it hard to capture a good picture of the contents. I moved around the desk to try from another angle.

The door to what I had already started to think of as the murder room opened and the white-haired gentleman called to Quinn. He went over to consult with him. I took another picture.

Quinn and the other man were discussing the time of death.

"I estimate he's been dead three to four hours. The housekeeper called 911 at six thirty?"

"A little after," Quinn said, glancing at his watch as if it would tell him when she called.

I looked at the time on my phone. It was ten minutes after eight.

Still listening hard, I turned on the video function and scanned the room, zooming in on the items displayed on the tables. I wanted to know what the spellbook club thought of Kensington Bosworth's magical collection, and I hadn't promised not to show anyone pictures of those items.

"So, the victim died between four and five," Quinn said. "Assuming death was instantaneous, or close to it."

"From that wound, I'd guess it was. We'll be able to say for sure after the autopsy."

So much for that last soup-and-sandwich supper.

"Thanks, Ed," Quinn said.

Ed Carrell. I recognized the name of the medical examiner from the paper.

I scrolled back to the photos of the evidence bag then visually scanned the other contents of the desk. A Rolodex sat next to the typewriter, and I leaned down to take a look. It was flipped open to a business card for a business ungrammatically called *How's Tricks.*

"Ahem." Quinn had rejoined me.

I tore my gaze away from the card.

"Get your photos?" he asked.

Showing him the best one, I said, "I'll send this to Dad tonight. But I still can't believe you seriously think Randy killed some poor old man."

Quinn's expression didn't change. "We'll explore all possibilities. You know that, Katie. But I must say, the victim was anything but poor. We'll investigate his finances, of course, but he was a member of one of Savannah's oldest families, a family whose wealth has only grown as time goes on."

"I didn't mean literally poor," I said. "More like pitiable. Because, you know, *he's been murdered.*"

"Oh." Quinn gave a nearly imperceptible shrug, then motioned with his chin. Obediently, I followed him out to the entryway.

"Thanks, Katie. Appreciate your help. Call me if you hear anything from your father about that statue."

"Okay." I wanted to say more, but Detective Quinn was already striding toward where the murder victim's secretary waited by the stairs. I started toward the door, then saw the blond woman still sitting in the same chair where she'd been when I walked in. Glancing over my shoulder, I saw Quinn's back was toward me. Casually, I veered toward the dining room and stepped inside.

The woman turned her head as I approached, bewilderment in her red-rimmed eyes. She wore a white chef's apron over a brown dress, and sensible shoes. Some of her hair had fallen out of its bun, so that lank tendrils clung to the sides of her heart-shaped face.

"Hello," I said. "You must be Mrs. Gleason."

She nodded but didn't speak.

"You found Mr. Bosworth?"

Her hand rose, and her fingertips brushed her lips before falling back into her lap. "In his office. On the floor."

I slid into the chair beside her, feeling torn. At least a dozen questions were ping-ponging around my brain. However, I couldn't bring myself to ask them of someone so obviously distressed. Mostly, I wanted to give her a steaming cup of tea steeped with lavender, chamomile, and licorice root to soothe the anxiety that hovered around her like an aura.

Anxious because she found him, or anxious because she killed him?

The uncharitable thought intruded before I could stop it. I pushed it away with an effort and leaned toward her. "Detective Quinn already spoke with you?"

Her hand dropped to her lap. "Briefly. He said to wait."

I felt my lips thin. "How long ago was that?"

She blinked. "I don't know. An hour?"

"Do you have someone to come get you when you're finished here?"

"Um, I guess my daughter could. But she doesn't need to do that. I can drive myself home." As she spoke, her words took on strength. "Really. I'll be fine."

"All right. I just—"

"Ms. Lightfoot, may I speak with you out here, please?" Quinn was standing in the doorway. His face was expressionless, but I could still sense his displeasure.

Popping to my feet, I said, "Sure thing. Excuse me, Mrs. Gleason." I touched her on the shoulder as I went by.

Back in the entryway, there was no sign of Malcolm Cardwell. I opened my mouth to ask where he was, but Quinn whirled around and hissed, "What do you think you're doing?"

My jaw set. "I was seeing if that poor woman was all right."

"That's all?"

"Of course." Never mind that my original intention hadn't been so altruistic. "She's obviously upset. Anyone would be, left in there for an hour, all by herself, with nothing to do but stew over finding her employer dead."

He took a deep breath and let it out before saying, "I'm going to talk to her now, and then she can go home." He gave me a pointed look and gestured toward the door. "You, on the other hand, can go home now."

"Right." I flashed a half smile and walked to the exit.

"Take care of yourself, Katie," he said from behind me as I yanked the door open.

Startled, I turned, but Quinn was already walking back where Mr. Bosworth's housekeeper waited in the dining room.

Declan still leaned against the porch column, only now his arms were folded over his chest, and his eyes had narrowed. He was watching the crowd gathered on the other side of the police tape, so he didn't see me at first. I followed his gaze and saw his attention was really on one person in particular.

Steve Dawes was chatting with a uniformed policewoman. She nodded at something he said, and he flashed a bright smile at her. Her body language shifted—a slight softening of her rigid posture. Charm practically oozed from the man's pores, and I knew exactly how it felt to be on the receiving end of it.

However, his clan of druids influenced business and political interests throughout the state, and they didn't respect the Rule of Three. I knew he was willing to do some things I didn't like, and he'd even dabbled in a bit of dark magic to try to convince me to leave Declan. So, of course, I was over my former attraction to Steve now.

Totally and completely over it.

Then he glanced up at me standing on the porch, and his brown-eyed gaze cut through the distance between us. I blinked, slightly stunned, and then my lips parted in surprise.

Oh, good Lord. Really? He's using some kind of spell to elicit information from that policewoman?

What was it, though? A glamour of some kind? His Voice?

I frowned at him and shook my head. He ducked his head sheepishly, then looked back at me with a grin. Then his expression became speculative, and I knew he was wondering why I'd been inside the house.

Declan turned to see what Steve was looking at and saw me standing a few feet behind him. He unfolded his arms, straightened, and strode over. "How'd it go?"

I looked up and met those eyes of blue I loved so, seeing quiet tenderness along with utter confidence. Sliding my arm around his waist, I said, "It was weird. I'll tell you about it on the way home."

"We have to run the gauntlet first." He nodded at Steve, who was watching us with avid interest. "Mr. Reporter has been working the crowd like a carnival barker."

"He's just doing his job," I said mildly.

Declan made a noise in the back of his throat.

Suddenly very weary, I rubbed one hand over my face. "Let's go."

We stepped off the porch, nodded to one of the officers keeping people back, and ducked under the yellow tape. Steve hurried over to meet us.

"Hey, guys," he said. "What's up?"

"Pretty sure you already know, or you wouldn't be here." Declan's words were clipped.

Steve's smile didn't quite reach his eyes. "Well, I know Kensington Bosworth is dead, but that's about it. Since the crime scene unit is here, I assume it wasn't from natural causes." He turned his attention to me. "And now I know it has something to do with our Katie-girl here."

The muscles in Declan's jaw flexed. He knew how much I disliked the nickname *Katie-girl*.

Steve continued, "Who apparently has a front-row seat." His head tipped to the side. "So. Tell me why you're here."

One side of my mouth turned up. "I don't think I'm supposed to be talking about anything going on in that house right now. And certainly not to a reporter."

"I've helped you out before," he said. "In fact, whenever you wanted my help, you got it, no questions asked."

I nodded. "And I appreciate it. Believe me, when I can tell you anything, I will. But right now, I just can't."

He glared at me for a few seconds, then his attitude softened. "All right. I get it. But what about off the record? Are you okay? Because you're obviously involved in another murder investigation."

Declan shifted his weight toward Steve. "Katie's fine. Quinn just wanted to consult her about something."

Steve's eyes widened. "Quinn is consulting you now? How did *that* happen?"

I looked down at the toes of my trail runners. "I sort of told him what I am."

When I looked back up, he was staring at me. "You told Quinn you're a witch."

"Yeah. And a lightwitch. And about Franklin Taite."

He let out a low whistle. "Why on earth would you do that?"

"He kind of saw me, you know . . ." I sighed. "Glow."

"Oh. Oh, wow. Well, yeah. I guess you'd have to explain that some way." He peered at me. "How did he take it?"

"With a grain of salt, I expect. He's a pretty down-to-earth guy, after all. But when he saw Bosworth's collection of—" I stopped, but his eyes had already lit up.

"Collection of what?"

"Off the record," I said. "Bosworth collected magical paraphernalia."

Steve started to ask another question, but I held up my hand. "That's all I'm going to say right now."

"But—"

"Nope," I said. "Maybe later." And then completely changing the subject, I asked, "How's Angie?" I was referring to his girlfriend, another witch. They'd been dating for about six months.

"Fine," he said.

But there was something in the way he said that single word. I would have pursued it, but I could sense Declan's impatience. Instead, I simply said, "Tell her hello for me," and turned toward where Mungo waited for us in Declan's truck. "And I promise I won't give any other reporter information."

"Better not," he mumbled, already scanning for someone else to question.

As Declan and I drove away, the WSAV news van turned the corner.

"Looks like Mr. Reporter is going to have some real competition," Declan said, flipping on his turn signal.

"Mmm-hmm," I said.

He glanced over at me, then returned his attention to the road. "What did Quinn want to ask you?"

"About the murder weapon," I said. "And like I said, Bosworth had quite the collection of magical paraphernalia. From different disciplines and from all around the world. It felt pretty weird in that house, let me tell you." Not to mention the protection spell around the house.

"What was the murder weapon?"

"A statue thingy," I said. After all, Quinn hadn't made me promise not to tell Declan, only not to show him the pictures I took of it. "But I don't know what it is. Something Native American. I'm going to ask my dad."

Declan nodded as he stopped the truck at a red light. "Good idea." Then he let out a whoosh of relief. "Boy, am I glad that's all it was. I was afraid you were going to get dragged into tracking down Bosworth's killer right in the middle of all the other stuff we have going on."

I didn't say anything.

He half turned in his seat and gave me a sharp look. "Katie?"

I made a face. "There's one tiny complication."

He waited.

"Quinn already has a suspect. Bosworth's secretary said there was an argument between him and the victim and that he seemed to have a special interest in what turned out to be the murder weapon." I licked my lips. "Also, the security alarm was turned off even though Bosworth always armed it. Since the suspect installed it, he might have been able to disable it."

Realization gradually dawned on my fiancé's face. "He thinks *Randy* killed Bosworth?"

I nodded.

The light turned green, and Declan slowly accelerated. "Well, we have to prove Quinn wrong then! Randy's a stand-up guy. He'd never kill anyone over money—or anything else."

"I know," I said quietly. "I don't know how, but we'll figure out how to help him."

So much for not getting dragged into this one.

Back home, I texted the picture of the murder weapon to my dad. I wasn't surprised when he didn't respond, though. He had an early flight and then a layover in Atlanta in the morning, so he'd probably already gone to bed. I considered texting Mama to make sure but decided against it. The mood I was in, the last thing I wanted was to explain to her that I seemed to have landed in yet another murder case— and no, I still didn't want my bridesmaids to wear tiaras during the wedding ceremony.

I did, however, call Lucy and tell her what had happened to Kensington Bosworth.

"Oh my," she said when I'd finished. "And Peter Quinn asked you to come to the house? That's unusual."

"I'll say. But he thought I could help. Who knows? Maybe I can. There's some kind of magic involved, for sure. The house was surrounded by a serious protection spell."

She tsked. "I can't believe we just saw Kensington this afternoon, and now he's been killed. Terrible. Just terrible." Lucy had the tenderest heart of anyone I knew. "Do you know anything about his family?"

"Not a thing," I said.

"Well, Mimsey will know something. She knows all the old families here in Savannah. I'll give her a call and mobilize the ladies. We can meet in the morning."

"Okay, but my bet is that Bianca either already knows or will know soon."

There was silence for several seconds, and then my aunt sighed. "Oh, dear. There's something you haven't told me, isn't there?"

"Afraid so," I said, and filled her in on what Bosworth's secretary had said about Randy.

"Well, that's just ridiculous," Lucy said. "That boy didn't kill anyone."

"I know. For now, all we can do is wait and see what Quinn does." A part of me hoped the detective would find another suspect, and fast. After all, he'd only begun his investigation. "Let's wait until we're all together to tell the ladies about Randy. I'll see you tomorrow."

"All right, honey," she said. "And don't worry. It will all work out."

I hung up and plugged in my phone on the kitchen counter. Declan had already gone into the bedroom, but Mungo trotted over and sat by my foot. I leaned down and gave him a scratch behind the ears.

"Lucy says it will all work out," I said. "I sure hope she's right."

He grinned a doggy grin. *Yip!*

Chapter 5

I'd never been one to sleep much. It wasn't insomnia, or at least not the enervating, debilitating version I knew some unfortunates suffered from. I went through my days with plenty of energy. By the time I moved to Savannah, I slept only a couple of hours a night. This was awesome for a baker, of course, as we regularly hit the kitchen at o'dark thirty. However, since I had learned I was a witch and began practicing my own spell work, the amount of sleep I managed had increased to three, sometimes even four, hours a night.

Most nights, that was.

That night wasn't one of them. My mind was awhirl with thoughts about Kensington Bosworth's murder, Randy being Quinn's prime suspect, and what the motive for killing the fussy old gentleman could possibly have been. Greed? Love? Revenge? Those were the classics. Or could it be magically motivated? I had a hard time imagining Mr. Bosworth as a sorcerer extraordinaire, but someone had cast that protection spell.

Whatever the reason, I was positive Randy was innocent. Along with the rest of the ladies in the spellbook club, I'd gotten to know him since he and Bianca had begun to date, and Declan knew him even better as a coworker. Randy Post was a good guy.

I finally gave up trying to get back to sleep around four o'clock and slipped out to the living room. There I donned shorts, T-shirt, and running shoes. Mungo watched from the sofa as I quietly filled a water bottle at the sink and tiptoed to the door. He didn't try to follow. A walk in the park was one thing, but he loathed running as much as he did dry doggy kibble.

After stretching at the bottom of the stairs outside, I swigged some water and took off toward the river. After a few blocks, my muscles loosened and my breath steadied. There were only a few vehicles on the streets at this hour and even less foot traffic. Night-lights glowed orange behind curtained windows, while the setting moon was a pale beacon in the mercury sky. The summer air, heavy with humidity and the scents of wisteria and night-blooming nicotiana, caressed my limbs as I moved through it.

Gradually, the rhythmic sound of my footfalls jostled my thoughts and concerns into some kind of order. I could count on my dad and Declan to deal with the carriage house renovation. My worrying about it wouldn't help a thing and would make what I had on my own plate more difficult. I simply had to try to let that go.

Sure. I could do that.

I hoped.

Cookie's baby shower was coming up, but the truth was Lucy was having a great time putting it all together. She didn't need my help at all. I'd still be available and would check in with her but could completely take that off my mental to-do list as well.

The wedding was pretty much in hand, other than getting the actual venue in shape—which I had just decided not to worry about. We had a few details yet to tend to. I still wanted to find the perfect gifts for my bridesmaids—the members of the spellbook club, naturally—and I still hadn't decided on what flavor of wedding cake I wanted. But I had a month, and I'd figure that out.

Somehow.

By the time I headed back to the apartment, I felt better about looking into Kensington Bosworth's murder. Of course, I wanted justice, and of course I wanted to clear Randy's name, but I also felt a strange urgency about the case that stemmed from the feeling I'd had in Bosworth's house. Why had it been surrounded by a protection spell? What was up with the collection of magical items? I'd felt a lot of power in that outer office, and the office beyond it. Some of it had to be latent energy from the items themselves, but there had been something beyond that. A force more than the sum of those parts.

And not all of that energy had been good, either.

The horizon brightened as I ran, the dawn bruising the sky deep purple, then fading to violet and red, and finally brilliant peach fingers of cirrus clouds reached toward me from the west. The sight energized me and gave me hope.

I'd talk to Randy. He would be able to shed some light on the supposed altercation between him and the murder victim, not to mention how someone might breach the security system. And Dad should be able to help us with the significance of the murder weapon. What was it called? Ginegosh? I'd never heard the term and made a mental note to look that up on the Internet.

What else?

Well, Mimsey would have some information about Kensington Bosworth. Mrs. Standish might be willing to fill in more of those details. No, strike that. I'd have a hard time *stopping* her from telling us more about him.

With the beginnings of a plan, I let myself back into the apartment. I was surprised to find Declan in the kitchen making coffee. The fragrance of freshly ground beans hit my nose and I nearly swooned.

"How was it?" he asked as I kissed him on the cheek and bent to untie my shoes.

"Good. It's always good. Clears my head. You should try it."

"No, thanks. I'll head to the gym before I pick up your dad," he said, blinking at me with sleepy eyes. It was quarter to five.

"What are you doing up so early?" I asked.

"Couldn't sleep."

"Randy?"

"Yeah."

I nodded. "A lot of that going around. I'm going to hit the shower."

I was pouring the batter for gooseberry muffins into tins when Dad texted me a bit after six. The loaves of sourdough had just come out of the ovens, and their thick crusts crackled as they cooled on their racks. Lemon cornmeal cookies filled another rack, and below them were black-and-white cookies, though I hadn't yet dipped them in their dark chocolate jackets. The scent of the maple scones in the oven joined the other good baking smells in the air.

Dad's text read:

An evidence bag? And is that blood? Good Lord, Katie—what have you gotten yourself into this time? But yes, that figurine looks like a totem of some kind. Algonquin, maybe Chippewa. We'll talk when I get there.

A totem. Of course.

Not like the big totem poles common in the Northwest, but a smaller version that still represented the animal qualities of a tribe or an individual. For example, my dragonflies represented adaptability and metamorphosis. Dad would know what qualities the fox and snake represented.

I was pouring buttermilk pound-cake batter into loaf pans when Lucy and Ben came in the back door of the Honeybee several minutes later. My aunt's feline familiar sauntered out of her designer leather carrier and took up her spot in the window of the reading area. Lucy went into the office to drop her things, and I heard her greet Mungo with affection before she bustled back out to don a blue-and-yellow chintz apron from the vintage collection that hung along the back wall of the kitchen.

The sound of the espresso machine signaled Ben's desire for more caffeine. I already felt jittery enough and declined when he called out to ask if I wanted a cup. This might be a long day, but after drinking

Declan's brew, I wouldn't dip into the really strong stuff until I needed it midday.

Lucy was already making the ganache for the black-and-whites when Ben joined us. He put his wife's green tea by her elbow and leaned against the door of the industrial refrigerator.

My aunt gave him a grateful glance, took a sip from the steaming cup, then looked at me. "The spellbook club will be here this morning."

"Thanks for calling them," I said. "I'm hoping Randy—"

The loud chirping of crickets erupted from Ben's pocket. He pulled out his phone and frowned. "It's Scott," he said, then, "Hello?"

Lucy and I exchanged glances. Uncle Ben had been Savannah's fire chief until his retirement three years before. That was when he and Lucy had brainstormed the idea of opening the Honeybee Bakery and had convinced me to quit my low-paying and utterly dull job as an assistant bakery manager in Akron and move south. Scott had taken Randy under his wing much the same way Ben had with Declan years earlier.

"You're kidding! In cuffs? That's just overkill." Ben pushed away from the fridge and went to stand by the window overlooking the alley. "Uh-huh," he said. "Right. And she was there the whole time?" And then, "Well, that's good news, I guess. Did he go home?" He listened for a few seconds. "Good man. Okay. Thanks for calling. I'll be in touch."

He hung up and turned to face us. "Detective Quinn picked Randy up last night and took him down to the precinct. In handcuffs."

Lucy's fingers crept to her lips. "Surely that wasn't necessary."

"Damn straight, it wasn't necessary. I don't know what Quinn's trying to prove but treating one of my firefighters like that . . ." He trailed off as he realized what he'd said. "Okay, not my firefighter, not anymore, but it wasn't like Randy was going to resist arrest."

"They *arrested* him?" I asked. Things were moving far too quickly and in the wrong direction.

Ben shook his head. "They questioned him for a few hours and then let him go."

Alarmed, I asked, "For a few hours? In the middle of the night? Without a lawyer?"

"He's no dope," my uncle said. "He called Scott, who called Jaida. She was there the whole time."

I let out a breath of relief.

A knocking on the front door drew our attention.

"Speak of the devil," Lucy said as she hurried to let Jaida in. Ben and I were right behind her.

Jaida French was a vivacious black woman in her middle forties, but this morning she looked about ten years older. She'd obviously had very little sleep, wore no makeup, and rather than her usual lawyerly attire, she wore jeans and a loose T-shirt that I suspected belonged to her partner—in law and in life—Gregory. She was one of Savannah's best defense attorneys, who also happened to be a member of the spellbook club. She specialized in all things tarot and had taught me a lot about how to use the cards for divination and in spell work. Her familiar, a Great Dane named Anubis, would be at home this morning.

"Coffee," she rasped, collapsing onto a bistro chair.

Ben hurried to the espresso counter to fill her request.

"Have you eaten?" Lucy asked at the same time I asked, "How's Randy?"

"No, I'm starving," she said. "And they let Randy go about an hour ago. I take it you heard what happened?"

"Ben just got off the phone with his boss," I said.

"His captain," Ben corrected me, followed by the screech of the steamer as he concocted Jaida's usual mocha latte.

I sat down across from her. "How bad is it?"

Lucy came back with a still-warm maple scone on a plate. She set it in front of our friend and pulled over a chair for herself.

"Not good," Jaida said. "But it could be worse. They don't have enough of a case to arrest him at this point, but forensics haven't come back yet. From what Randy told me, his prints very well might be on the murder weapon. Apparently, it's some kind of Native American figurine, and he'd asked the victim if he could look at it when he was there putting in the security system." She took a bite and rolled her eyes. "This is fantastic. Thank you." She swallowed. "The security system is another problem. There was a master code Randy used when he was working on it. You're supposed to wipe that when the installation is complete, which he insists he did. But he can't prove whether he did that right after the installation as he claims or after killing Bosworth, which is what Detective Quinn is positing."

"Great," I said.

She took another bite and nodded. "I know."

There was a pounding on the door, and we looked up to see Bianca standing on the sidewalk. I moved to let her in as Ben brought Jaida her coffee.

Out of all the members of the spellbook club, Bianca looked the most like the stereotypical version of a witch. She practiced traditional Wiccan spell casting and had an avid interest in moon magic. Tall and willowy, she had jet black hair that reached most of the way down her back, and translucently pale skin. This morning, however, her brilliant green eyes were red-rimmed and puffy. Like Jaida, Bianca's usual fashion sense had been eclipsed by circumstances. I'd never seen her wear yoga pants in public, and I was pretty sure that was an orange juice stain on her far-too-warm-for-July sweatshirt. However, she still carried a Coach handbag, and a little white face with a black Zorro mask peeked out of it when she set it on a chair: her ferret familiar, Puck.

Lucy sprang up to give her a hug. "Oh, honey."

"You okay?" I asked.

Bianca's jaw set in a determined line. "So you've heard."

"From Scott," I said. "How's Colette?" I asked, referring to her eight-year-old daughter, who absolutely adored her mother's boyfriend.

"At a friend's house for the night," Bianca and Jaida responded at the same time. "She doesn't know anything about what's going on yet," Bianca went on.

Ben brought her a cup of coffee, and there was another knock. This time it was Mimsey Carmichael. My uncle glanced at the big clock on the wall as he went to let her in.

"It's nearly seven. Might as well open up," he said.

Mimsey bustled in as soon as he unlocked the front door. Short, pleasingly plump, and looking nowhere near her actual age of eighty-one, the spellbook club's informal leader had owned Vase Value for decades. So, it wasn't surprising that she focused on flower magic, along with color magic and dabbling in a bit of divination with her pink crystal shew stone. Today she wore a sensible skirt and matching top in light blue, and a light blue bow perched on the side of her white pageboy haircut. I knew she'd deliberately chosen that color because it represented tranquillity and protection. Her familiar was an obnoxious parrot named Heckle who, thank goodness, usually preferred his perch in the flower shop to coming to the Honeybee.

She took one look at the four of us huddled around the little bistro table and shook her head. "Now, ladies. We simply mustn't despair. Kensington Bosworth has passed through the veil to the next plane, and we cannot help him anymore. However, Bianca's beau is another matter."

I raised my eyebrows at Lucy, who shook her head. Mimsey hadn't found out about Randy being a suspect from her.

Mimsey went on. "Don't look so surprised, Katie. News like this travels fast. Bianca called me on her way over here."

"Cookie, too," Bianca said.

"Good," the older witch said. Now, let's move into the library and discuss next steps."

The door opened, and three customers came in and

headed toward the register. Cookie Rios was right behind them, talking animatedly on her cell phone.

Lucy jumped up. "It appears we're all here. You all go stake a claim in the reading area. I'll be with you as soon as I can."

Bianca, Jaida, and I stood as Lucy went to stock the display case with the baked goods that had been cooling in the kitchen and help Ben with the customers. Mimsey led the way to the Honeybee library. Lined with shelves that held all manner of titles for our patrons to peruse at their leisure, it also boasted a big poufy sofa and matching chairs upholstered in jewel-toned brocade.

Cookie trailed behind, still on the phone.

"All right, then. Eleven it is. Thanks for being flexible." She hung up and looked at me. "I was supposed to show a house this morning, but my client's pretty easygoing. I just hope we don't lose our chance at this one."

"Sorry." I grabbed the RESERVED sign and hung it by the entrance to the reading area, so we'd have a modicum of privacy.

Her jade-colored eyes widened. "No, no! That's not what I meant. There's always something, you know? And if the spellbook club needs me, I'm here."

Though she'd moved to Savannah from Haiti when still a child, a slight accent still flavored her words. The youngest member of the spellbook club at twenty-six, she practiced Wiccan magic with the rest of us but had lately begun to delve back into her family's voodoo traditions. She was recently married, and even more recently pregnant. In her second trimester, she was still slender beneath her yellow sundress except for her healthily expanding middle. Her dark hair fell in thick waves around her shoulders, and brightly colored plastic bangles were stacked on her wrists.

As we settled in the reading area, Lucy brought in peppermint tea for Cookie and cups of plain black coffee for Mimsey and Bianca. I shook my head in response to her questioning look, and she returned to help Ben with the early customers.

Mimsey folded her hands on her lap and turned to me. "Katie, Lucille shared the information you gave her on the phone last night, so we know the situation. Is there any more news?"

I nodded. "The police picked Randy up for questioning last night. Jaida stepped in to help."

"Right," Jaida said, apparently feeling better after getting some food and caffeine in her system. She filled the others in on what she'd told us.

When she was finished, Mimsey nodded again. "Well, it could be worse. I do wish Detective Quinn would just take our word that he needs to look elsewhere, but soon enough we'll have a better suspect for him."

I made a noise.

"Now, Katie," she said. "You know darn well you've been called again." No matter what I said, she believed I would always step up to my calling as a lightwitch.

Oh, who was I fooling? Even Peter Quinn had called me. Literally. And I'd already decided to do what I could.

So instead of protesting, I said to Mimsey, "Lucy

said you knew Kensington Bosworth. What can you tell us about him?"

She took a sip from her mug and settled back on her chair. Her feet didn't quite reach the floor. "I didn't know Kensington terribly well. He was quite a bit younger than me, you know. At least fifteen years. My youngest sister went to school with his sister, though, and I know a bit about the family. Fifth generation, old Savannahians. His grandfather traveled a great deal, and rumor was he collected odd things from around the world. Kensington's father apparently continued the tradition."

Things had slowed down at the register, and Lucy came over and sat next to me on the sofa.

I took my phone out of my apron pocket. "His collection might strike a little closer to home once you see it." I found the video I'd taken while Quinn had been talking to the crime scene technician. I held it out and everyone leaned forward. "These things were displayed in his outer office, and apparently there were more in his personal office. I didn't see those, because, well . . . he was still in there."

There were sober looks all around.

"So, he collected magical items," Jaida said thoughtfully. "Is that why Quinn called you?"

"I'm sure of it. I mean, there was also a Honeybee Bakery bag in the kitchen, but I think he saw this stuff on display and thought, *Gee, do I know any witches? Why yes, yes, I do!*"

"Even though many of these items were probably inherited," Cookie said, taking the phone and watching the video again. "I don't know about you, but I've never run into Mr. Bosworth in any of our magical circles."

We all shook our heads and murmured agreement.

"Quinn specifically wanted me to look at the murder weapon," I said.

Jaida gave me a sharp look. "You've seen it?"

"In an evidence bag, yes. And I took a picture to show my dad. He texted me this morning and confirmed it's a piece, maybe from the Chippewa tribe. Specifically, a totem."

Bianca's lips pressed together, but she didn't say anything.

"Where's the picture you took of it?" Cookie asked, beginning to scroll through my photos.

Gently, I took the phone away from her. "I promised not to show anyone."

"Why?" Jaida demanded.

"Because Quinn asked me to promise."

"Because he thought Randy was involved," Jaida said.

"Yes," I said.

"Well, he's already talked to Randy about it, so I don't think he'd care if you showed us now."

I hesitated, then shook my head. "A promise is a promise. Remember the Rule of Three. I don't need any blowback if I break it."

Bianca glared at me.

Mimsey nodded. "Of course, dear. We understand."

But I wasn't so sure Bianca did.

Chapter 6

"What else can you tell us?" I asked Mimsey.

"Not a lot. He had money, of course. I assume his sister does, too. If she's still with us. I don't know what happened to her. I'll call Marcella and ask if she knows."

"Is Marcella your younger sister? The one who went to school with Kensington's sister?" I asked.

"Yes. She's the youngest of the three. Mimsey, Nessarose, and Marcella. Nessarose is two years younger than me. Lives in one of those RV communities near Sedona. Marcella was a bit of a surprise to Mummy and Daddy, though. She's only sixty-three," she said.

"All witches?" I asked.

"To varying degrees." She made a face. "Nessarose has more flair than talent, but certainly likes to dress the part down there in Arizona."

I felt a twinge of envy. My mother and father had kept my gifts from me, and as a child I'd never known why I felt so different. I would never regain the time

I could have spent learning about the Craft and herbal magic.

A speculative expression settled on Cookie's face. "I wonder who gets all that lovely, lovely money."

"Mr. Bosworth's attorney should know," Jaida said. "Though it's doubtful a lawyer would divulge that information to anyone prior to filing for probate."

"Whoever it is might tell the police, and Quinn might tell me," I said, then shrugged. "Or not. I'm not sure."

Jaida took a deep breath. "Okay, Mimsey is going to call her sister about Bosworth's sister. Katie can check with Quinn about his attorney, and I'll put out feelers among my colleagues as well." She looked at me. "What else?"

"I thought I'd go see Mrs. Standish," I said. "She seemed well acquainted with him. In fact, she was right on the edge of divulging some gossip about Mr. Bosworth yesterday. Remember, Lucy?"

My aunt nodded. "She's bound to know something, and she loves to dish. I'll go with you to see her this morning after Iris comes in for her shift."

"Excellent," Mimsey said.

"I'd like to talk to Randy, too," I said. "See what he can tell me about the security system."

"I already asked him a ton of questions along those lines," Jaida said.

"Still, we need to talk with him. He might tell us something he didn't tell the police."

Bianca's eyes filled with tears.

I put my hand on her arm. "It's going to be okay."

She pulled her arm away. "You can't know that."

I withdrew my hand and looked down. She was right, of course. Just because I'd successfully investigated some crimes in the past didn't mean I'd be able to do it again this time. Meeting her eyes again, I said, "Well, we're going to do the best we can."

"What about this secretary of Bosworth's?" Bianca asked. "What's his name?"

"Malcolm Cardwell," I said.

"I'm going to go see him after I drop Colette off at summer art camp this afternoon."

"Um, he struck me as a bit . . . difficult," I began. "I don't think—"

"I want to talk to the man who accused Randy of murder," she insisted.

"Now, honey," Mimsey said.

Bianca glowered at the older woman.

Mimsey gave her a gentle smile in return.

"Listen, y'all," Bianca drawled. Suddenly, despite the orange-juice-stained sweatshirt, she was all elegant Southern charm. It was as if she'd flipped a switch. "I promise I'll behave myself. I simply wish to ask the gentleman a few questions."

I quirked an eyebrow. "He's kind of a stuffed shirt. I bet he'd respond to that Southern belle thing of yours."

"*Thing?* Bless your heart, darlin', but I haven't a clue what you mean."

"Uh-huh." I looked at my watch. "My dad will be here around ten, but then he and Declan will head over to the carriage house this afternoon. Let's try to track down Mr. Cardwell's address and drop by around two o'clock or so. If you don't mind my coming with you, of course."

Actually, Bianca looked relieved. "Thanks."

Cookie was typing on her phone. "Six-eighteen Fallow Road," she said.

"What?" I asked.

"I remember the name. Malcolm and Suzanne Cardwell recently bought a four-bedroom house. I didn't sell it to them, but my colleague did. I just checked our internal database at the office to get the address. It's faster than looking it up online or going over to the courthouse."

Mimsey grinned. "Nice work, dear." She beamed around at all of us. "It sounds like we have our action items all lined up."

I stood. "I'd better get a little more baking done before we start, then."

At eight, Iris came in and got right to work making breakfast sandwiches for a group of four tourists. At eight thirty, Lucy phoned Mrs. Standish, apologizing for breaching etiquette with such an early call. We were both crowded into the office, me in front of the computer, looking up *Ginegosh*, and Lucy perched next to Mungo on his club chair. Though she wasn't on speaker, I could hear every word Mrs. Standish said.

"Please, think nothing of it! Skipper and I would be delighted for you to come by the house. Anytime. Right now, in fact. I'll be able to give you a treat for once!" Then her voice lowered, but not so much that I couldn't still hear her. "Now, tell me, Lucy. Does this have anything to do with Kensington's death?"

"You know about that already?" Lucy asked.

Sighing, I shut off the monitor and swiveled the desk chair to face her. There was nothing remotely related to the term *Ginegosh* on the Internet. I could only hope Dad would have an idea what the name meant.

"It was right there on the front page of the *News*!" Mrs. Standish boomed. "Terrible, terrible tragedy, of course. But there was mention of a special consultant to the police, and lo and behold, there was your Katie in the background of the picture."

I whirled around to turn the monitor back on. In seconds I'd brought up the online version of the *Savannah Morning News*. Sure enough, Steve's article was front and center, along with a photo of the house surrounded by police tape and Declan and me on the front porch. It must have been taken right after I'd come back outside after talking with Quinn.

Great.

Lucy finished the call and hung up. "If we leave now, we should get back before Declan and your dad get here."

"I'll drive," I said.

"Deal." She stood.

Mungo moved to the edge of the chair and tipped his head to the side.

"You want to come?" I asked.

He gave a soft *yip!* and jumped down to the floor.

Back out front, I set Iris to making up a batch of green tomato muffins that Lucy and I had recently concocted. It was a riff on classic fried green tomatoes with a little thyme sprinkled in to give whoever ate them courage and a positive attitude.

Because really, who couldn't use a little more of that in their lives?

Thyme could also be used in love and protection spells, to attract money, and to promote intuition and sleep. As we left, I heard Iris muttering over the mixing bowl, "Thyme plus heat in this yummy treat for folks to eat, oh, so sweet . . . no, that's not quite right. Um . . ."

Grinning, I left her to it. The words didn't matter so much as the focused intention, and she obviously had that handled.

Outside, Mungo allowed me to attach his leash to his collar, and we set off with Lucy for my car. Once inside the Bug, I blasted the air-conditioning and turned toward Bull Street. I'd never been to Mrs. Standish's home, but Lucy had delivered food there for an Animal Welfare Society fund-raiser.

In between my aunt's murmured directions, we chatted about wedding cakes.

"Do you want to go with something more like a handfasting cake than a traditional wedding cake?" Lucy asked. A handfasting was the neo-pagan version of a wedding.

My brow wrinkled. "How would that be different than a traditional wedding cake?"

"Turn left at the next light," she said. "Handfasting cakes are often less formal, but not always. And they typically have some kind of Celtic or Wiccan imagery on them."

Most of the guests weren't remotely pagan, and Declan wasn't, either, so we'd decided to have a straightforward ceremony presided over by Judge Matthews.

"Well, I like the idea of decorating the cake with

Celtic symbols, but I keep coming back to the image of a simple three-tiered cake decorated with fresh flowers. I'm thinking gerbera daisies. So, I have a good idea of how I want it to look. The problem is that I don't know how I want it to *taste*."

"You love carrot cake, and it's one of the most popular flavors for wedding cakes," she said.

"I adore carrot cake. And devil's food cake. And red velvet cake. And German chocolate cake . . ." I trailed off.

"Sometimes tiered cakes have a different flavor for each level," she pointed out.

"I know," I grumped. And I did. "But I'm having trouble choosing only three flavors."

She laughed. "How about coconut? Or a hummingbird cake? Caramel pecan? Strawberry?"

I groaned. "Stop it!"

We crossed into a new block, and Lucy pointed at a stately gray-brick home on the other side of the street. "That's it."

I pulled my car to the curb, and we all got out. Mrs. Standish had the door open before we were halfway up the walk. She wore a brilliant white caftan, a matching white turban, and white sandals with rhinestones. Other than a slash of lipstick the same dark red as her nail polish, her face was free of makeup.

"Hello!" she sang out, waving us in.

"Is it all right that I brought Mungo along?" I asked.

"Of course! Does he eat caviar?"

I blinked. "Um. I don't see why not."

"Excellent. Come along, then."

We hurried inside, and she quickly shut the door behind us. I could see why she wouldn't want to let in the heat, but after only a few seconds I felt a shiver threaten the back of my neck. The house was like an ice locker.

"Come back to the sunroom," she said. "Dean is waiting for us there."

We obediently followed her through a spacious living room with high ceilings and skylights that let in abundant light. I'd assumed Mrs. Standish would furnish her home with antiques and fussy knickknacks, so I was surprised to see the light wood furniture was spare and avant-garde with a Scandinavian flair, and the rugs and pillows had simple patterns and boasted bright, primary colors.

"Here we are, dears!"

She led us into a round, glassed-in room with a view of the swimming pool in the backyard. Here the furniture was white wicker decked with yellow chintz pillows, all surrounded with flowering plants in huge pots. Skipper Dean, wearing white slacks and a blue linen shirt, lounged beneath an arching bougainvillea. In front of him, a table held a sweating pitcher of fresh orange juice, miniature bagels, lox, cream cheese, capers, red onions, minced hard-boiled eggs, and yes, a lovely pot of shimmering black caviar. Mungo immediately went to sit by Dean's foot and was rewarded with a pet on the head and a nibble of bagel spread with cream cheese.

"Hello, little guy," Dean said. "Lucy, Katie, please have a seat. We're so glad you could visit this morning."

"Thanks for letting us barge in so early." I settled

in a chair flanked by two pygmy orange trees loaded with fruit.

"Nonsense." Mrs. Standish filled a plate and sank onto a chaise lounge. She waved her hand at the table. "Please have a bite."

Suddenly very hungry, I obliged.

"Now." She set her plate aside and folded her hands. "How can I help?"

Lucy and I exchanged glances.

"You know what happened to Kensington Bosworth, right?" I asked.

Mrs. Standish nodded. "At least what was in the paper. Why were you there?"

"Um," I hedged. "Detective Quinn thought I could help with a question he had."

She leaned forward. "And could you?"

"That remains to be seen." I considered exactly what to tell her and decided the truth, or at least part of it, would be the best course. "The problem is that the police suspect Randy Post of killing Mr. Bosworth."

Her eyebrows raised so high they disappeared beneath her turban for a moment. "Now, why on earth would they suspect him?"

Lucy spoke up. "Apparently Mr. Bosworth and Randy argued. Something to do with payment for the security system Randy installed. As I recall, you mentioned something about how you hoped Mr. Bosworth wouldn't balk at the bill."

Mrs. Standish nodded emphatically. "Kensington was rich as Midas, but he had a miserly streak in him. As did his daddy and granddaddy. Not so much with causes, but with people. Philanthropy was a family tradition, but they were terrible about paying the help. I imagine that secretary of his was underpaid, and I heard he'd cut back the housekeeper's hours."

The housekeeper, Mrs. Gleason, who'd found the security system disarmed and then her employer dead in his office. I thought again of the grilled cheese sandwich she'd been going to make for Mr. Bosworth's supper and added a chat with her to my list.

"Heaven knows it's hard enough to find a good housekeeper," she mused. "I desperately miss my Alda since she got married and moved away. Happy for her, of course! But we've had to make do with a service, and it's just not the same."

"I see," I said. "You mentioned something about how Mr. Bosworth wasn't giving to charity the same way."

Now her head swung back and forth. "Indeed, he wasn't. He used to be so good about contributing to my animal causes, but in the last two years he gave only a pittance in comparison to his earlier generosity. I heard rumors through the grapevine that he had become involved with some shady characters."

"Really? Like who?"

"I'm afraid I don't know the specifics." She grimaced. "Such a shame. Apparently, he short-shrifted the other charities he'd avidly supported before and was donating to someone new."

"What charities were those?" Lucy asked.

Mrs. Standish looked blank.

"He gave to organizations that promoted Native American cultural preservation," Skipper Dean said.

He'd been so quiet that I'd almost forgotten he was sitting there.

"And there was an organization that returned pilfered treasures to their homelands in Egypt and the Middle East," he continued.

"Well, dog my cat!" Mrs. Standish exclaimed. "I had no idea."

Dean gave her an affectionate smile.

"Could he have been under some kind of financial strain?" I wondered.

"Lord, no. The man was loaded," Mrs. Standish said. "Though he once joked that he hoped to spend the majority of his fortune before he died. At least I assumed it was a joke. His heirs would have been very sorry if that had happened."

I scooted to the edge of the chair and leaned my elbows on my knees. "Do you know anything about his will or his heirs?"

"Not really," she admitted. "He and his sister, Florinda, inherited the family fortune. Kensington got more money than Florinda, though. His daddy was a sexist pig, you see. But she still got quite a lot. In the millions, certainly." She took a bite of bagel, chewed, and swallowed. "She lost it all, though."

I frowned. "*All* of it?"

"Mmm-hmm." Her voice lowered a fraction. "Had a bit of a gambling problem, you see."

"Ah," Lucy and I said at the same time.

"I imagine she'll be awfully happy to get any money Kensington left her," Mrs. Standish said. "I just hope she doesn't gamble that away, too."

Cookies and Clairvoyance

"He didn't leave her any money, honeywaffles," Skipper Dean said.

Honeywaffles? Really? I stifled a smile.

Her head whipped around. "How do you know that?"

He shrugged. "We were chatting at a fund-raiser recently. I try to be a good listener."

My lips twitched. He'd had plenty of practice, considering his housemate.

"Well!" she brayed. "Tell us what you know!"

Another mild smile from Dean, and then, "Kensington said his sister had found a balanced life, and he didn't want to upset her by dumping a bunch of money in her lap."

Lucy and I exchanged glances.

As if.

Dean noticed. "No, he was serious. She had indeed suffered from a gambling problem, and giving her money was only going to upset her equilibrium. He felt it was a kindness not to burden her with temptation. However, he did leave some to her son."

My ear perked up at that. "So, his nephew?"

"Indeed." Mrs. Standish leaned forward and reached for another bagel with one hand and the caviar spoon with the other.

Skipper Dean didn't know the name of Florinda's son when I asked.

Mrs. Standish held up one finger as she finished chewing and swallowed. Then she said, "Florinda divorced her first husband when her son was still a teenager. I believe she's remarried since then, but we

don't exactly run in the same circles anymore. . . ."
She trailed off.

Skipper Dean cleared his throat. "Edna, what was
Florinda's first husband's name?"

She looked thoughtful, then brightened. "It was
Bundy! I remember, because I thought he was such a
cad, and at the time I wondered if he could have been
related to that murdering sociopath, Ted Bundy."

My jaw slackened in surprise, but she didn't notice.

"Of course, he wasn't actually a serial killer—or at
least if he was, they never caught him!" She grinned.
"But I do remember that name. Kensington's nephew's
last name must be Bundy."

"I love Mrs. Standish to death," I remarked to Lucy
as we drove back to the Honeybee. "But she is one
odd duck."

She smiled and nodded. "One of my favorite odd
ducks."

Chapter 7

Lucy and I came back into the bakery through the alley. Right away I heard a familiar voice.

"Dad!"

I ran out to where my father sat talking with Declan and Uncle Ben. Mungo was fast on my heels. My father stood up and held out his arms for a big hug.

"Hey, kiddo," he said in that deep, warm tone that always seemed to make everything all right.

Smiling, I stepped back. Someone had once remarked that he looked like Lorne Greene from the western series *Bonanza*, and if I squinted I could see it. He had a strongly planed face and warm brown eyes. His thick white hair waved above his ears, and summer or winter he wore a chambray shirt, jeans, and boots. I'd inherited a darker shade of my mother's red hair, green eyes, and freckles, but I had my father's mouth and deeper coloring.

"How was your flight?" I asked.

He held out his hand and rocked it back and forth. "You know—air travel. But it's worth it to see you."

A nod at Declan. "And this guy here. On the drive in from the airport, he filled me in on what happened to your customer. It looks like you've gotten yourself into another fine mess." He bent to pet my familiar, who had completely ingratiated himself with my father when we'd visited at Christmas.

I rolled my eyes at the Laurel and Hardy quote and gave him another hug when he straightened. "Thanks for coming to help out."

His eyes twinkled. "Always happy to help my favorite daughter."

"Mmm." I was an only child, so he was trying to be funny again. "Speaking of help, and messes, what can you tell me about that picture I texted to you?"

"Right. The totem. Do you have a larger version of that picture? It's a bit difficult to make out the details."

"Come into the office," I said. "We can take a look on the computer monitor."

I took out my phone and quickly sent the picture to my e-mail account. He followed me back to the tiny office, where I brought up the photo. He sat down, pulled a pair of reading glasses from his shirt pocket, and leaned forward.

"Mmm-hmm," he murmured, and zoomed in a little closer. "Hmm."

"It's apparently called *Ginegosh*. I tried looking that up online but got nothing."

"Mmm-hmm," he said again, then leaned back and took off his glasses.

"Mmm-hmm, *what*?"

"Ojibwe for 'fox' is *waagosh*, and the word for 'snake' is *ginebig*. My bet is that *Ginegosh* is a combination of the two, since those are the only two animals in this totem."

I stared at him. "How did you know that?"

He shrugged. "The Ojibwe, aka Chippewa, speak a native language that's similar to Shawnee. As do the Cheyenne and some other tribes. They're, shall we say, sister languages, but not the same. A few years ago, I worked with a Chippewa tribe member who was looking for some help, and I became interested in the similarities between the languages."

"What kind of help?" I asked.

Afraid of how people might take it in our little town of Fillmore, Ohio, my mother had insisted that my parents stop practicing magic in order to protect me when I was very young. Since Lucy had told me about my hereditary gifts, I'd learned that my father helped my mother with a bit of spell work, and that she was practicing regularly again, but I knew next to nothing about his shamanic practices.

"She was ill," he said simply. "There was misplaced negative energy left over from a bad relationship, and I helped her remove it, so she could get better."

"Really?" I asked, fascinated. "Will you tell me more about how you do that kind of thing?"

His face lit up. "Sure, if you're interested."

"Oh, believe me. I'm interested." I looked at my watch. "But right now, the lunch rush is about to start. Can you tell me anything else about this piece?"

"Other than there's a hefty dose of blood on it?" He made a face. "Not really. It was probably made for someone specifically, perhaps as a gift. It likely represents a particular family, kind of like a coat of arms would in England or tartan plaid patterns represent Scottish clans. To the best of my knowledge, there isn't any kind of registry for Native American totems like there are for those systems, though. I can tell you that foxes represent cleverness and strength, and snakes represent wisdom and renewal."

"A good combination," I said but couldn't help looking at my watch again. "I'd better get back to work."

Sure enough, there was a line at the register. Lucy was ringing up purchases, and Iris was whipping up coffee drinks.

Declan and Ben were standing by the front door talking, and we wended our way toward them.

"Any luck?" Declan asked.

"Dad can tell you about it," I said. "I need to call Quinn and fill him in." I looked at my dad. "Thanks."

"I hope it helps," he said.

"Sky, how about we head over and drop your luggage at Ben's, and then I'll show you the progress at the carriage house?" Declan asked.

My dad nodded. "I'll see you later, Katie. Sounds like Lucy and Ben are planning a barbeque this evening."

I looked at my uncle, who grinned. "Burgers on the grill. Just the five of us."

"Perfect," I said. "We'll be there."

And hopefully, we'd know a bit more about Kensington Bosworth by then.

After the lunch rush settled down, I went back into the office and called Detective Quinn. The phone rang four times, and I expected to get his voice mail. Then he picked up.

There was a short silence before he mumbled, "Hlo. . . ."

"Oh, God. I woke you up. I'm so sorry."

"Who is this?"

"Katie Lightfoot," I said. "I can call back."

"No, no." He cleared his throat, and I heard him take a drink of something. "Did you find out anything about the murder weapon from your father?"

I repeated everything Dad had told me. When I was done, Quinn made a hmphing noise. "Chippewa for 'fox' and 'snake,' you say. That's interesting enough, I suppose."

He didn't say the other thing I knew he was thinking—that Randy had shown an interest in the Ginegosh totem and his fingerprints were probably on it.

"Do you know anything about who inherits Mr. Bosworth's money yet?" I asked.

Quinn sighed. "Katie, I know I asked for your help, but you can stop now. We have this investigation under control."

"Because you think Randy did it."

Silence.

"Are you even bothering to investigate anyone else?"

"Of course," he snapped. "We aren't complete incompetents."

"Yes. I know you're very competent indeed. But Quinn—" I paused to carefully consider my words. "The police have been wrong before."

More silence at that, then a sigh. "And you've been right. You're not going to back away from this case, are you?"

"Probably not. Sorry. Randy is my friend."

Another sigh. "Don't do anything stupid," he said. "And don't get hurt."

"Okay."

"And let me know if you find out anything."

"Quid pro quo?"

"If I find out something that seems . . . relevant."

"Like who the money goes to?" I persisted. "Because 'relevant' seems awfully subjective."

"We'll see. We haven't heard back from the lawyer yet."

"Well, it didn't go to Bosworth's sister, Florinda. He was afraid she'd gamble it away like she did the inheritance from their father. That much I was able to find out already."

Quinn swore softly under his breath. "Maybe I should put you on staff."

I allowed a little laugh. "Nah. I'm way too busy here at the bakery. Go back to sleep, Detective Quinn. I'm sorry I woke you."

We hung up, and I turned my attention to the computer again. There was no match when I entered *Florinda Bosworth* into the search engine. Then, because Florinda was such an unusual name, I tried searching for that plus *Savannah*.

Turned out that Florinda wasn't such an unusual name after all, at least not in my town. A total of eight records came up, and one of them was for Florinda Bundy from decades before. If I had a staff like Quinn did, I'd have them start calling each one. On the other hand, Quinn probably already knew her current last name from Bosworth's records, which I didn't have access to. Or he'd found out from Malcolm Cardwell.

The very man Bianca and I were about to go see.

I closed the search engine and found the picture of the Ginegosh totem was still open on the computer. On impulse, I grabbed my phone back out of my tote bag and, not having its USB cord with me, mailed myself the rest of the photos and the video I'd made in Bosworth's outer office. After I downloaded them from e-mail, I perused each one on the larger screen.

Such an eclectic collection of magical items. I wonder if he ever used any of them, or if someone else did it for him.

Because I had definitely felt something protecting the house, and it hadn't been Randy's security system.

Then I saw the picture of the datebook on the desk. I'd skipped by that photo a couple of times already because the glare from the desk lamp had obscured the details on the plastic evidence bag. However, it perfectly captured the page of Mr. Bosworth's weekly planner, albeit upside down. Quickly, I cropped out the rest of the photo, rotated it so the writing was right side up, and enlarged it. Doing so lost some of the resolution, but I could still make out what it said.

Tuesday, he'd had a dentist appointment. In the margin, there was a note that had a line through it. By zooming even more, I made out the words, "Hermetic Order of the Silver Moon."

What the heck is that?

I scribbled a note.

The only other thing written in the datebook was a name: Caesar Speckman.

"Katie," Lucy called from the kitchen. "Bianca's here."

"Be right there," I called back, quickly jotting the name on a Post-it note and sticking it to the side of the monitor.

I looked over at Mungo, who bounded up from his prone position to stand on the chair. "I'll follow up on Mr. Speckman later. You stay here and take care of things while I'm gone. Okay?"

He whined and sat back.

"I don't know how receptive Malcolm Cardwell will be to dogs," I said. "Besides, you know how Bianca drives."

He blinked, then ducked his head under his paw.

I laughed. "Exactly."

Bianca wasn't really a bad driver. I was sure that if I drove a cherry red Jaguar convertible, I'd want to take corners a bit too quickly, too. She was fast but had great reflexes.

And truth be told, I loved riding in her car.

My friend had showered and changed into a flowing gauze dress and ankle-strap sandals. Her thick black hair was braided and coiled into a chignon on the back of her head, and she wore a delicate silver choker with a single pearl in the middle. All she was lacking was a crown of flowers to be the May queen.

The GPS guided us to 618 Fallow Road. Admittedly, I kept a firm grip on the edge of my seat, out of Bianca's sight, for most of the ride, but a part of me wanted to *squee!* when she whipped through a roundabout or made a sharp turn. On the way I filled her in on what Dad had told me about the Ginegosh figurine.

"Well, it makes sense that Randy would be interested in it," she said. "I don't know why Detective Quinn can't see that."

I nodded. "Right?" And then I thought of the entry in Bosworth's datebook. "Say, you don't happen to know anything about something called the Hermetic Order of the Silver Moon, do you?"

Her forehead creased. "Nuh-uh. It sounds like something I'd be interested in, though."

It did indeed, given her predilection for moon magic. I'd been thinking that it might be an organization devoted to exactly that.

Malcolm Cardwell's house was in Heritage Overlook, a newer neighborhood of quite nice but nearly identical homes. Number 618 was a mushroom green split-level surrounded by a big lawn strewn with toys. Two boys and two girls between the ages of nine and three were running through an old-fashioned sprinkler that fanned the air with glittering droplets of water. We could hear their laughter from three houses away. A small park with brightly painted playground equipment took up most of the block across the street.

Bianca pulled to the curb behind a Ford Expedition with stick-figure stickers of a family of six on the back window. She turned off the engine, and we got out. The strains of a jazz saxophone emanated from the garage, punctuated by the thump, thump, thump of a stand-up bass.

On the sidewalk, she cocked her head to listen. "I know that song from the radio. It's a local band."

"Unless Ben puts it on at the Honeybee, I don't listen to a lot of jazz," I admitted.

"Well, I do, and that's the Eclecticats. Whatever his faults may be, Malcolm Cardwell apparently has good musical taste."

As we walked up the sidewalk toward the door, the kids abandoned their play and came running over.

"Hi!" the girl who appeared to be the oldest said. "Who're you?"

I smiled. "I'm Katie and this is Bianca."

"Oh." She grinned. "I'm Max. You want to talk to my mama?"

"Actually, I'd like to see your—"

The front door opened, and a very pretty and very pregnant black woman came out.

"Mama!" the little girl yelled. "These ladies want to talk to you."

The woman waved her hand good-naturedly and started down the steps. The kids took off for the sprinkler again as Bianca and I hurried to meet her.

"What can I do for you?" she asked, her tone easy-going though there was a soupçon of dismissal beneath the words.

She thinks we want to sell her something.

I held out my hand. "I'm Katie Lightfoot, and this is Bianca Devereaux. Your husband is Malcolm Cardwell?"

The music coming from the garage stopped, then started up again.

She shook my hand. Her tone was puzzled as she said, "Yes. I'm Suzanne Cardwell."

I smiled and gestured toward the squealing kids. "Are all those yours?"

Suzanne rolled her eyes at the sky, but when she looked back at me they were smiling. "Every one of them." She patted her belly and laughed. "And another one obviously on the way. Then I think we'll take a break. Like, forever."

So, the stuffed shirt I'd met in Mr. Bosworth's house had four, going on five, children under the age of nine, and was married to this lovely woman? If there had been a bubble over my head, it would have been filled with scratched-out preconceptions.

"Oh!" Suzanne said. "You're not from WVAN, are you?"

I shook my head. "Though I wouldn't be surprised if you've been visited by a news crew or two."

"News crew? But the interview . . . wait a minute. Is this about what happened to Malkey's boss?"

Puzzled, Bianca and I nodded.

"Oh. Well, that's different. The band is supposed to be interviewed on television later this week, so I was a little confused." She shook her head. "Awful what happened to Mr. Bosworth. Just awful. Hang on. I'll get Malkey." She turned and strode over to the garage, showing remarkable grace considering how far along she was. She opened the side door, stuck her head inside, and said something.

The music stopped. Moments later, the garage door rolled up to reveal four men, a keyboard, drum kit, and three brass instruments on stands. At the back, Kensington Bosworth's private secretary was putting the stand-up bass I'd heard from the street on its stand.

"Ohmagod," Bianca breathed. "That's them. He's a member of the Eclecticats."

Now the reference his wife had made to a television interview on the local PBS station made more sense.

"Don't go all fangirl," I murmured.

Bianca shot me a look, then stepped forward as Cardwell came out to the driveway.

"Take ten," he called over his shoulder. "Lemonade's in the kitchen. Suzanne? You mind?"

"Got it," she said, and hurried after the men who were heading for the house.

He came over and stopped in front of us. He looked very different from the man I'd met the night before. He wore a ball cap, an Allman Brothers T-shirt, board shorts, and flip-flops. The glasses were gone, too. I suddenly wondered if he'd been wearing the suit and tie because he'd been on the way to a band gig. His whole demeanor away from Mr. Bosworth's house was different, too, with more of a casual cast to his shoulders and a wry quirk to his lips.

Then his eyes widened a fraction as he recognized me. "You're the police consultant from last night."

Bianca side-eyed a look my way. I ignored her.

"We met last night," I confirmed. "I was—we were—wondering if you'd be willing to talk to us a little about your boss."

Chapter 8

"I already answered the detective's questions," Cardwell said slowly.

"Of course." I paused to consider what kind of trouble I might get into if he thought I was there on police business. Which, in a way, I was. But not officially. A fine line, indeed. Best to stick as close to the truth as possible.

I smiled. "Sorry to bother you at home, Mr. Cardwell. But when I saw that collection of Mr. Bosworth's, I just had to know more about it."

"Oh, that stuff," he said dismissively. "He was fascinated by anything related to the occult. Was always reading up on magic and sorcery and how it's been used in different cultures through the ages."

"You said he was working with a dealer in town," I said. "Could you tell me who it was?"

Cardwell gave a little nod. "Caesar Speckman."

My lips parted in surprise.

"Has that souvenir shop How's Tricks down on the waterfront. You've probably seen it."

No, but I've seen his business card in Bosworth's Rolodex.

"Souvenirs? Like for tourists?" Bianca asked.

Cardwell nodded. "He plays on Savannah being the most haunted city in America. Works with one of the companies that does ghost tours for out-of-towners. His other shtick is cheap magic tricks."

"But Mr. Bosworth's collection was anything but cheap," I said. "At least from what I saw."

"Speckman is savvier than his tourist trap might make you think. He has a side hustle dealing in the kind of thing Mr. Bosworth was interested in."

"Did your boss, um . . . you know . . . ?" I twiddled my fingers in a hocus-pocus gesture.

He understood. "Nah." Then he paused and looked into the distance as if remembering something. "Well, maybe. I did catch him sprinkling a bunch of salt around in a circle one time. He said it was borax for ants, but it looked like salt to me. Plus, it was in the middle of the room, not around the edges like you'd apply pesticide. Anyway, the way he was acting reminded me of my great-auntie. She was a Gullah root doctor."

Bianca and I nodded. The Gullah were descendants of West African slaves who lived along the coastline of South Carolina and Georgia. Many of them still practiced their own particular brand of witchcraft.

A shrug. "Anyway, who knows what the old man did when I wasn't in the house. I was only there from nine to two during the week." He waved a hand toward the garage, where the other band members were trickling back from the house, lemonade glasses in hand. "Decent hours that made it easy to play music in the evenings and still spend time with my family. The guy could have been trying to raise zombies from the dead, for all I cared."

"So, you weren't close," I said.

"He was my boss. I called him Mr. Bosworth, and he called me Mr. Cardwell, and we both called Olivia Mrs. Gleason. He didn't really need a secretary, to be honest. But he hated technology, and I think he found the idea of someone typing up his letters and putting phone calls through for him nostalgic. I did my job, and he gave me a paycheck." Cardwell didn't exactly seem broken up over Bosworth's death.

Keeping my tone casual, I said, "Word has it that Mr. Bosworth wasn't the most generous employer."

He frowned. "He was tight with his money, all right. But not very many people are willing to work the shorter hours I am, nor can they operate a typewriter or spend all day away from a computer—or want to. We negotiated a fair wage, and he gave me time off whenever the band was traveling or had a daytime gig."

"Mrs. Gleason, the housekeeper," I said. "Her first name is Olivia?"

He nodded but didn't say anything, his expression becoming speculative and then hardening. I had a feeling that he wouldn't talk to us much longer.

I suddenly changed the subject. "And just to follow up, Detective Quinn was going to contact Florinda Bosworth to let her know about her brother's death." That was probably true.

Cardwell blinked. "Okay."

"He didn't ask you for her current surname or address? I'll need that." Which was absolutely true.

Looking a little less sure, he shook his head. "Her last name is Daniels, and she lives in Pooler. That's all I know."

"Back to your boss's collection," Bianca said. Her Georgia accent was on steroids. "And that statue called Ginegosh. Can you tell us anything about it?"

His eyes narrowed as he turned toward her. "What did you say your name was?"

"I didn't. It's Bianca," she drawled. "Bianca Devereaux."

"And . . . why are you here?" He looked pointedly at me. "In fact, I'm not sure . . ." He trailed off.

I sighed, but before I could say anything, Bianca took a step forward and held out her hand. He took it automatically.

She gave him a warm, engaging smile. "I'm here to find out why you accused my friend of murder."

He stared at her, then pulled his hand away. "I didn't accuse anyone of murder."

"Oh, but you did. You told the police that Randy Post had an argument with your boss, that he coveted that particular piece of statuary in his office, and that because he had installed the security system, he had to have been the one to break in and kill Kensington Bosworth." The sweet smile remained on her face the entire time she spoke. "Now, I am ever so curious about what your problem is with Mr. Post."

He looked flustered. "I didn't have a problem with him. I only met him a couple of times."

"Then why did you tell the police to arrest him?"

"I didn't! I only said—" He glanced at me. "Well, I did suggest that the police speak with him. I thought perhaps he'd know how someone could have bypassed the system he put in."

I gave him a look. "That wasn't the way I heard it."

She took another step toward him, and Cardwell took an involuntary step backward. "Well, they did speak with him." Her tone was still pleasant, yet somehow daggers dripped from the words.

"Bianca," I said.

"For several hours," she continued. "He is a respected Savannah firefighter, and now he is the main suspect in Kensington Bosworth's murder, and it's *your* fault."

Cardwell didn't look away, and his shoulders became as ramrod straight as they'd been when he'd introduced himself the night before. "No. It's not my fault. They're not going to convict him if he didn't do it. I was right to tell them what I did." He looked at me. "Listen, I don't really understand why you're here. I'm happy to call Detective Quinn and answer any other questions he might have."

"No need," I said brightly. "We'll let you get back to your band practice, okay?"

I grabbed Bianca's arms and turned her toward the car. She tried to pull away, but I didn't let go. "Come on," I said in a low voice.

She gave in, and we walked toward the street.

"I still can't see how anyone besides the installer could have gotten past that security system," Cardwell called after us.

Bianca whirled around and glared at him. He

stood in the middle of his yard, hands on his hips. Behind him, his bandmates had come back out of the garage and watched with interest.

"Come *on*," I said.

Bianca and Cardwell locked eyes for a long moment, then she turned away and marched to the driver's side of the Jaguar. She slammed the door and revved the engine. I jumped in, and we roared off.

"Bianca," I said when we were a block away.

Then I saw the tears in her eyes and fell silent. I remembered how I'd felt while I was trying to clear Uncle Ben's name back when the police had thought he'd killed Mavis Templeton. Instead of berating her for alienating Bosworth's secretary, I reached over and squeezed her shoulder.

"Do you think Randy's home?" I asked. If so, he was probably fast asleep after the night he'd had.

Bianca glanced at the clock on the dash. "He's probably at my house by now. He was going to take a nap and then come over before I have to go pick up Colette from art camp."

"You mind if I come by and have a chat with him?"

She hesitated, then shook her head. "No. I think that would be a good idea."

Bianca's husband had left her and their young daughter when he found out Bianca had become interested in magic. Since then, she had developed quite a talent for the stock market, a combination of her own gift with numbers and money that she occasionally augmented with a bit of spell casting. She had used some of her growing fortune to start Moon Grapes, her wine shop on Factors Walk, and she had bought a house in Haversham Woods. The upscale neighborhood was in the middle of Savannah, close to downtown, Southside, and the Oglethorpe Mall. Bianca often talked about how quiet it was, and Colette had made a lot of friends in the Woods.

I admired the mix of traditional and contemporary architecture as we wended down the elegant streets. The homes were larger than most this close to downtown, with big yards and lots of street parking. She pulled into her driveway and parked behind Randy's car. I paused to let Lucy know where I was via text then got out of the Jaguar. Bianca had already started toward the house, worry coming off her in waves.

Inside, her home was airy and open, with ten-foot ceilings and lots of windows. The woodwork was meticulous, from the crown moldings to the carved stair banister, and wide heart-pine planks made up the floors throughout. The living room boasted a Tennessee stone fireplace, and double doors opened out to an enclosed patio behind the house.

Randy, drinking iced tea, sat on the leather sofa. He wore shorts and a wrinkled T-shirt, and his face reflected a deep weariness. His expression brightened as we walked in, though, and he was instantly on his feet and across the room to take Bianca into his arms.

"Hey, babe," I heard him murmur.

She clung tightly to him for a few seconds, then broke away, her eyes glistening.

Randy looked at me, and his face flushed. "Hi, Katie."

107

I grinned. "Hi." Then the smile fell from my face. "Sounds like you had a rough night."

He nodded. "You could say that."

Glancing at Bianca, I said, "So, I don't know what Bianca has told you about the spellbook club . . . ?"

"Pretty much everything. At least I think so." He looked at her, and she nodded.

She'd told us when they'd had that conversation. Lordy, had she been nervous. I didn't blame her after what had happened with her no-good husband, and I was glad to see Randy seemed at ease with his new girlfriend's witchy nature.

"And about how sometimes I, er, get involved with certain homicide cases with their help?" I asked.

Another nod. "Uh-huh. Declan has mentioned it once or twice, too, though he doesn't talk about it with the others at the station." He licked his lips. "Please tell me that's why you're here."

I moved over to an upholstered rocking chair and sat down. "It is. I'm sure you're exhausted, not to mention sick to death of questions, but would you mind chatting for a few minutes?"

"Not at all." He went back to the sofa, where Bianca joined him. "I need all the help I can get, Katie."

"Well, I can't guarantee anything, but I'll do what I can. First off, tell me about this argument you had with Kensington Bosworth. Was it just about money, or did the Ginegosh figurine come up?"

He shook his head. "Not at all. I did talk to him about the little statue, but that was a couple of days earlier. It was a perfectly civil conversation. I wanted to know why it was called that, and he didn't know.

108

He didn't seem to know anything about it. It was just another piece in his weird collection."

I started to bristle at his assessment of Bosworth's interest in the paranormal, but then had to agree. The collection was all over the place, and even I thought it was odd.

"Why did that piece in particular grab your interest?" I asked Randy.

"My family has a similar statue that was handed down for generations, but we don't know where it came from."

"It's probably a family totem," Bianca said. "Katie's dad says the name probably comes from the Chippewa words for fox and snake, kind of mashed together."

Randy looked intrigued. "Is that so? Huh. I have some Chippewa blood, that's for sure. Our statue is a fox with a beaver tail."

"You should ask Dad about that," I said. "He's going to be in town for a week. He'll know the significance of the beaver in your family totem. He told me the fox represents cleverness and strength."

"Your dad is Chippewa?"

"Shawnee. A fourth, I think." I tried to steer the conversation back. "You touched the statue?"

"Yeah. I handled it, all right. Just while we were talking about it in Bosworth's office, but unless his housekeeper is really diligent, my prints are still on it."

I exhaled. "Well, maybe yours aren't the only ones."

He didn't look encouraged by that.

"Okay, tell me about the argument you had with Bosworth," I said.

"It was about payment for the security system. See, the company I work with sells the system and then arranges for a freelance installer like me to put it in. I set my own rate for each job, and I invoice it myself. Well, Bosworth had paid for the system already, but he didn't think I spent as much time putting it in as he'd expected, so he didn't want to pay all of my bill. He got pretty upset about it." Randy grimaced. "And loud. I'm sure his secretary heard us. It didn't help that I lost my temper and threatened to sue him if he didn't pay up." He sighed, and Bianca squeezed his hand. "I don't generally have much of a temper, but I was tired, and well, he just made me so *mad*."

"It sounds perfectly understandable to me," I said. "This was a standard security system?"

"Sure. I've put in dozens of them. No big deal."

"And from what I understand, there's some kind of master code that you use to turn it on and off while you're working with it."

He nodded. "And then I have the customer create their own code. After that, I can't use the master. Bosworth had been using his own code for almost two weeks."

"So, it automatically goes away when the new owner creates their own code?"

"Yup."

"Then why are the police all het up about you using the master code to get inside the house?"

His lips twisted in discouragement. "They think there's some kind of back door the company knows

110

about to get in if they need to. Which might be true. But if so, they don't give that code to me."

"So how else could the killer get in?" But even as I wondered out loud, I had a few ideas.

As did Randy. "Easy. Either they knew the code, or Bosworth simply turned off the system and let them in."

"In which case, it was probably someone he knew," I said slowly. "Or . . . who else would he have given the code to?"

"Well, the housekeeper and the secretary both had it. . . ." He trailed off, looking thoughtful.

I leaned forward. "Do you think either of them had a reason to want Mr. Bosworth dead?"

Randy took a deep breath and gave a little shake of his head. "Really, I'd have no clue. How could I? I was in and out of there in two days."

"And during that time, you saw them both interact with their boss?"

"Sure, a few times. And with each other. Everything seemed copacetic."

One side of my mouth pulled back as I thought about that. Something could have been going on within the household that no one knew about.

"Malcolm Cardwell doesn't live on site. And I assume the housekeeper doesn't, either." I was thinking out loud.

"Olivia? No. Her daughter lives with her. Divorced. Dropped by once when I was working. She's around your age, Katie. Pretty. Nice, too."

I looked at Bianca, but she didn't seem to mind her

beau calling another woman pretty or nice. Rather, she emanated a quiet confidence sitting there beside Randy, who was several years younger than she was. My friend had always been confident, but this was different. This was confidence in them as a couple.

In love.

The realization warmed my heart. It also made finding the real killer feel even more urgent.

Continuing to think through what I knew already, I said, "So, Olivia Gleason found the body. She called the police, and then she called Malcolm Cardwell. The alarm was off when she got there. Malcom Cardwell thought that was odd because his boss was religious about keeping the system armed. However, either or both of them could be lying."

Randy shrugged. "I suppose. I can tell you that Mr. Bosworth seemed very relieved to have the protection."

I remembered the energy that had surrounded the house, how strong the spell had felt as I moved through the front door. Magical protection in addition to a practical security system.

What had Kensington Bosworth been so afraid of?

Chapter 9

We left Randy to take a shower, and Bianca dropped me at the Honeybee before going to pick up her daughter. It was nearly four thirty when I got back to work.

I went into the office to store my tote bag but stopped in the doorway when I saw Mungo. He glared at me from his club chair and managed to infuse his obvious displeasure about my tardy return with a sense of betrayal.

"How do you do that?" I entered the room and dumped the tote, then knelt in front of him. "I'm sorry. You probably would have loved running through the sprinkler with the Cardwell kids."

His mouth turned down in a doggy frown.

"I'm late because I went to Bianca's to talk to Randy."

He made a little moaning noise in the back of his throat. He loved going to Bianca's house. She kept a supply of organic, grass-fed jerky on hand just for the canine familiars in the spellbook club.

"Can I make it up to you with a ham and cheese sandwich?"

His eyes brightened.

"I suppose you want it grilled."

Yip!

"Shh. Okay, I'll be right back."

Shaking my head, I went out to the kitchen to make the world's tiniest grilled ham and cheese sandwich. Then I cut it up into bite-sized pieces—terrier bites, that was—and took it back to him on a plate.

Instant forgiveness.

While he ate, I pulled out my phone and texted Quinn with a question that had occurred to me on the way back from Bianca's.

Didn't want to wake you again, but was wondering if there was anything missing from Bosworth's collection? As in, could robbery have been the motive?

I sent it and returned to the kitchen with Mungo's plate, which was already licked clean.

"You let him push you around," Lucy said from where she was wiping down the counter.

"I do," I admitted. "Of course, Honeybee never bosses you, does she?"

Lucy made a face but didn't answer. She didn't need to, because we both knew her familiar could be a bit of a princess at times.

Iris had already mixed up the sourdough levain for the next day's bread and put it into pans to rise overnight. Now she was mixing up the dough for the spice cookies Lucy and I had recently developed. I would come in the next morning and bake up the cookies first thing for the daily special. We often tested out new recipes as daily specials, and I was hoping the spice cookies would prove popular with the customers.

The scent of allspice filled the atmosphere around where she worked. It was one of my favorite spices not only because of its complex flavor, but because it could be magically tapped to attract money, love, energy, and luck.

"I saw that you added the calendula cookies to the menu board," Iris said happily, and did her little two-step. She had developed that one on her own after she found out that the flowers, sometimes known as pot marigold, were not only edible, but magically promoted happiness and harmony.

"They were a big hit," I said. "Delicious, and the flecks of golden petals dusted with vanilla sugar are a work of art."

She grinned. "Thanks."

"Feel free to come up with more recipes that incorporate flowers," Lucy said. "I can see a whole table covered with plates of colorful, flower-infused cookies at the next event we cater."

Iris started the big standing mixer, licked a bit of molasses off her finger, and came over to where Lucy and I stood. "Can I ask a question?"

"Of course, honey," my aunt said. "What is it?"

"You're investigating another murder, aren't you, Katie? You and the others?"

I gave Iris a hesitant nod as I considered how much to tell her.

However, she continued before I had a chance. "Why don't you just use your, you know, *powers* to solve crime? I mean, you're witches, right? I know

115

I'm just learning, but you're, like, the real thing. Can't you just—" She waved her hand in the air. "Make the bad guys turn themselves in or something?"

Lucy and I looked at each other.

"Well," I said. "I asked that once, too. Right after I found out I was a hereditary witch. And you know what Mimsey told me?"

Iris shook her head.

"She said that real magic isn't like that. You can't just wiggle your nose like they do on television and—*poof!*—something disappears. See, our kind of magic is a tool we can use along with our brains and our intuition and good old hard work in order to track down the truth." I laughed. "And then she told me, and I think these were her exact words, '*There is no abracadabra cure-all to crime solving. If there were, every law enforcement agency in the world would be clamoring to use our skills.*'"

Iris quirked her mouth to one side, obviously unimpressed with my answer. "I'm not that silly, Katie. I don't think you're going to snap your fingers and some bad guy will appear in a puff of smoke. But that detective is using your skills, isn't he? And you know how to do spells that would tell you who killed someone, don't you?"

I grinned. "Tell me who killed someone? Um, not really."

There was, of course, good old-fashioned divination à la Mimsey's pink shew stone or by another method. However, no one in the spellbook club was particularly good at it—especially me. And even when

I had managed to make a divination spell work, the results had been hazy at best.

"What about tarot cards?" Iris asked.

"Yeah, I get what you're saying, but a tarot spread isn't exactly like a police lineup."

"Okay, whatever. It just seems like you ought to be able to do *something* magical to find the killer." She turned back and started putting the last batch of baking pans into the dishwasher.

I looked at Lucy, who shrugged. "Mimsey's right." She went back to wiping down the counter.

Of course, Mimsey is right, I thought. *But what if Iris is, too?* The universe seemed to hand me the opportunity to find justice in cases that involved magic. Was there more I could bring to those situations now that I more or less knew what I was doing as a witch?

Everything seemed to be under control in the kitchen, so I went out to check the display case. Lucy followed me. The bakery was nearly empty, and we would officially close in about fifteen minutes. Ben had already tidied the coffee counter for the next day and was tugging the café curtains closed over in the reading area.

"Those green tomato corn muffins flew out the door," she said. "We might have to add them to the regular roster."

"We need to take something else off the menu, then," I said, eyeing the tray where the muffins had been.

She sighed. "I know. I just want to offer people everything we can."

I laughed. "Me, too. But even with Iris' help, we can only do so much. Let's add the muffins while green tomatoes are plentiful—I'll put them on the produce order from the farm—and take the ginger-snaps off the menu until fall. That's when people will want something that warms from the inside."

"You're perfectly right," she said. "Let's do that." Then she leaned close and asked in a low voice, "Did you find anything out?"

"Lots of things, but I don't know if any of them are helpful," I said. "It turns out—" The door opened, and I fell silent when I saw who had come in the bakery.

"Peter," Ben said, his hand outstretched as he approached Detective Quinn. Not one to hold a grudge, he seemed to have completely forgiven Quinn for once trying to convict him of murder.

Quinn shook my uncle's hand. "Ben, how are you?" Then, without waiting for an answer, he asked, "Is Katie around?"

Ben nodded to where I was already walking toward the reading area. It was empty, and there was only one customer sitting on the other side of the bakery, so we'd have some privacy. Quinn nodded and joined me. He sank into one of the overstuffed chairs and regarded me as I perched on the edge of the sofa.

"You look like you feel better," I said.

His eyes shone clear gray, and the shadows below them were gone. Even the silver in his hair appeared to gleam a little more brightly.

"I do. A little shut-eye will do wonders." He tipped his head to the side. "I got your text and was in the neighborhood."

Since his precinct was only five blocks away, that was likely true.

"I see," I said in a neutral tone. I couldn't tell whether he was peeved or not.

He held my gaze for several seconds, then seemed to make a decision. "The victim's secretary provided us with a list of items in the collection you saw, a list that Bosworth himself put together for insurance purposes. He says it's up to date. I've had someone at the house most of the day, checking to see if anything is missing. So far they haven't found anything."

"That's very efficient," I ventured.

One eyebrow slowly rose. "Yes. We sometimes manage that."

"I didn't mean—"

He cut me off with a wave of his hand. "I also spoke with the victim's lawyer. He felt it would be a breach of trust to tell me who benefited from Bosworth's death, but he also wants justice for his client. To that end, he put everything else aside and filed for probate today so that we could get access to that information without his betraying attorney-client privilege."

"Because it's now public record," I said eagerly. "And? Or are you going to make me go find out for myself?"

He looked amused. "No. I'll tell you."

I blinked but had the good sense to keep my mouth shut. Quinn wasn't often in a sharing mood.

"You're right—Bosworth's sister didn't get any-thing, but her son does inherit, and quite a lot. Plus, he inherits the entire collection of paranormal items. Other than the chunk of change that goes to Dante

119

Bundy—that's the nephew—several philanthropic organizations around town receive the rest of the money."

"Hang on. *Dante* Bundy?"

"Yes. Why?"

"Because last night when I obeyed your abrupt summons to the murder victim's home, I saw a car parked on the street a few houses down. It had a custom license plate that read 'Dante.'"

The corners of his mouth turned up, and he pulled his notebook out of his pocket. "You don't say. What kind of car was it?"

I squinted as I tried to remember. "A BMW. I couldn't tell you what kind, though. It was dark blue, I think."

"Anyone in the car?"

"Honestly, I was distracted and didn't notice. Dang it." Could I have seen the murderer and not realized it?

Nah. He wouldn't stick around for hours after killing his uncle. Would he? But then why was his car there?

"Don't worry. I'll look into it," Quinn said. "We collected the license plate numbers on vehicles that were parked on the street within a two-block area."

Feeling somewhat encouraged, I said, "The philanthropic organizations that Bosworth left money to—animal welfare, Native American heritage groups, and a group that restores stolen Middle Eastern artifacts?"

He looked surprised but nodded. "You have good sources. But more money goes to another group—the Hermetic Order of the Silver Moon."

I stared at him. "I saw that name in his datebook."

Quinn frowned. "You snooped through Bosworth's datebook?"

"No, I did not. I simply saw it when I was taking the pictures of the Ginegosh statue. At least I assumed it was Bosworth's. It was on his secretary's desk, though. Could it have been Cardwell's? Wouldn't Mr. Bosworth have kept his datebook on his own desk?"

And that would mean Malcolm Cardwell had something to do with the Hermetic Order—

Quinn cut off my line of thought with, "That was Bosworth's datebook on the secretary's desk, all right. I checked." He made a note, then sat back with a thoughtful expression.

"*Hermetic Order of the Silver Moon* had a line drawn through it," I said slowly. "Do you think that could mean he'd changed his mind about leaving them money?"

One shoulder lifted then dropped. "Hard to tell. His lawyer did mention that Bosworth had an appointment to see him next week. Katie, do you know what the Hermetic Order of the Silver Moon *is*?"

I shook my head. "Do you?"

"They don't have a website. There is one mention of it on the Internet, and that states that it's a charitable foundation. However, we couldn't find any evidence that they actually give money away, and they aren't registered with the state of Georgia as a nonprofit. There's no information about where they're located or who works there or who they benefit."

"How can that be? How much did Mr. Bosworth leave them?"

Quinn gave me a figure.

I whistled. "And only one mention of them on the Internet."

"On the regular Internet. We have a guy who knows how to navigate the dark web, and he's working on it. And of course, we're looking for banking records. Nothing so far. The name, though, it strikes me as . . ." He reddened.

"Something a witch might recognize."

"Well, yes. Do you think you could find out more about it?"

"I'm happy to make some inquiries." I was betting someone in the spellbook club would know, but if they didn't I'd check in with Steve and his druid clan.

He looked relieved, though I couldn't tell whether it was because I agreed to help or because he'd found it difficult to ask.

"Um." He looked down.

"Yes?"

"I've given this a lot of thought, and I'm going to ask you for another favor. You don't have to do it, of course, and it's not official, but I thought I'd check, and like I said—"

"Oh, for heaven's sake," I interrupted. "What?"

He took a deep breath, then, "I tracked down the victim's sister and told her that her brother had been murdered. She thanked me very much and shut the door in my face."

I winced. "Maybe she was too upset by the news to talk about it."

"I didn't get that impression." He looked wry. "I

think she just doesn't like cops. However . . ." He trailed off with a meaningful look.

"However, you think she might talk to me," I finished.

His lips pressed together, and his eyes widened in a look of exaggerated speculation. "Could be."

"I'd need an excuse to go see her," I said, thinking about that for the umpteenth time. I'd already intended to go talk to her, but there was no reason to tell Quinn that if he hadn't guessed it already. "I'll figure something out," I said.

"Thanks, Katie." He stood and shot his cuffs to expose the perfect white shirtsleeves at his wrists and took a few steps toward the door.

I rose to my feet as well. "Quinn?"

He turned back.

"It sounds like you're really investigating all angles of this case. Does that mean Randy Post isn't your primary suspect anymore?"

His face was impenetrable. "I always investigate all angles of a homicide."

"I . . . I know," I stuttered. "I didn't mean . . ."

He relented. "There is still a long way to go on this one, and I can't know what else we'll find out. But right now, Mr. Post remains at the top of the suspect list. We're still waiting on forensics, though."

I sighed. "Okay. Thanks, Quinn. I'll let you know if I find anything out."

His expression softened. "Remember the rule: be careful and don't put yourself in a situation where you could get hurt."

I nodded. "Believe me. It's one of my favorite rules to live by."

Running late, I quickly drove to Declan's apartment only to find he'd already put together a gorgeous panzanella salad with tomatoes, cucumbers, bell peppers, and basil from the garden at the carriage house, along with a sprinkle of savory kalamata olives. The air was redolent with the scent of the toasted sourdough bread he'd used to make the croutons.

"That's the perfect thing to go with Ben's burgers. You are a saint." I quickly kissed his cheek and flew into the bedroom to change out of my workaday skirt, T-shirt, and sneakers into a grass green sundress with tie straps at the shoulder and a full skirt. I'd been told the color complemented my hair, but more important, it was the coolest thing I owned. I added sandals with barely-there straps that I planned to ditch the second I hit the door.

Lucy loved the rooftop garden of their town house in Ardsley Park, and Ben was grilling. It was July, but I knew she'd want to entertain outside, so I was going to be prepared for the evening heat.

Declan drove. On the way, I barely got a word in edgewise as he raved about how terrific my dad was.

"He just marched in there and started asking everyone questions. Then he inspected what's already been done, and Katie, he really knows what he's talking about. He even fired a guy!"

"Wait, what?" I asked, alarmed. "Dad went in and fired someone who is actually working on the carriage house when we're having trouble finding people who can get everything done before the wedding?"

"It's okay, hon. Really."

"No! It's not okay, Deck." Suddenly the weight of the last few days came crashing down and I could hardly breathe. "I thought Dad would help. I thought—"

Declan reached over and took my hand. "It *is* okay. I promise."

Something about the way he said it made me pause. I took a deep breath as he pulled to the curb in front of my aunt and uncle's. "All right." Another deep breath. "Sorry."

He laughed and brushed his finger across my cheek. "No need to be. Just trust me."

I nodded. "I do."

"And soon enough we'll both be saying those words, in our own backyard, behind our new old house."

Chapter 10

Pots of herbs and flowers lined the walkway to the front door and crammed into every space in the entryway. Living in a town house, Lucy didn't have a proper yard, but as a hedgewitch, she couldn't help but grow things. There were culinary herbs and decorative flowers, as well as plants with magical properties. Of course, all plants have magical properties of some sort. She regularly changed out the decoration on the front door and the newest was a spray of angelica planted in a half pot firmly affixed to the door at eye level. Since angelica was an herb of protection and antitheft, it was the perfect choice for the entry to their home.

We entered without knocking. I kicked off my sandals and called out, "Hello?"

"We're in the kitchen," Ben called back.

Mungo dashed past us and into the living room, where Honeybee greeted him as if they didn't spend almost every day together in the bakery. They touched noses, and then my familiar bounded after my aunt's more elegant one, heading for the back of the house.

The living room felt spacious thanks to the vaulted ceilings that were studded with skylights. Tall windows let in even more light, giving it an airy feeling. Hanging ferns added to the atmosphere, and ivy crept up the brick wall around the fireplace. Rugs in bold, geometric patterns set off the glowing cherry-wood floors, and comfortable furniture was arranged in conversational clusters.

The pungent scents of bacon and vinegar rode the air and became even stronger when we entered the kitchen. Glass-fronted cupboards lined the walls, showing off Lucy's collection of stoneware. Bundles of dried herbs hung from the ceiling, and the big wooden table invited casual eating and long chats.

Ben was tossing together hot bacon and green bean potato salad, and I realized I hadn't eaten a proper meal all day. That wasn't a shocker; since I worked in a kitchen, I tended to snack and taste test a lot. Today I hadn't been in the kitchen enough to do even that, so now I was salivating like Pavlov's proverbial dogs.

Declan's eyes widened when he saw the giant burgers piled on a platter, all ready to hit the hot grill. I didn't blame him. Ben added plenty of Old Bay Seasoning and chopped Vidalia onions to his burgers, and he didn't skimp on the size. In between her regular tasks at the Honeybee, Lucy had baked up a batch of fluffy buns to serve the burgers on. My dad sat at the table, carefully removing the silk from ears of

127

corn and rewrapping the husks around them to keep them from burning while they cooked on the grill.

His face lit up when he saw me. "Will you look at all this?" He spread his arms wide to take in the waiting feast.

"Holy crow." I put the bowl of panzanella on the table. "Do you think we have enough food?"

Lucy's eyes twinkled. "Just trying to make Skylar feel welcome. We're grilling fresh peaches for dessert, drizzled with rosemary honey."

Beside me, Declan groaned.

Ben stepped forward. "What can I get everyone to drink?"

The verdict was ice-cold beer all around. Once we had that handled, Lucy directed us to grab whatever we could and take it up to the rooftop.

"The table is already set up there," she said.

I'd been about to suggest we eat inside, out of the heat, but it would have been futile. Lucy saw the look on my face as I picked up the bowl of peaches. "Don't worry. It's nice and cool up there. Ben rigged up a little treat for us."

Thoroughly curious, I followed behind as everyone trooped up the stairs to the third floor, Mungo and Honeybee trailing behind. Lucy opened the door, and we walked into an oasis.

Ben had installed retractable awnings that shaded the entire rooftop area, as well as a series of misters that were spraying their cool fog all around the patio.

"Oh, this is lovely," I breathed.

My aunt gardened entirely in containers. There were at least a hundred potted plants on the roof.

They ranged from the long wooden boxes that hung along the railing on the street side to ficus trees in giant planters on either side of the doorway to a flat of herb starts on the potting bench. There were subtle magical touches from spells my aunt had cast out here, just as I cast spells in a section of my own garden behind the carriage house. A tiny glass fairy peeped over the lip of a terra-cotta container, and the edge of a coin gleamed from beneath a scented geranium. I knew many of these plants were spells themselves, maturing into fruition, and some of them had items buried near the roots.

An orange batik tablecloth covered the wrought-iron table, and soon it was loaded with all the food we'd carried up. Ben got the grill going, and the rest of us collapsed onto chairs.

"To Sky." Declan raised his bottle of pale ale.

"Hear! Hear!" Lucy chimed in.

Dad rolled his eyes, but I could tell he was pleased.

"I started to tell Katie about what happened at the house," Declan said. "But then I decided to leave it to you."

"Well, first off," my dad said with a shrug, "I fired your stonemason."

I stayed calm. At least if the new fireplace in the living room didn't get done, it wouldn't affect the wedding. Maybe we could cover it with a tapestry or something for the reception.

Ugh.

"He was using substandard materials and charging you for the ones he should have been using instead. I caught it in time, though."

"You should have seen the guy's face when he realized he was talking to someone who knows about construction," Declan crowed, not minding in the least that he was admitting he knew next to nothing about being a general contractor.

Lucy tsked.

Ben made an approving noise, then started attacking the grill with a wire brush.

"The good news is that I made some calls to one of the suppliers I use at the hardware store, and he recommended someone who lives in Rincon. That's close, isn't it?"

"Sure," Declan said.

"I have a call in to him."

I felt my shoulders relax. "Oh, Dad. Thank you."

"That's why I'm here," he said. "And you don't have to wait to get started on the bathroom tile, either."

"You know someone who can start right away?" I asked, daring to hope.

He pointed a thumb at his chest. "Sure. I did our bathroom in the basement, and you know how picky your mother is."

I did know. "Really? That would be great."

"I'll start tomorrow. Oh, and the fixtures that were back-ordered?"

"Yeah. I think we have to pick out new ones if we want to get them in time for the wedding."

"Nonsense," he said. "I called another supplier, and they're on the way. You just have to cancel the other order."

We continued to chat while Ben cooked the corn

and burgers on the grill with a bit of help and advice from Declan and my dad. When they were finished, we loaded up our plates and dug in. There was silence for a full minute.

Then I sat back in my chair. "This is so delicious."

Murmurs of agreement all around, then Lucy turned her attention to me and asked, "What did Quinn want to talk to you about?" Since they were hosting dinner tonight, Lucy and Ben had left the bakery while the detective and I had still been chatting.

"You'll never believe it," I said. "He asked for my help."

"Again?" Declan asked with surprise.

I poked him in the arm. "Yes, again. He wants me to go talk to Mr. Bosworth's sister."

"Why?" Lucy asked. "I mean, you wanted to anyway, but I assume Quinn doesn't know that."

"She shut the door in his face," I said. "I don't know that she'll be able to tell me anything useful, but her son does stand to inherit a pile of money, plus his uncle's paranormal collection."

"Oh, really?" Lucy asked.

"Quinn found out and told me."

She leaned forward. "Well, Mimsey stopped by when you were out this afternoon. She heard back from her sister, who told her that she'd lost track of Florinda over the years."

"That's okay. Bosworth's secretary said she lives in Pooler and her last name is Daniels now. I got her address from Quinn."

"Oh, that's good. Marcella did tell Mimsey one

thing. There was absolutely no love lost between Kensington and Florinda. In fact, she absolutely hated him."

"Skipper Dean made it sound like Mr. Bosworth didn't leave money to his sister as a kindness, given her gambling problem," I said thoughtfully.

My aunt shrugged. "Maybe they're both right. Maybe she hated him, and he was still trying to save her from herself. What else did Detective Quinn tell you about Kensington's money?"

I took a sip of beer and grimaced. It had already warmed in the bottle. "Some money goes to his usual charities, but a bunch of it goes to something called the Hermetic Order of the Silver Moon. It's a foundation that supposedly funds charities, but there's no other information about them. Have you ever heard the name?"

Lucy and my dad looked at each other. She shook her head, but he said, "Not exactly. I've heard of the Hermetic Order of the Golden Dawn, though."

"Pretty similar," Declan said, and reached for more corn.

Dad said, "Golden Dawn was a secret magical society in the late nineteenth and early twentieth centuries. It was formed by three Freemasons. They had a tradition of initiation and hierarchy like the masons, but unlike the masons, the Order admitted women on par with men. They explored and taught many aspects of the occult, like ritual magic, spell work, and tarot as well as alchemy, astrology, and astral projection. Some say much of modern Wicca is based on the

132

teachings of the Golden Dawn. I have no doubt there are still a few active chapters around."

"Light magic or dark?" Lucy asked.

My dad shrugged. "Gray, as are a lot of societies like that. Possibly self-serving in some cases."

Like the Dragoh druids, out for money and power. Not inherently evil, but certainly not too worried about high morality.

"But you've never heard of the Silver Moon people?" I asked, looking around the table.

They all shook their heads, even Ben, who had been looking a tad bored with our discussion.

"Okay, I'll see if Steve knows anything about them."

That was met with stony looks from Declan and Ben.

"He might be able to help," I protested.

Declan pushed back from the table. "Excuse me," he said. "I think we left that rosemary honey for the peaches downstairs."

When he was gone, my dad lifted one eyebrow. "Careful, Katie."

"Steve's my friend," I said. And when Lucy gave me a look, I added, "And I know just how far to trust him—and how far not to."

I ate one last bite of juicy tomato and sat back, thoroughly sated. "So, any idea how I can get Florinda Daniels, née Bosworth, to talk to me?"

"To offer your condolences?" Lucy said.

"Mmm," I said noncommittally. "Why would I, a complete stranger, come see her out of the blue to tell

her how sorry I am for her loss? Because her brother
was a customer at the Honeybee?"

She made a face. "Good point."

Dad grinned. "Didn't you say her son inherits that
magical collection you keep talking about? Now, you
couldn't be expected to know that, right? As Bosworth's sister, she'd be the logical one to inherit. Tell
her you've heard of it or even seen it, and you want to
buy it. Or part of it. Or you represent people who are
interested in taking it off her hands."

"You." I pointed at him. "Are a genius."

He grinned. "Tell you what, tell me some of the
things that are in the collection, and I'll come with
you as the buyer."

"I can do better than tell you," I said. "I can show
you a video I took of part of it. Will you be able to
break away tomorrow morning?"

"Early afternoon would be better. I'm dropping
Declan at the firehouse in the morning, and he's letting me use his truck while he's on his forty-eight-
hour shift. I want to be at the carriage house when
the drywaller shows up."

"Okay. That works," I said.

"I'll pick you up at the bakery after the lunch rush.
So, oneish?"

Ben waved his hand. "Iris is working almost full-
time since she's off school for the summer. We can
spare Katie whenever you want her."

"Okay, I'll be there at noon," Dad said.

Declan came back with the rosemary honey and a
container of vanilla ice cream, and Lucy and I began
grilling the peaches for dessert. We were eating them

when I remembered something else I'd been going to ask.

"Does anyone know Caesar Speckman?"

Lucy and Declan shook their heads, but Ben said, "The guy who has the magic and souvenir shop?"

"Yeah. How's Tricks. I've never been in. In fact, I can't remember even seeing it."

"He's a member of the Downtown Business Association," Ben said. "We struck up a conversation at one of the meetings. He invited me to drop by the shop, so one day when I was in the neighborhood, I did." He rolled his eyes. "It may have started out as a magic shop, but now it's crammed full of stuff for the tourists. You know—peach everything, T-shirts, *Bird Girl* statues, guidebooks. Lots of stuff about the ghosts of Savannah. There were still some magic tricks in the back, but they looked pretty dusty."

"Interesting," I said. "Because Malcolm Cardwell said Speckman dealt in paranormal items. Called it his 'side hustle.'"

My uncle shrugged. "Nothing I saw in his shop looked like the authentic stuff I've seen you and Lucy use in your work. However, if Bosworth was fascinated with the paranormal, maybe he was into stage magic as well."

Stage magic? Maybe. But I don't think so. I do think I'd like to visit Caesar Speckman's shop myself, though.

Chapter 11

"Okay, so after one day we already have some real suspects that must have better motive to kill Kensington Bosworth than Randy ever could." I held up my hand and began ticking them off my fingers. "His sister, Florinda."

We were on our way back to the apartment. Declan flipped his turn signal and asked, "What's her motive?"

"Resentment, maybe? Or perhaps she didn't know that she wasn't in the will and was hoping for a windfall. Hey! What if she fell off the gambling wagon and owes a bunch of money?"

He gave me a sideways look. "You shouldn't sound so happy about something like that."

Chastened, I slumped in my seat. "Yeah, you're right. I should wait until I meet her before I start making judgments."

"And maybe not even then," he said mildly.

I brightened. "Or Florinda might have known all

along that she wouldn't get any money in the will, but she killed her brother so her son would benefit."

"Hm. Who else?"

"Her son, of course. Dante Bundy. He does inherit, and money is always a good motive. Plus, that Thunderbird you saw when we went to the crime scene? Well, I saw a car parked behind it with 'Dante' on the license plate. Coincidence?"

He smiled. "Probably not. Does Quinn know?"

"Yep. He's looking into it. I bet if Dante showed up at Mr. Bosworth's door, he'd turn off the alarm to let in his nephew."

"Good point. Okay. Who else? You think one of his charities wanted their donation faster and hired someone to kill him?" He was grinning.

"Very funny," I said. "Though the Silver Moon people sound awfully fishy, and they did get more of the philanthropic money than any of the other organizations."

He gave a kind of facial shrug. "There is that. You really going to ask Steve about them?"

"You know he's a druid, right?"

He grimaced. "Yeah, yeah. Big deal."

"It's not a big deal. It's just that he might know about another secret society in town."

A snort at that. "Some secret society he belongs to. Everyone knows about the Dragohs."

"Not *everyone*. They're still a secret clan. Sort of."

"Whatever."

I sighed. "Listen, do you want me to have someone else ask him? Cookie, maybe?"

There was a long silence as he actually considered that. "Nah. You have to do it. He won't tell anyone else. Who else is on your suspect list?"

He pulled into his parking space and turned off the engine.

I held up my hand, three fingers up. "So far those three, four if you include the Silver Moon people, plus there were two people who knew the code for the alarm system: Malcolm Cardwell and Olivia Gleason."

He got out. I opened the door, and Mungo sprang to the ground. I followed, holding the bowl the salad had been in. Declan scooped up my familiar and carried him up the stairs. Once inside, he turned on the lights, put Mungo down, and turned to me.

"Did you get any gut feeling when you talked to the secretary?" Just a hint of an Irish brogue flavored the question.

"No. . . ." I drew the word out. "He seems pretty aboveboard."

"And you haven't talked to the housekeeper, Gleason, right?" The accent was stronger.

Watching him with narrowed eyes, I said, "Not yet."

He had a funny look on his face.

"What is it?" I asked. "Declan?"

No response.

"Declan! You're scaring me. Is Connell telling you something?"

Something flashed deep behind his eyes, and suddenly I knew I wasn't looking at Declan anymore.

"Aye and begorrah!" Connell shouted, and Mungo growled. "I've been trying to tell yer man—"

"Connell!" I broke in. "How dare you! We have an agreement. If you're going to break it whenever you want to, then it's not really an agreement at all. How am I to know when you're going to get it into your head to show up in Declan's body?"

Never mind that he didn't technically have his own head.

"Oh, stop bein' such a fussy woman," he roared. "I've been trying ter get himself to warn you off this murder investigation, but yer man doesn't seem ter want ter listen. Wants ter save his friend, you know, so maybe that's getting in the way of his listenin' ter me. I've not been subtle, lass."

I rolled my eyes. "I can imagine. But still—"

"No, Katie!" He held a finger up inches from my face, and I flinched. Declan would never do that, but it was his hand and his blue eyes that were flashing. My heart started to race, and a cold sweat broke out on my brow.

"You must believe I don't break our agreement lightly," Connell continued in a lower tone. "*You must be careful.*"

My fear turned to anger. "Why?" I demanded. "What do you know?"

He glared at me for a long moment, then his shoulders slumped, and the glare was replaced with confusion mixed with concern. He reached out and rubbed his thumb along my jaw under my ear, a strangely tender gesture. "'Tis what I don't know, lass."

"Connell . . ."

His hand dropped, and he shook his head. "Thar's somethin' different about the magic involved wi' this murder. Somethin' fierce." He licked his lips. "Somethin' dangerous."

"But . . ." I trailed off as his face underwent another subtle change.

Suddenly Connell was gone.

"Declan?"

He blinked. "Oh, my God, Katie. I'm so sorry."

I shook my head. "Don't be. Connell has my best interests at heart." My emotions were mixed, but I knew that much was true.

Declan took a deep breath. "He does. I've never felt him like this, Katie. He's . . . I think he's afraid."

A shiver ran down my back.

"Maybe you should leave the rest of this investigation to the police."

I stared at him. "But what about Randy?"

"Randy's a good guy. You're the love of my life. Of the two, I'm pretty sure you know who I'm the most concerned about."

With a small smile, I kissed him. "Thank you. And thank Connell. But I haven't had any feelings of danger so far."

Declan's brow wrinkled. "Does that mean you're not going to stop?"

I grimaced. "I believe Connell. I do. Something's not quite right about this one, and I don't just mean that a man was killed. But Quinn asked for my help with Florinda. At the very least, I'm going to talk with her."

He sighed. "At least your dad is going with you tomorrow. I'm going on shift, and I'd rather you didn't go investigating things on your own."

"I can take care of myself."

"You know what I mean."

I smiled and let it go. I didn't like the implication that I was some delicate flower that needed to be protected, but I knew he was on my side.

Long after Declan had already started snoring, I was still staring at the ceiling.

Something different about this magic. Something dangerous.

Continuing to investigate after Connell had made such an effort to warn me felt wrong, but so did abandoning the investigation altogether. How could I just walk away?

At two a.m. I woke with a start and sat straight up, looking wildly around the darkened bedroom. Mungo sprang to his feet at the end of the bed and stood staring at me.

After a few seconds, I realized there was no imminent danger. I'd been dreaming about Iris asking why witches couldn't solve crimes with magic. In the dream, I'd been thinking about how sometimes psychics do help solve crimes. And on that note, I'd woken myself up.

I swung my legs over the bed, lifted Mungo to the floor, and padded out to the living room, thinking furiously. I wasn't a psychic. I didn't have the Sight. In fact, I was crap at workaday divination, even though I'd tried it a few times, both alone and with the help of the spellbook club.

However, I was pretty good at spell work. So were the other ladies in the spellbook club. Plus, I was a catalyst *and* a lightwitch.

And you could create a spell for just about anything.

Right?

So . . . why not?

Why not cast a spell that would give me the Sight?
Not forever, of course. That would take some bigger
magic than I had in mind, and I couldn't be sure of
the repercussions. I mean, I didn't really want to walk
around seeing ghosts or the future all the time.

I just wanted to be clairvoyant long enough to
know who killed Kensington Bosworth. Then I would
tell Quinn, and he could take it from there. That way
I could fulfill my calling as a lightwitch in Kensington
Bosworth's murder investigation, and at the same
time remove myself from the danger Connell had
warned me of.

Quickly, I gathered several of my spellbooks, a
notebook and pen, and my laptop. Settling onto the
sofa, I sketched out an idea of what I had in mind.
When I was done, I sat with it for a few minutes, then
pulled Mungo onto my lap.

"What do you think?"

His brown eyes shone with approval.

"Okay, then. I'll e-mail the ladies, fill them in on
the latest, and see if they can meet after the Honeybee closes tomorrow evening. They can bring supplies, too."

He licked my chin, and I opened my e-mail program.

That night, I slept nearly four delicious hours.

The next morning in the bakery, I made up another
batch of green tomato muffins, but the spell I mur-

mured as I mixed in the thyme had a different emphasis than Iris' had the day before. I was boosting the ability of thyme to augment intuition. Then I added nutmeg and extra cinnamon to the spice cookie dough Iris had already mixed up the previous afternoon, adding an extra *oomph!* to their ability to promote psychic abilities.

I added the extra bits of power only to the treats I planned to use in the clairvoyance spell that evening, and not to the baked goods that would be available to the public. It was benevolent magic, certainly, and only a part of the larger spell I had planned for the evening, but I'd put a lot of focused intention into those treats. It was possible that particularly susceptible customers might find themselves with some kind of temporary Sight, and not everyone would relish such a thing.

When I was finished with the special treats for our evening gathering, I tucked them out of the way on the back counter and got to work on the rest of the day's baking.

After the morning rush, I went back to the office and found myself searching on the computer for Caesar Speckman and How's Tricks—I itched to correct it to How *Are* Tricks every time I saw it. The more I thought about it, the more I realized Speckman might be able to give me important information about the paranormal collection that I was supposedly going to Florinda Daniels' home to discuss that afternoon.

Besides, if things went according to plan, I was going to learn who the murderer was that very evening.

A quick trip to a touristy souvenir store wouldn't hurt anything. Even Connell would have to agree with that.

Or maybe he wouldn't, but I pushed that aside.

Speckman's shop didn't have a website, but there were plenty of favorable reviews on travel sites from customers who had been on vacation and looking for Savannah-centric tchotchkes to take back home. The entrance was off an alley that I couldn't remember ever being down. But Ben knew where it was.

"Hey, Katie. Here are the candles you asked me to bring."

I looked up to see Cookie standing in the doorway. "Hi! Thanks."

She stepped in and handed me four purple votives in glass holders. I put them on the shelf above the filing cabinet, indicated she should take the desk chair, and moved Mungo aside so I could sit beside him on the club chair.

"Don't mind if I do," she said, maneuvering down to a sitting position. "Is everyone in for tonight?"

"Mimsey and Bianca for sure. Jaida probably, but I'm still waiting to hear. And Lucy, of course."

"Well, I love the idea of gaining temporary Sight," she said. "Say, I sold that house I showed yesterday morning, so I decided to take today off from the office. You guys need any help in here?" Cookie had worked at the Honeybee for a while before she was married. The early hours hadn't agreed with her, but she knew the ropes.

I started to shake my head, then stopped. A grin

spread across my face. "I think things are under control here, but do you want to go shopping?"

She quirked an eyebrow. "Shopping?"

"For souvenirs and magic tricks." I explained that I wanted to check out Caesar Speckman's establishment. "I could use the company."

"I'm game," she said, struggling to a standing position. "Let's walk."

Surprised, I asked, "You're serious? In this heat? In your condition?"

"Heat, schmeat," she said. "I grew up in Haiti. Come on."

"Well, okay. Mungo, you coming?"

He lay down, put his chin between his paws, and gazed up at me soulfully.

"You sure? It's only ninety-three or so out there."

A couple of blinks, then he firmly shut his eyes.

I laughed. "Guess he decided his time would be better spent napping."

Cookie reached into her bag and drew out her own familiar—a red, black, and yellow–striped king snake. "Rafe doesn't mind the heat, do you, honey?" She kissed him behind the eyes, and he flicked his tongue at her three times.

I managed to suppress my instinctive shudder. "Let's get going. And don't let Rafe scare the customers on the way out."

As we walked, I told Cookie what I'd learned about Caesar Speckman.

"I don't know if he'll be able to help, but if he was

finding items for Mr. Bosworth to add to his paranormal collection, maybe Caesar knows whether he actively practiced sorcery."

"Just because someone deals with magical artifacts doesn't mean they engage in the Craft themselves," she pointed out.

"True," I agreed, and thought of Connell's warning again. "We'll tread very lightly."

It was only a few blocks to River Street from the Honeybee, but I was ready to get out of the heat by the time we descended the stone steps from Bay Street. Following the directions Ben had given me, we turned left, and several paces farther along discovered a short alley. The sign for How's Tricks hung over a doorway in the middle, perpendicular to the wall, like a tavern sign.

"I've never noticed this before," I said. "Probably walked by it dozens of times."

Cookie frowned. "Me, too."

Our footfalls seemed loud on the oyster-shell tabby, echoing off the high brick walls on either side. We stopped in front of the closed door and looked at each other. It was solid wood, and there were no windows.

I grabbed the handle and pushed.

A welcome rush of cool air greeted us, and we stepped inside. The air smelled like dust and coffee. Not a sound breached the walls, and when the door closed, the silence was so thick I could almost touch it. I sent out my senses, anticipating that they'd encounter some kind of paranormal power. After all, the place was ostensibly a magic shop. However, I didn't feel more than a hint of magic, and even that felt very old—possibly left over from the days when the bricks had first been laid.

Then my eyes adjusted from the bright sunshine outside to the soft fluorescents above, and I took in my surroundings. It wasn't a large space, perhaps fifty feet by seventy-five. The place was packed, though. A few shelves overflowed with tourist guides and maps, while another offered stuffed toys—including several of the tour trolleys that ferried visitors around Savannah's sights. Still more shelves were stacked with commemorative mugs and shot glasses. Brightly lit cases boasted jewelry and candy. There were rotating displays of postcards, refrigerator magnets, and one stacked with half-sized Georgia license plates emblazoned with popular first names. A whole section of the shop was devoted to items related to what locals simply called The Book—*Midnight in the Garden of Good and Evil* by John Berendt. In another area, there were miniature replicas of some of Savannah's well-known statuary, including *Bird Girl*, *Waving Girl*, the African American Monument, and James Oglethorpe, the founder of the colony of Georgia himself. T-shirts hung on the wall behind the register at the back, many of which advertised local sports teams.

"Good heavens," Cookie breathed. "You should have warned me."

I laughed. "It is a bit much, but I'm sure the tourists love it. So many keepsakes to choose from!"

"Mmm-hmm," was her murmured response. She walked over to the jewelry case. "Some of this stuff is pretty nice, actually. A lot of sterling silver."

Joining her, I scanned the contents. One necklace in particular snagged my attention. It was a round locket with a smooth silver face. It was larger than most lockets, however, perhaps an inch and a half across. An idea began to form in my mind.

Footsteps sounded from beyond the open doorway behind the counter. Seconds later a man entered the shop from the back, completely engrossed in the electronic notebook he held in his hand. When he looked up and saw us standing there, his eyes widened in surprise.

"Oh!" His gaze flicked over our shoulders to the front door, and he frowned. "I'm so sorry. I didn't hear you come in."

"No worries," I said, walking toward him. Cookie trailed behind me.

He wasn't much taller than me, with a bit of a paunch and the beginnings of jowls that would only grow more severe as he aged. His wispy blond hair was cut short and beginning to gray. Khaki Dockers and a T-shirt with the Savannah Bananas logo made him look kind of geeky, which wasn't helped by the bright white sneakers on his feet. His eyes were blue behind rimless glasses and held frank curiosity.

"Ladies, may I help you find something?" he asked. "Are you visiting from out of town?"

Cookie and I exchanged glances, then I shook my head. "Actually, we both live here in Savannah."

His eyebrows rose for a moment. "Oh? I usually don't get a lot of local traffic in here."

"I'm Katie Lightfoot. My uncle is Ben Eagel," I

said. "We own the Honeybee Bakery. He told me about you. If you're Caesar Speckman, that is."

"That's me!" he said. "Ben's a good guy, a real good guy. Like him a lot." Then an amused expression crossed his face. "What did he say about me?"

I shrugged. "Just that he knows you from the DBA, and that he's been here in your shop." I looked around. "I bet you do a lot of business in high tourist season. He did mention something else. . . ."

Cookie stepped in. "Magic tricks. Katie is looking for some for her nephew, and Ben told her this would be the place to get them."

"Um, for Declan's nephew, actually." I was an only child and wanted to avoid an obvious lie. Plus, Declan did have a twelve-year-old nephew who would probably love to perform tricks for his friends.

"Of course! I know just the thing you're looking for. Come with me, ladies."

We followed him into a back corner of the shop.

"Here we are. What do you think?" he asked. "Cards? Cups and balls? Coins? Or there's scarf magic, or the ring trick. Here's a whole set with all of that and more." Standing on tiptoe, he grabbed a dusty box from an upper shelf and handed it to me.

"I bet you could sell us some real magical items," Cookie said.

I shot her a sideways look, but she ignored me.

He smiled. "You mean tricks for adults rather than children? I don't—"

"No," she said. "I mean the real deal."

I cleared my throat.

"I'm not sure . . ." He trailed off, looking apologetic.

"Do you sell genuinely magical items?" she asked.

A chill ran down my back. My friend was using her Voice to elicit a truthful answer from the magic-store owner. Hers was more powerful than the other spellbook club members—except mine. However, I was careful not to use my Voice unless absolutely necessary because it had caused so much grief when I'd used it in the past. In fact, I'd nearly killed Declan with it once. That kind of thing can ruin a relationship pretty darn quickly, and I was lucky he'd forgiven me.

Speckman stared at her. "Genuinely magical?" Then his gaze sharpened.

Uh-oh. Cookie's Voice usually lasted longer. *So much for treading lightly.* I nudged her with my elbow.

She gave him an innocent look and put her hand on her belly, as if to distract him with her condition.

It didn't work. "So, you want the real thing, huh?" His eyes narrowed, and he looked between us. "Who the heck are you, really?"

I held the box of magic tricks in front of me as if it were a shield. "As I said, I'm Katie Lightfoot, Ben Eagel's niece. And this is Cookie Rios."

He sighed. "And you fancy yourself witches."

Chapter 12

Cookie started to protest that we were real witches, but I cleared my throat.

"Something like that. And we heard you were Kensington Bosworth's magic dealer," I said.

Caesar looked surprised, then frowned. "I see. You knew Kensington?"

"He was a customer at the bakery," I said. "And I've seen some of his extensive paranormal collection." No need to mention that I'd seen it after he'd been killed.

"Is that so? And he told you I procured some of the items for him?"

I smiled and kept my mouth shut.

He smiled in return. "And now you wish to use my services. Wonderful!"

Cookie opened her mouth to speak again, but I beat her to it. "Perhaps. What can you tell us about Kensington's magical practice? His collection was quite eclectic. Did he focus on practicing one particular kind of magic?"

Caesar Speckman gave a little laugh. "I wouldn't know. The poor guy was all over the board. Little bit of this, little bit of that. He'd talk about how he could use his collection to tap into real magic, but I never believed it. I mean—" Then he seemed to catch himself. "Not that I don't believe! No, indeed. If you want me to find something for your, er, rituals or whatever, I'd be happy to do my best."

He doesn't believe in magic. He's just a businessman.

I exchanged looks with Cookie.

"When did you start working with Mr. Bosworth?" I asked.

His eyes drifted to the ceiling as he thought. "On a regular basis? About two years ago. Before that, I'd found a few items for his father."

"Um . . ." I trailed off.

Caesar smiled. "Yes?"

"His house was very well protected." I took a deep breath and plunged on. "Magically, I mean."

"Oh?" His smile faltered, and he looked uncertain.

"Do you know anything about that?" I asked.

"Um, not really my bailiwick, you know? But I do believe, yes sirree! Maybe ol' Kensington managed a bit of real magic after all." He spoke encouragingly, as if talking to children.

It was really irritating.

"It wasn't enough. He knew it wouldn't be," I said. "He had an alarm system installed."

Caesar quirked an eyebrow. "Is that so?"

"Two weeks ago," I said. "Any idea what he was so afraid of?"

"The usual, I suppose," he said. "Robbery. After all, his home was chock-full of valuable items."

Which was exactly what Malcolm Cardwell had said. Maybe they were both right. Maybe the shielding I'd felt around Bosworth's home had been a simple, everyday precaution. But had he done it himself, or had he enlisted help from someone else? Cardwell thought he'd seen his boss casting a salt circle, but Speckman didn't seem to think Bosworth had possessed any power.

Then again, Speckman didn't appear to believe in real magic at all, despite his lame claim to the contrary. Valuable ceremonial items, along with cheap stage tricks, were just a way to make money.

"So, do you see anything your nephew would like?" The shop owner's eyes twinkled. "Or was there something else you really wanted me to find?"

I realized I was still holding the box labeled JUMBO MAGIC TRICK SET. "This looks perfect."

Disappointment flashed across his face. "That's a good one. Lots of variety. Come along then. I'll ring you up."

We were being dismissed. I guessed I was lucky he'd answered my questions at all, even after Cookie used her Voice on him. Not that he would have necessarily known, of course. Even if he was as big of a believer in magic as he claimed.

I paid for the magic tricks, and he came out from behind the register and walked Cookie and me to the door. We went out to the alley, and he firmly closed the door behind us.

"Hey, hang on a sec," I said to my friend. "I forgot

my wallet in there." I turned and went back inside, while she waited by the entrance to the alley.

Caesar Speckman was only halfway across the shop. He turned back when I entered, an irritated look on his face.

I hurried toward him. "Say, there is something else I wanted."

His expression instantly became solicitous.

"I was wondering if you could get more of those silver lockets." I pointed to the one that I'd seen earlier in the jewelry case.

He leaned down to take a look, then nodded. "How many do you need?"

"Six."

"I'll make a call. Can I reach you at the bakery?"

I assured him he could, thanked him, and hurried back out to where Cookie leaned against the corner of the brick wall. Patting my tote bag, where my wallet had been the whole time, I said, "Got it."

She nodded, and we resumed walking toward the riverfront.

"Did you think it was strange that no one came in the entire time we were there?" she asked. "I mean, I know it's not high season, but there are still a lot of people in town. You'd think someone would want a souvenir or two."

"Yeah, but the place isn't exactly located where there's a lot of foot traffic."

"I wonder how he even makes a living, then."

"Probably why he has a side business finding items for collectors," I said. "And apparently he's linked up with one of the ghost tour companies."

"It sounds like he lost a good customer in Kensington Bosworth," she said. "Hardly a motive for murder. If anything, he'd want to keep the guy alive so he could sell more stuff to him."

I made a sound of agreement, but I was still thinking about those lockets. If Caesar could get six of them, I'd found the bridesmaid gifts I'd been looking for. The lockets were silver, a potent metal that provided security and protected from outside spells, plus they were large enough that I could concoct individual herbal spells and place them inside for each of the ladies of the spellbook club.

Perfect.

When we got back to the bakery, Iris was standing on a stepladder behind the register. She'd cleaned off the tall chalkboard where we listed menu items and was halfway through rewriting it, taking off the discontinued pastries and including the new additions, like red velvet whoopie pies.

"Hey, Katie. I found some muffins and cookies in the back corner in the kitchen," she said as I walked by. "Do you want me to put those in the case?"

"Nope. That's a special order. I'll wrap them up and get them out of the way."

"Okeydoke." Using green chalk she started drawing a vine around the outside of the board, and I continued into the kitchen to store the treats I'd made specifically for the spell that night out of harm's way.

"Oh, and Mimsey came by," she called. "She brought some flowers you ordered. I told her to put them in the fridge. Hope that's okay."

"Of course," I said.

She looked like she wanted to ask a question, then seemed to think better of it. I let it go without comment.

Iris was a hard worker, and she'd taken very well to the hedgewitchery we—Lucy mostly—had been teaching her in the last year. She knew the ladies of the spellbook club were witches, and sometimes I saw a look in her eye when she knew we were meeting that told me how much she wanted to join us. I felt torn. On one hand, everyone liked her, and we wanted to encourage her in magic. On the other hand, at six members, we worked very well together.

Either way, I wasn't going to tell her what I was planning for later that evening. I needed to be able to focus completely, and I wanted everyone else to as well. I loved Iris to death, but that night I didn't want any distractions.

Stowing the magic set in the office, I wondered whether Declan's nephew would like it. If so, I could check that Christmas present off the list.

Dad walked in a little after noon. He looked freshly shaved, and his hair was still wet.

"Sorry I'm late," he said. "I stopped by Ben and Lucy's to take a shower. Couldn't help starting in on the bathroom tile this morning. I think I can get it done in a couple of days."

"Oh, man. I can't tell you how happy that makes me." I gave him a big hug.

He laughed. "Well, then you're going to like the rest of my news, too. The stonemason is a real master. He's going to have to fix some of the work the other guy did, but it shouldn't be a problem. A little unexpected cost, but worth it, believe me. Plus, I got the drywall guy going in the kitchen, and it will be ready for paint in three days. The framers will finish up the closet this afternoon, and then they can get back to finishing up the garage."

I felt my eyes inexplicably fill with tears. "Oh, Dad. You are amazing. Thank you."

His lips curved in a gentle smile. "This stuff is why I'm here, honey. I'm only too glad to help." He ruffled my hair as he'd done when I was a kid. I ducked away as I had then, too. "You ready to go see this murdered fellow's sister?"

I nodded. "Let's go."

Dad drove us to Pooler in Declan's truck while I navigated. On the way, I told him about my plan to cast a spell that night to confer temporary clairvoyance.

"I've been in too many scary situations while following my 'calling,'" I said. "This time, I'm going to try an end run. I mean, if it works, then I'll have done what I set out to do—bring justice to Kensington Bosworth's killer and wipe Randy right off of Quinn's suspect list. And if it doesn't work, no harm, no foul, you know?"

He looked sideways at me, then returned his attention to the road. "Then why are we going out to see the sister?"

"Because Quinn asked me to."

"I see."

"And because I don't know if the spell tonight will work or not," I admitted.

"Do you want a little advice?" he asked.

"Sure."

"When you're casting this evening, ask your totem for help, too. You don't have to do it out loud if you don't want to, just incorporate the request silently into your spell. Your animal is strong. She can help."

"My animal is an insect."

"Do you respect her any less for that? You don't need a bear or a puma, Katie. All beings have their strengths."

"Of course. I'll be sure to ask my dragonfly for help."

I didn't tell him anything about Connell's warning. See, Dad didn't know Connell existed. Even if I had wanted to try to explain who—or what—he was, it wasn't my story to tell. It was up to Declan whether he wanted to confide in my father or not.

Florinda Daniels lived on an acreage outside of town in a ranch-style home accessed by a well-maintained dirt road. Two horses grazed in the field behind, and chickens pecked around the edges of the fenced front yard. The house was neatly painted white with green trim, while the outbuildings were all bright barn red.

Dad stepped down from the truck, stretched his back, and stood with hands on hips regarding the house. The door opened, and a golden retriever bolted toward us, barking furiously. Dad murmured something as it got near, and it fell instantly silent. Tail wagging its whole back end, it cocked its head and eagerly nosed his hand. He leaned down, slid his fingers beneath its collar, and massaged the back of the dog's neck.

"That's a good way to make a friend for life," said the woman who had followed the retriever out the door. "I hope Jackson didn't scare you. He's a bit enthusiastic about letting us know when we have visitors, but he's a gentle soul."

A sleeveless collared shirt topped her Wrangler jeans, and scuffed paddock boots protected her feet.

Dad gave Jackson another scrub under the collar and straightened. "He certainly is. An old soul, too."

She smiled. "Not everyone notices. I'm Flo Daniels." Her words flowed like smooth honey. I could see the resemblance to her brother. However, despite her Southern tones, she didn't strike me as a belle from an established Southern family.

I introduced myself and stuck out my hand. We shook.

"And this is my father, Sky."

She held her hand out to him next, her gaze frankly assessing. It was a little disconcerting to see a woman give my dad the kind of once-over she was giving him. Then she looked at me and stepped back.

"No one just happens onto our property by accident. You must be looking for my husband."

"Actually, we're here to see you."

She looked surprised. "Me?"

"You," I confirmed.

"All right." She waited.

I looked at Dad, and something passed between us. She already liked him. With an infinitesimal nod, he stepped forward. "I understand there was a terrible tragedy in your family."

Florinda stared at him.

He tried again. "I'm so very sorry to hear about your brother."

Finally, she blinked. "You're obviously not a friend of his." Now her expression was skeptical. "Because if you were, you'd know I'm not sorry he's dead."

No love lost between them.

My father's face remained impassive as he held her gaze.

She turned pink. "I mean, I didn't *want* him dead or anything. I'm not *happy* he's gone. I'm just not, you know . . . sad."

He nodded. "Well, I must say that makes the reason I'm here a bit easier."

"The reason . . . why?"

"I'm only relieved that I'm not being too cold-hearted by coming here so soon after your brother's death. You see, I was interested in his very eclectic collection of paranormal items from around the world. I was wondering if that collection would be yours now, and if you might be interested in selling all or part of it."

Smooth, Dad. I didn't know you were so expert at lying.

After a few seconds of hesitation, she said, "Perhaps this is a discussion better had over drinks in the cool shade."

She led us to the front steps, then we followed her along the wraparound porch to the more spacious covered porch at the back of the house. There, three fans hung from the ceiling, which I noticed was painted the same haint blue as Kensington Bosworth's house. Florinda waved us toward wooden Adirondack chairs softened with plump pillows.

"I'll be right back with some tea."

"Thank you," we murmured in unison.

When she returned with a pitcher and three glasses on a tray, we were sitting and looking out at the rolling green pasture and the meadow speckled with wildflowers beyond. Jackson the retriever had taken a position at my dad's feet, resting his chin on the toe of his boot.

"It's beautiful here," I said as she handed me a glass.

Her face brightened, and she softly said, "And peaceful. I love it here. All my life I'd been waiting to find a place that felt like home, and I knew the moment I stepped into the yard out front that this was it. Not exactly what I was brought up to prefer, but there you go." She sat down and turned her attention to my dad. "Jackson really likes you. That goes a long way with me. So, tell me, Sky. You've heard about that ridiculous collection the men in my family have been obsessed with for generations."

He nodded but didn't elaborate.

"Well, I'm sorry to disappoint you, but I can't sell it to you. Believe me, if I could, I would. The whole kit and kaboodle. However, my brother didn't leave it to me. In fact, he didn't leave me anything at all." An undertone of bitterness threaded her words. "Not that I care for myself, you understand. But my husband works so hard, and while we're doing fine, I think he might have been counting on my brother leaving us some money. It would make life easier to know there was a nice nest egg to retire on."

She passed her hand over her eyes and turned to look out toward the horses. "My son never really forgave me for losing the money I inherited when Papa died, but I only really found happiness after it was gone." She turned back to my father. "That's who you need to talk to, Sky. That's who Kenny left the collection to. Dante always wanted more money, lots more money, and now he's got it. Kenny paid for a fancy boarding school and after that, Dante's college education, but he's never done anything with it. I blame the friends he made at the university. Those boys came from deep pockets, indeed. Entitled, you know? I certainly do. I was just like them growing up. Heinrich Dawes was even more indulgent than my father was, though."

I blinked. "Your son went to school with Steve and Arnie Dawes?"

She looked sardonic. "You know of them, then. Well, of course you do. Family like that. And that Powers boy."

"Victor Powers's son?"

He was, among other things, a Georgia politician on the rise.

"The very one." Her gaze returned to the grazing horses. "Dante so wanted to be part of their little clique, but he never really fit in. He blamed it on not having a trust fund like they did, but I'm not so sure. Maybe that was why he was drawn to trouble. He had several run-ins with the law back then. The police were at my door far too often during those years." Her shoulders hunched. "They still make me nervous."

Which explained her reaction to Detective Quinn when he came to see her.

Florinda continued. "My son was prelaw, you know, and Kenny would no doubt have paid for law school, but Dante chose not to continue his education. Now he drifts from job to job. In truth, he just doesn't like to work." She sighed. "And now, depending on how much Kenny left him and whether he sells that bunch of occult nonsense, maybe he won't have to."

Suddenly she drew in a breath and looked back at us. "Oh, my heavens. I've been going on and on. How rude! I'm so very sorry." Then she smiled at my dad. "You are simply too easy to talk to, Sky."

My lips twitched.

Dad smiled back at her. "Thank you. I'll take that as a compliment."

She batted her eyelashes. I'd never actually seen anyone do that in real life.

"Oh, it's meant as one, believe me." Her smile widened. "If you'll leave me your phone number, I'll let Dante know you're interested in Kenny's collection." Suddenly, she frowned. "Of course, I don't know how much of it was stolen when he was killed. I always told Kenny that having all those things right there in the house was an invitation to thieves, and now look what happened. Murdered for what are essentially just trinkets."

Dad and I exchanged glances.

"Oh, dear. Is that what happened?" I asked, even

though Quinn had said nothing was missing from Bosworth's collection.

She stood. "Well, it must have been robbery. My brother wasn't my favorite person, nor I his, but he didn't run around making enemies." She made a face. "Or at least not enemies who would kill him, you know?"

We rose as well. "Thank you very much for speaking with us, Flo," my dad said.

"Of course. Why don't you just text me your number, and I'll get back to you." Dad pulled out his phone, and she rattled off her own number.

Florinda walked us out to the truck. She turned to Dad. "I'll be in touch, Sky."

"Excellent," he said, and climbed behind the wheel.

Florinda watched us go, arms crossed. A plume of dust followed us out to the main road. Dad turned onto the asphalt. "Do you have time to stop by the carriage house before getting back to the bakery?"

I shook my head. "Not if we go talk to Steve Dawes, which is exactly what we need to do now."

"I saw the look on your face when she said his name. Who's Arnie?"

"Steve's little brother. Or he was. Arnie and Declan were roommates and went through training together. From what I've heard, Heinrich Dawes had a fit when his son decided to be a firefighter instead of joining the family business. Maybe he was right. Early in their careers, Declan and Arnie were at a fire where Arnie broke protocol, going in alone and without a safety line. He got lost, and he died that day. Steve has blamed Declan ever since."

Dad whistled. "Rough."

"Yeah. It was. I was surprised that Dante Bundy went to school with Steve and Arnie, but the look on my face might have been when she mentioned Victor Powers. Remember when I told you about the Dragohs? The druid clan Steve belongs to?"

He nodded.

"Victor Powers is their leader, and his son will eventually take his father's place in the clan. I want to ask Steve what he knows about Dante Bundy and whether he has connections to any real magic."

"And about the Hermetic Order of the Silver Moon."

"That, too."

"Well, I must admit I'm a little curious about this reporter friend of yours, and the carriage house will still be there in another couple of hours," Dad said. "Just point me in the right direction."

Chapter 13

The *Savannah Morning News* building boasted an impressive central rotunda. As we approached from the parking lot, I noticed how it combined with the brick pavers, divided windows, and the wrought-iron fence to give the relatively new edifice the feel of old Savannah. Inside, the classical architecture continued. Above, the balustrade-lined walkway looked down on the main entrance. Dad paused to admire the huge compass rose set into the terrazzo floor—a hint at Savannah's nautical history—while I approached the reception desk and asked the young man sitting there for directions to Steve's office. I'd seen his Audi when we parked, so I was pretty sure he was on the premises.

The receptionist frowned and picked up the phone. After a hushed conversation, he directed us to what turned out to be a conference room. Steve was waiting for us inside. He wore cargo shorts and a LIFE IS GOOD T-shirt with flip-flops.

"Hey, Katie-girl."

I grimaced.

He grinned. "About time you stopped by. My cubicle isn't exactly private, so I thought talking here might be better." He stepped forward to give me a hug, then appeared to change his mind when Dad followed me into the room.

I closed the door. "Steve, this is my dad, Sky Lightfoot. Dad, this is Steve Dawes."

Steve stepped forward and enthusiastically pumped my father's hand up and down. "Very glad to meet you, sir. I've heard a lot about you."

Dad gave him a small, speculative smile. "Mmm. I've heard a bit about you, too."

Steve appeared flustered for a moment, then quickly regained his composure. "Well! To what do I owe this surprise visit?"

"Let's sit," I said.

"Sure." He stepped to the other side of the conference table in the middle of the room and turned a chair around backward. Straddling it, he leaned his forearms across the back.

"What do you have for me?" he asked.

"Actually, the question is, what do you have for me?" I slid onto a chair across from him, and Dad sat down next to me.

Steve frowned. "Seriously?"

"What do you know about Dante Bundy?" I asked.

His expression didn't change a whit. Not so much as a blink.

"Come on," I said. "I know you went to school with him."

The skin seemed to tighten across his face. "I did. But I'm not going to tell you a darn thing unless you

167

give me something first. I know you. I know you have information about this case, and I want it." He shrugged, and his expression relaxed. "Or at least some of it."

I tipped my head to the side and smiled at him. "You know I'm trying to get to the truth behind a tragic death. You said it yourself the other night: You've always helped me when I needed it."

His lips twitched. "Katie Lightfoot, are you flirting with me?"

"No!" I stole a look at my dad, who did not appear in the least amused. "But you know darn well why I'm asking about Dante Bundy. He was Kensington Bosworth's nephew. I assume that's not news to you."

"Hardly. The guy never shut up about it. I mean—" He stopped. Shook his head. "Come on. Give me something. Anything. Does Quinn have his sights on any suspects?"

That meant he didn't know about Randy being picked up and questioned by the police. Interesting. Well, I sure as heck wasn't going to be the one who told him. However, I didn't feel bad telling him something that was already public record.

"Dante Bundy inherited a bunch of money from his uncle Kensington." I paused, then plunged ahead. "And that whole collection I told you about. Which, come to think of it, you probably already knew about. Right?"

Steve didn't answer the question. "Are you saying Dante is a suspect?"

"Not officially," I hedged. "That's why I want more information about him."

He sighed and looked at my dad. "Was she like this growing up?"

Dad nodded. "Pretty much."

Steve looked briefly at the ceiling, then back at me. "Okay, okay. Yes, I went to school with him. He hung out with me and my friends for a few months, but it didn't last."

"Why not?"

"He was a wannabe."

"Wannabe rich kid?"

"Yeah, that was part of it. But he wanted to join another group that I'm a member of. I wasn't then, of course. Arnie was still alive then and had agreed to take on the family, er, obligations in that group."

"Dante wanted to be a Dragoh?" I asked in surprise.

Steve's eyes flashed.

I waved my hand in the air. "Dad already knows about your druid clan. The question is, how did Dante know? And did he know specifics?"

"Some," Steve answered in a tight voice. "Not everything."

"How did he find out about you?"

"Not from me or any of my friends. Someone else told him."

"Is Dante trained in magic?"

"Why?"

"Well, there was a pretty powerful protection spell around Mr. Bosworth's house. Or didn't you notice when you were there?"

He sighed. "I noticed. But I have no idea whether Dante currently practices anything besides his golf swing. We pretty much cut him off after he brought up joining the clan." He looked at Dad. "One does not join the Dragohs. One is born into the Dragohs."

"Mmm. So I understand," he said drily. "But back in the day, Dante apparently didn't know that."

"Maybe," Steve said. "It's not like we talked to him about it."

"What about the Hermetic Order of the Silver Moon?" I asked.

He stared at me. "What do you know about that?"

"Mr. Bosworth had some kind of connection to it."

Suddenly, he stood and began pacing back and forth. "That's impossible. What kind of connection? For how long?"

I leaned back in my chair and regarded him. "I don't know the answers to any of those questions. In fact, I don't even know what the Order is, other than it's some kind of foundation Kensington Bosworth left money to."

He stopped. "Foundation! Where did you get that crazy idea?"

"From Quinn. But there's very little information available about it."

Dropping into his chair, he stared out the window. "No kidding."

"Steve, please. What is the Hermetic Order of the Silver Moon?" I pleaded.

Turning back, he distributed a look between us. "I could be wrong. I mean, maybe there is a genuine group with that name, though how that could be, I can't fathom. But the Order I've heard of, and I've only heard rumors, used to be a druidic clan here in town."

"Geez. How many of them are there?" I asked.

"Only one now," he said tightly. "The Silver Moon druids and the Dragohs were, shall we say, rivals. We're still here. They aren't."

"You make it sound like the Jets and the Sharks," I said.

He didn't smile. "You're not far off."

"Huh. And now they're . . . oh, good heavens. You're not going to tell me the Dragohs actually, you know, *eliminated* the Silver Moon druids." I couldn't quite bring myself to say the word *killed*.

Steve shook his head. "No, nothing like that. We, um, discouraged potential new members from joining their clan. That was back in the 1950s. The Order died from attrition."

"Was Kensington Bosworth's father a member?"

"I have no idea," he said. "But my father might know."

"If he was, then maybe Kensington was also a druid." The idea was a little hard to imagine, but not impossible. I'd learned that power flowed behind some of the most mundane appearances. "In fact, I wonder if the Silver Moon druids ever really went away," I said slowly. "Maybe they were just good at keeping a low profile."

"The Dragohs would know if there were still any Silver Moon druids around." Steve's mouth turned up in a small smile I found disturbing.

"Are you sure?" I insisted.

The smile remained for a few more seconds, then his lips thinned, and he abruptly stood. "If you'll excuse me, I have some phone calls to make."

Dad and I rose, and I opened the door.

Steve followed us out to the hallway. "I'll get back to you if I find anything out. Sky, nice to meet you." Without waiting for a reply, he turned and went back into the conference room and closed the door behind him, his cell phone already in his hand.

"What do you think?" I asked Dad as he drove out of the parking lot.

"I think if there are rival druid gangs involved in this case, I want you out of it."

"Yeah. Well, if things go well tonight, I'll be able to identify the killer and Quinn can take it from there."

"Yes, but will he?" he asked.

I rubbed my eyes, suddenly tired. "I can only hope so."

It was nearly three when we got back to the Honeybee. Dad dropped me off in front, then left to check on the progress at the carriage house. I hurried inside, full of apologies for being gone for so long, but Lucy waved them away.

"We managed just fine," my aunt said in a mild tone, then glanced toward the kitchen. "In fact, Iris is nearly done with tomorrow's prep."

I followed her gaze and saw our employee madly chopping dried apricots for the marmalade scones that would be the next day's special. She finished and scooped them into a lidded bowl, swaying her hips in a dance shuffle as she stowed the bowl on a back counter.

172

"She's in a good mood," I said.

Lucy nodded. "She's got a date tonight."

"Ooh." I grinned. "Details?"

"You'll have to ask her."

I went back to the office and stowed my tote bag, gave Mungo a scritch and a kiss between his ears, then joined Iris. She had moved on to scrubbing down the appliances, still doing her little two-step as she moved from the range to the industrial sink.

"I love it when you do that," I said.

She grew still and looked up at me with a puzzled expression. "Clean?"

"No. That dance thing." I pointed to the floor at her feet.

Her face reddened. "Oh, God. How embarrassing."

"Really? You always look so happy when you do it. It makes things cheery around here."

Her blush deepened. "I didn't realize I did it." She bit her lip, then seemed to make a decision. "See, my dad taught me how to dance when I was little. I mean, really little. At first, I stood on his feet, and he held my hands."

"That's sweet."

"It was. And it made me happy, every time we danced. The last time was my middle school graduation." She took a shaky breath. "Then he got sick and, well, you know."

I nodded. Iris' father had passed away when she was thirteen. She still lived with her stepmother, Patsy, while going to school at SCAD.

"I guess it's one of the ways I hold on to him."

"Dancing with him made you happy, and now when

you're happy, you dance. Makes perfect sense to me. I didn't mean to make you self-conscious. Please don't stop just because I said something."

She smiled. "Well, when you put it that way."

"I hear you have a date," I said.

Her head bobbed. "Oh, Katie, he's amazing! I met him in my illustration class, though he's actually majoring in sound design."

"He's cute?"

"Katie, that's so shallow!" But then another huge smile broke out on her face. "He's gorgeous. Tall and thin with thick brown hair." She looked up at the ceiling with a dreamy expression. "He wears it in a modern pompadour." Her feet shuffled a bit. This time she noticed and stopped. Then she shrugged, gave a little giggle, and danced over to the refrigerator with her cleaning supplies.

Laughing, I went to check in with Lucy and Ben.

Iris left early to get ready for her big date, and at four thirty I went back to the office to review my plan for the evening. Admittedly, I was taking a shotgun approach to the spell. That meant using every aspect of magic that the spellbook club members specialized in. My own contributions were the baked goods imbued with strong kitchen magic.

I heard voices out in the bakery. The ladies were arriving. However, there was one more thing I needed to do before joining them. It had been forming in my mind all day, and now I took a piece of blank paper out of the printer tray and carefully wrote out the spell I wanted to invoke.

Mungo watched with interest. When I was done, I read it out loud to him.

Future, past, and present Sight
I will gain this summer night.
Psychic powers come to me
Plain the murderer to see.
As we cast, our will be done
And once I know
The Sight is gone.
This single fact
Is all I need.
The case is cracked
For this we plead.
So mote it be.

When I was done, he tipped his head to the side as if trying to make up his mind.

"Yeah, I know. Not exactly beautiful poetry, but it gets at what I want to accomplish. Think it will work?"

He jumped to the floor and trotted to the open doorway. Then he turned and looked over his shoulder at me.

Yip!

Chapter 14

The ladies had all gathered in the library area. They'd already cleared the sofa and chairs to the sides, moved in one of the bistro tables, and on top of it had assembled the things I'd asked them to bring. Ben finished closing the café curtains, gave me a peck on the cheek, and left. Lucy took off her apron and slipped out of her Birkenstocks. Barefoot, she drew the floor-to-ceiling curtain across the entrance to the reading area, shutting it off so that passersby couldn't see inside if they happened to glance in the front door of the bakery.

Inside the book-lined space, the light was hazy and blue, almost like twilight despite the heat of the day outside. The air was cool as well, which added to the illusion. The only sound was the quiet hum of the air-conditioning in the background, a low and soothing white noise that canceled the sound of traffic out on Broughton Street.

It didn't cancel the rumble of a big engine going

down the alley out back, though. I realized it was probably a truck delivering to one of the retail spaces in the block, then put it out of my mind altogether and gathered the muffins and cookies I'd made that morning. I put them on a tray along with a pitcher of fresh lemonade from the refrigerator and six small glasses. Lemons resonated with the energy of the moon and were particularly useful in summertime spells. Besides, we needed something to wash down the magical treats.

"Ladies," I said as I put the tray down on the coffee table. "Thank you for coming. I've made a few special goodies to help direct our spell this evening."

They exchanged glances, but everyone reached for a muffin or a cookie and a glass of lemonade.

"Happy to be here, honey." Mimsey wore indigo slacks and a blouse covered with indigo and lavender flowers—colors that tapped into psychic awareness and intuition. Despite her words, a tiny frown creased her forehead.

"What's wrong?" I asked.

Her lips pressed together. "I'm just not sure about this spell you have in mind. Clairvoyance isn't something to be trifled with."

I half smiled. "No, it's not. And I know you don't think we can use magic to solve a crime, at least not directly." I hesitated, then plunged on. "I'd like to try, though. You see, Connell showed up last night."

There were surprised looks all around.

"Oh, Katie." Lucy's forehead was creased with worry. "I thought that was over."

"Apparently, it's not entirely over. He apologized like crazy, of course, but he felt it was necessary to warn me."

Now my aunt's eyes widened in alarm. "Warn you? Of what?"

I shook my head. "He wasn't very specific. He wasn't being coy. I truly think he didn't know more than he told me."

"Which was what?" Jaida demanded. She was wearing khaki capris and a sleek red tank top.

"That there was something strange about the magic in this case. Something dangerous. And that I should leave it alone."

Silence descended on the group.

"But you don't want to abandon Randy," Bianca finally said in a quiet voice. "This is your solution?"

I nodded.

"I don't know. Mimsey's right. What if you're stuck being clairvoyant as a result of this spell? We're a pretty powerful bunch, you know." Bianca bit her lower lip, then turned her intense green-eyed gaze full on me. "I'd have a hard time living with it if you were permanently given the Sight."

"Oh, for heaven's sake," Cookie said. She looked especially young tonight with her hair in a ponytail and no makeup. "What would be so wrong with that? Being able to tell the future? Win the lottery? Heck, I'd take it." A speculative look settled on her face after she spoke the last sentence.

"You don't even want to know whether you're having a boy or a girl," Bianca pointed out.

"Clairvoyance visits everyone differently, Cookie.

You could see far more than you want to," Mimsey said. "Sometimes the Sight isn't even visual. It could be something heard or felt instead. It could be the future or the past or one of several possible presents. Clairvoyance isn't just intuition, and it's not always controllable. Katie could be saddled with violent visions or visited by ghosts—benign or otherwise. Her everyday life could be affected with an overlay of another plane that exists alongside ours. Most people who were born with the Sight have learned over a lifetime how to control it, at least somewhat. Katie might not be able to."

Cookie stared at the older witch, then at me. "Oh. I guess I never really thought about what it would be like to suddenly gain the Sight." She took a breath and looked around at the others. "Maybe this *is* a bad idea."

Lucy took a deep breath. "I agree. I don't think you should go through with this, Katie. When you e-mailed us about what you wanted to do, I tried to convince myself that it would be okay. I've seen how you've grown in the Craft, how readily you've tapped into your innate abilities, and how your magic has grown. Even so . . . this might be too much."

I chose my next words carefully. "Given Connell's warning, I can't think of another option. And Lucy, I think you know deep down that we can do this. If you weren't my aunt, you might not question it at all."

She made a face but didn't deny it.

"Furthermore, there's no guarantee that if I—if we—stop investigating Mr. Bosworth's murder that I'm suddenly scot-free." I took a deep breath and continued. "As Bianca said, we're pretty powerful together. We ought to be able to control the spell, especially as a group."

Lucy met my gaze, then pressed her lips together and seemed to make a decision. "Okay. We can at least hear what Katie has in mind."

I smiled my gratitude at her. "Let's take a look at our tools."

We gathered around the bistro table.

"I'm thinking of a burning spell." I pointed to the silver bowl in the middle of the table. It was about ten inches in diameter and embossed with interlinked pentagrams. "In Bianca's cauldron." I glanced over at her. "Thanks for bringing it."

"Of course."

My aunt nodded. "A burning spell makes sense. That was one of the first spells you ever cast."

"Right. And we can tap into everyone's capabilities. Jaida, what tarot card did you decide would be best for tonight?"

She reached down to the table and turned over the card she'd brought. It was from the classic Rider-Waite tarot deck and depicted a woman in a blue robe with a cross on her chest and a horned crown on her head. She sat in front of a veil decorated with what looked like apples, but I knew were pomegranates. They were sacred to Persephone, the queen of the dead.

"The High Priestess," she said. "She represents the subconscious and hidden mysteries. She maneuvers between the here and now as well as accessing deeper psychic information we're usually not privy to."

"Perfect," I said. "Mimsey?"

She picked up the vase of blossoms she'd retrieved from the fridge. "Jasmine and magnolia are both conducive to increasing psychic awareness." She gave a little laugh. "Not to mention, they smell heavenly, and I always have some on hand for flower arrangements."

Breathing deeply of their scent, I said, "Sounds just right for tonight. Thanks."

She nodded and turned to Lucy.

My aunt picked up a small earthenware bowl and removed the openwork lid. "Potpourri that I made from plants I've grown and dried in my herb room at home. All promote intuition or psychic connection."

I leaned forward and took a whiff. "Smells lovely. What's in it?"

"Bay leaf, honeysuckle, and lemongrass. A few rose petals. A sprinkle of sage." She grinned. "And a little incantation to trigger them."

"A spell within a spell. Nice."

Bianca's hair, worn long and loose tonight, shielded her face as she leaned down to the table. Brushing her hair over the shoulder of her flowing gauze tunic, she straightened and held up a smooth white rock with a sheen like a pearl. "I cleared this moonstone in the light of the full moon. Thought it might come in handy."

I touched it with the tip of my finger. Moonstone was a conduit for intuition and prophecy. "Thank you."

She held my gaze for a long moment, then nodded and returned the stone to the table with the other items.

"Well, I brought the candles, at least," Cookie said with a shrug.

I wondered if she felt a little left out. "Purple candles, vital for invoking the circle."

She suddenly grinned and held out her hand. "Right. And here's a little extra protection for the circle."

I took the vial she held. "What's this?"

"Black salt. Not the fancy stuff from Hawaii that people cook with. This is witch's salt, mixed with scrapings from a cast-iron pot and the ashes of burnt walnut shells. Oh, and a little patchouli."

"Patchouli," I repeated.

She shrugged. "It's in the recipe."

I turned the vial and watched the salt flow from one end to the other. "Wow."

"Thank you, Cookie," Mimsey said. "That will indeed strengthen the circle." She looked at me. "And that will help keep the spell contained. But even so, how do you plan to direct the spell so that you get the information you desire—the identity of Kensington Bosworth's killer—rather than whatever information the universe might randomly reveal to your newfound and hopefully temporary Sight?"

Reaching into my pocket, I took out the spell I'd written and handed it to her. She perused it carefully, then handed it to Jaida to read.

"Yes," Mimsey said thoughtfully. "Yes, I think that might do it."

Once they'd had a chance to read it, the other ladies nodded their agreement.

"Okay, then. Shall we get started?" I asked.

"Absolutely," Lucy said.

I glanced over to where Mungo, Honeybee, Puck the ferret, and Rafe the king snake waited by the window. The familiars would stay outside the circle but be ready to assist us if needed.

Jaida, Cookie, Bianca, and Mimsey each picked up a purple votive in a glass holder, then went to one of the four compass points and placed the candle on the floor. They stepped back to the central table. Lucy took the vial of black salt, walked to the eastern candle, and began sprinkling the dark crystals on the floor. She continued deosil, or clockwise, around to the southern candle, then to the western one, the northern one, and finally she ended at the eastern candle again and closed the salt circle.

She returned to the table, picked up a lighter, and handed it to Mimsey. The older witch nodded and went to the eastern candle. Bending down, she lit it, then straightened and said, "We call upon the archangel Raphael and the element of air to aid us in this endeavor."

"So mote it be," we all murmured.

Mimsey continued to the southern compass point, lit the candle, and said, "We call upon the archangel Michael and the element of fire to aid us in this endeavor."

"So mote it be," we responded.

And so it went with the western candle, calling upon Gabriel and water, then Uriel and earth to the north. Mimsey completed the circle again at the east, then joined us.

"Jaida," she said. "You begin."

Nodding, Jaida gently picked up the High Priestess card and placed it in the cauldron. Next, Mimsey pinched off a sprig of jasmine and three magnolia petals and added them to the pot. Lucy picked up her container of potpourri and tipped a little in. I nodded to Bianca, who placed the moonstone next to the silver vessel, adding to the spell but not to be burned. Then I unfolded my spell again and held it out, so everyone could help me read it out loud.

Future, past, and present Sight
I will gain this summer night.
Psychic powers come to me
Plain the murderer to see.
As we cast, our will be done
And once I know
The Sight is gone.
This single fact
Is all I need.
The case is cracked
For this we plead.
So mote it be.

"Above, below, and within," Mimsey said.

I added the paper to Bianca's silver bowl and struck a wooden kitchen match. The others joined hands around me in yet another circle. I lit the contents in the cauldron, then gripped the sides of the table and closed my eyes.

Waiting. Willing.

Then I remembered what Dad had said and silently called out to my totem.

Dragonfly, please aid this endeavor however you can.

There was a flutter of wings at the edge of my

consciousness, then it stilled. Nothing else happened for several long seconds. Then the hum of the air conditioner seemed to grow fainter. The atmosphere thickened around me. I opened my eyes and could see the others standing, hand in hand, watching me with intense expressions of hope and worry. However, there was something different about them. They didn't appear as solid as usual. I blinked, and they became a little more transparent. Then I realized their lips were moving, chanting something, but I couldn't hear them.

In fact, I couldn't hear anything at all. But that was okay. Everything was okay. Except I was supposed to be looking for something. Learning something. What was it?

Movement outside the circle drew my attention.

Nonna!

My grandmother, as I remembered her from when I'd last seen her alive when I was nine years old, stood by the bookshelf. Her long red hair was streaked with white and twisted into a loose braid that coiled around her head. Laugh lines framed her mouth and eyes, while her round cheeks were smooth and pink. Her green eyes seemed to glow in the twilight of the room as she turned her gaze on me. The familiars were all staring at her, and it occurred to me to wonder whether they could always see the spirits around us.

I smiled in relief and waved. My grandmother would protect me. "Hi, Nonna! It so good to see you," I said. Or I thought I said. My lips moved, but if I made a sound, I couldn't hear it.

Usually, I only heard my grandmother. I'd never seen her like this. The spell was working!

She waved back at me. Except it wasn't a wave, really, and her face was stern. She was holding up her hand like a crossing guard. Then the other one came up. She made a pushing motion.

And her lips were moving. I shook my head. "I can't hear you, Nonna. I'm sorry."

She didn't stop, though. She kept repeating words over and over. I squinted, trying to read her lips.

"Stop . . . Danger . . ."

A feeling of dread settled upon me as I realized she was trying to warn me of something.

"Must stop! Now! Katie . . ."

Her eyes pleaded with me.

"I don't know what you want me to do!" I shouted.

And finally, I could hear her.

"Stop the spell. Break the circle. Your magic is feeding the wrong spell!"

Fear stabbed through me. I didn't know what to do. Except—

Quickly, I moved to where Mimsey and Lucy held hands. Grabbing them, I forcibly pulled them apart. As their fingers parted, my ears filled with sound.

A loud *pop!* in the cauldron was followed by a flash of light and a whoosh of smoke. Mungo began barking, a high and desperate sound that chilled my blood. Honeybee caterwauled. Rafe hissed. Puck ran around the circle, trying to get to Bianca. Then suddenly he ran inside and up her skirt and arm to her shoulder.

He ran inside.

I had only a split second to realize I'd succeeded in breaking the circle. Then everything went black. I felt myself begin to fall. Gentle hands eased me down to the floor.

"She's passed out!" Lucy said. "Call 911!"

But I hadn't passed out. I was still conscious. I blinked rapidly, and my vision began to return.

"No," I moaned.

Mimsey kneeled beside me. "Ladies! The Sight has overwhelmed her. Come help—"

"It's not that," I broke in. "I'm okay."

Only I wasn't. Something was wrong.

Really, really *wrong*.

No. Something was really, really *gone*.

I gasped and struggled to sit up. "No!" Looking wildly around, I saw them all staring at me. "This can't be." I was panting like a terrified animal.

Lucy grabbed my shoulders. "Katie, *what's wrong*?" she demanded in a shrill tone I'd never heard her use before.

"It's gone," I said.

"What's gone?" Mimsey asked, looking just as worried as my aunt.

"My magic," I whispered. "I can't feel my magic anymore."

Chapter 15

"Nonsense!" Mimsey said briskly. "Witches don't just up and lose their magic. Come along, Katie. Let's get you off the floor."

Obediently, I let them haul me to my feet and lead me to the sofa. Nonna wasn't in the Honeybee anymore. At least I couldn't see or hear her. The spellbook club members were their good old solid selves again, which was a relief. However, there was an absence.

A lack. A gray dullness to everything.

It was as if water had been drained from a bowl of pebbles. Like the pebbles, I remained. Like the water, my magic had flowed away, leaving unfilled gaps in my being.

How could this have happened? What, exactly, did happen?

I tried to wrap my mind around it, to remember the details of the spell. Had we done something wrong?

Wait. Nonna had said something.

"Your magic is feeding the wrong spell."

What spell? Someone else's spell?

"Is everyone else all right?" I asked, afraid that whatever had happened—or *whoever* had happened—had stripped their gifts from everyone in the coven.

They looked around at one another.

"I feel fine," Lucy said slowly. Honeybee jumped on the arm of the sofa and rubbed her head against my aunt's arm.

"Me, too," Bianca said, reaching over and brushing my hair back from my temple.

The others murmured agreement.

"Of course, we feel fine!" Mimsey said. "And you will, too, Katie. Just rest here for a bit. This must be the aftermath of the spell."

"I don't think so," I said slowly.

"We heard you talking to someone," Bianca said. "Did you learn the identity of Kensington Bosworth's killer?"

My eyes filled with tears as I shook my head. "No. I was talking to Nonna." I looked at Lucy, who had never been visited by her mother, though Nonna had shown up to chide my mother at least one time that I knew of.

My aunt frowned. "What did she say?"

"She . . ." I hesitated. "She told me to stop the spell. That's why I broke the circle. She said something about danger. I don't know what. I couldn't actually hear her. Which is weird, you know? Because usually I can *only* hear her, yet this time—"

"What kind of danger?" Cookie broke in. She came

over and perched on the edge of the sturdy coffee table. Rafe had twined his yellow, black, and red–striped body around her forearm.

A tear spilled over onto my cheek. "I don't know. She said, '*Your magic is feeding the wrong spell.*'"

The ladies looked at one another anxiously, and suddenly Mimsey didn't appear quite so sure of herself.

"I should have listened to Connell." I tried unsuccessfully to keep the quaver out of my voice.

Lucy sat down next to me and put her arm around me. "You didn't do anything wrong, honey. You only wanted to do good."

Bianca hugged herself and turned away. I wanted to tell her not to blame herself, that I would have tried to clear Randy even if he hadn't been her boyfriend, that I really did believe in seeking out the truth, that Quinn really had needed me.

But I didn't. Because without my magic, I wasn't a witch anymore, was I? And Quinn needed a witch for his paranormal cases, not just some random baker.

Oh, God. What if I can't bake anymore? That was part of my gift.

I let out a sob and clamped my hand over my mouth.

"Now, hang on," Mimsey said. "Mungo, come here, please."

Mine was the only familiar present who hadn't joined us. He stood by the bookshelf, his head cocked to one side as if he couldn't figure out what was going on. When Mimsey called him over, he didn't budge.

"Mungo, honey?" I pleaded.

Slowly, he crossed the room and stopped by my foot. I patted the sofa cushion beside me. Instead of jumping up and snuggling with me like he normally would, he sniffed my leg and backed away.

"Please?"

But that was gone, too. Our connection. That thing where I knew what he was thinking. Where he knew what I was talking about. The magic that intertwined us.

He whimpered and ran out of the reading area toward the kitchen.

"No," I sobbed. "No."

I choked out the word again and again from the bottom of my broken heart.

I don't know how long I cried. There were a lot of tissues thrust at me, and hot drinks and cold drinks. Finally, Lucy made me swallow a shot of the bourbon we used in our pecan pies, and that did the trick.

Shakily, I blew my nose. "I'm sorry, everyone."

"Don't be silly," Bianca said, worry creasing her brow.

Jaida sat down across from me. "Can you tell us what happened during the spell?"

I closed my eyes and tried to remember. Carefully, I told them everything I could remember, ending with, "I really thought it was working." My throat felt tight again. "I really thought I could learn who killed Mr. Bosworth."

"Declan is on his way," Lucy said. "And I left a message for your dad."

"What? Declan can't leave work. I mean, I'm not sick or anything."

I saw the others exchanging looks. I was already

too upset to care, though. And heck, I could see how they'd see losing my magic as a kind of sickness.

But maybe not terminal.

"Do you think this could be temporary?" I asked, suddenly daring to hope.

Cookie said, "Geez, I sure hope so. It must really suck not to have any magic."

Mimsey spared her a glare before saying, "That's entirely possible, honey. Let us see what we can find out. I think for now you should go home and take it easy. Draw a nice hot bath. Throw in some Epsom salts and some lavender. Go to bed early."

Great. The last thing I need is to stare at the ceiling for hours on end.

A loud pounding on the front door distracted me. It was Declan. My dad must have picked him up at the firehouse in the truck, because he was right there beside him, one hand cupped around his eyes as he peered through the glass.

My aunt hurried to let them in, and I got up and followed her. Seconds later, Declan enfolded me in a hug. I sighed into his shoulder and closed my eyes, letting myself feel like I was six years old for a few moments.

Then I pushed away. "Lucy told you what happened?"

He nodded. "I don't really understand, though."

"Any hint from you-know-who?" I asked.

Grimacing, he shook his head. "I wish there was, but he's silent. Sky, what do you think about what Lucy told us?"

Dad, who had been watching our cryptic exchange

about Connell with puzzled interest, frowned. "She said you lost your magic, Katie. How can that be?"

"I don't know. But it's—" I swallowed. "It's gone."

His forehead wrinkled as he tried to figure out exactly what that meant.

I got it. I really did. As Mimsey said, witches don't just suddenly lose their magic. And in fact, not just witches, but everyone possesses magic of some kind, and though it might be masked in some people, it didn't just go away.

Not unless . . .

"A hex," I said slowly, and looked around at everyone. "Maybe someone put a spell on me."

Mimsey's eyes lit up. "If that's what happened, then we might be able to find a counter spell. Ladies, we've got some research to do. Katie, Declan can take you home. Wait to hear from us."

I convinced Declan I'd be okay and to go back to work. He resisted until Lucy told him I'd be spending the night at their town house. I quickly agreed. So, after a long kiss and a reluctant wave, he left with Dad. The members of the spellbook club had already hurried away to start their research, and Lucy began cleaning up the Honeybee reading area. I insisted on helping, though I probably wasn't that useful. By then a thick numbness had settled into my psyche, and over and over I found myself staring into space as I tried to put together what had happened to me.

When everything in the Honeybee was tidy and prepped for the next morning, I braced myself and went back to the office. Mungo was sitting on his chair rather than lounging, watching the door as if he expected me to come in and give him a darn good explanation of what was going on.

"Sorry, buddy," I sighed. "You were there. You saw Nonna, too, didn't you?"

He looked puzzled.

"After that, I don't know what happened. But the spellbook club is on it, and I'm hoping we find a solution soon. Don't give up, okay? I need you on my side."

He jumped to the floor, came over by my foot, and sat down. I picked him up, and he nosed my chin, then gave it a hesitant little lick with the very tip of his tongue.

It was better than nothing. "Thanks, little guy."

At Lucy and Ben's, we ate a cold supper of ham sandwiches and fruit. It was a quiet meal for the most part, punctuated by spates of forced chitchat that kept falling back into silence. By eight thirty, Mungo and I had retired to the fold-out sofa bed in Lucy's herb room, since Dad was staying in their guest room. I sat propped up against the pillows, flipping through my aunt's collection of spellbooks to see if I could find anything that might help.

"Your magic is feeding the wrong spell."

What kind of spell had Nonna meant?

There were protection spells, which would be too late, and reversal spells, which would help now—only the ones I found required that you know exactly what kind of spell you were reversing. None of the books contained a hex that resulted in someone losing their magic. There were spells to block magic, to send it back to the user, and to dissipate a spell, but nothing like what had happened that afternoon.

Still, I was sure someone was responsible. Over and over, I thought of what Connell had said about the magic in this case being strange somehow. Being dangerous. Well, he'd been right.

It has to be dark magic. No wonder I can't find it in Lucy's spellbooks.

There was a knock on the door.

"Come in." I closed the book on my lap as the knob turned.

My dad stuck his head in. "Hey, honey. How're you doing?"

I shrugged. "At least I'm not bawling my head off now. That's progress from earlier today."

He came over and sat down on the edge of the bed. Mungo went over and nosed his hand, which Dad rewarded with some good ear scritchin's.

"I'm sorry you're hurting," he said.

I managed a wan smile.

"I've never heard of anything like this happening."

Waving at the pile of books beside me, I said, "You're not the only one."

"Still, I think I might be able to help."

I stared at him, feeling another seed of hope begin to sprout. "Really? How? What do I need to do?"

He shook his head. "Not tonight. I need to prepare. And I need to talk to your mother."

Rubbing my eyes, I groaned. "I haven't told her."

"Don't worry. I'll handle it."

"She'll probably think losing my magic is for the

best anyway." I couldn't keep the sarcasm out of my voice.

"Now, Katie."

"She never wanted me to know anything about my gift. She hid it from me. And now it's gone. I barely got a chance to practice the Craft, Dad! Because of her." I knew I wasn't being fair. Truthful, yes, but not really fair.

"Your mother did what she thought was best," he said. "And you know how she feels now. She's happy for you."

I opened my mouth to speak, but he shook his head again and reached over to tousle my hair. "Keep a good thought, okay? It's important. Don't add any more negativity to this if you can help it."

Slumping, I nodded. "Okay. I'll try."

Certain I'd be awake and fretting all night, I was relieved when I conked right out and slept until Lucy woke me at six the next morning.

Almost. Because I'd come to believe my sleep disorder was related to my magic, and now, just like my magic, the sleep disorder was gone.

It didn't help that after all that rest, I felt exhausted as I drove to the Honeybee.

Chapter 16

Of course, I went to work. Not because I particularly wanted to, but because I didn't know what else to do. However, since I'd slept in, we got a late start, and from the get-go I could feel myself just going through the motions.

Measure, stir, mix.

Dollop or roll or knead. Whatever the recipe called for next.

Put it in a pan. Put it in the oven. Put it on the rack. Put it in the display case. Put it in a bag and watch the customer carry it out the door.

No incantations. No spell work. No helpful nudges toward money or love or happiness.

Two loaves of sourdough bread collapsed into rock-hard lumps while they were baking. The whoopie pies came out lopsided. The banana muffins tasted like soap.

"Nonsense!" Lucy said, echoing Mimsey from the day before. "They taste just fine."

However, I noticed she put them in the back of the

bottom tray in the display case, where few customers would notice them.

At quarter after ten, the phone on the wall rang. Ben scooped it out of its cradle.

"Honeybee Bakery. Sweet or savory, we've got you covered."

I rolled my eyes. He was always trying out new ways to greet our callers.

"Caesar! Well, hey there. How're you doing?" He chuckled. "Or should I say, how's tricks?"

That got my attention. I put down the rolling pin I was holding and turned toward my uncle.

He caught my eye and waved me over. "Good, good. Glad to hear it. . . . Yep, everything's going well here. Slow season and all. But winter is coming." He laughed. "Right. For us, that's a good thing." He glanced at me. "Yep, she's right here. Hang on a sec."

I took the receiver. "Hello?"

"Hi, Katie. It's Caesar Speckman. I went ahead and ordered those lockets you wanted. They'll be here tomorrow."

"Oh," I said. "Um, thank you."

"Don't get me wrong. You don't have to take them if you've changed your mind."

Had I changed my mind? I'd wanted to give the members of the spellbook club herbal spells within those silver lockets as bridesmaid gifts. Now I couldn't cast the spells.

Discouragement spread across my shoulders like a heavy blanket. I took a deep breath and forced myself to straighten. Dad was right. I needed to stay positive.

Besides, they were lovely lockets, regardless. Maybe Lucy could help with the spells.

"I'll take them. Thank you for ordering them so quickly."

"No problem. I just tacked the lockets onto an order I already had with the jewelry company, and they were able to add them at the last minute. The UPS delivery is usually around noon, so you can pick them up tomorrow afternoon if you want."

"Sounds good. I'll see you then," I said.

We hung up, and I went back to rolling out the dough for full-moon sugar cookies. Lucy had already mixed the iridescent white icing and set out the lavender-infused sugar to decorate them with when they'd cooled.

The lunch rush was busier than usual when Dad showed up. He waited patiently in the reading area while I fetched pastries, Ben took orders at the register, and Lucy worked the coffee counter. Iris had a dentist appointment and wouldn't be back until later in the afternoon.

Finally, I was able to grab a couple mugs of dark roast brew and join my dad. I set a plate with two cream scones slathered with butter and peach freezer jam down in front of him, and he reached for one with an appreciative *mmm*.

After he'd demolished half of one and chased it with a swallow of coffee, he said, "I talked to your mother."

"What did she say?" I took a swig out of my own mug and braced myself.

"She's terribly worried, of course. You're her little girl."

I gave him a wry look.

"Don't be like that. She was going to call you, but I told her to wait until after tonight." His eyes glinted.

"Why tonight?" I asked.

"Katie, would you be willing to go on a journey to find your magic again?"

I remembered what he'd said the night before. "*I might be able to help.*"

The sprout of hope began to grow. Trying to tamp down a flare of excitement, I asked, "What kind of journey?"

"A shamanic journey, with me as your guide."

"Oh, Daddy," I said, and threw my arms around his neck.

He patted my back. Then I saw several customers watching us from the bistro tables and sat back on the sofa.

"I don't know if it will work," he said. "But it's worth a try. I've helped people in situations that echo yours, people who have become ill because they've lost their spirit. You're not ill, but—"

My chin bobbed up and down in a fierce nod. "But that's what it feels like. Like my spirit is gone."

His eyes held worry and love. "Let's meet tonight, then. After dark, at the carriage house."

"The carriage house?" I asked in surprise.

"Yes. All the workers will be gone, and we'll have privacy in the backyard. You already have the gazebo set up for spell casting, and that energy will feed into our journey, as will the energy of your gardens, magical and otherwise."

Anticipation arrowed through me. Dad was going

to fix everything, and as a bonus, it would be in my favorite place in the world to practice the Craft.

"I'll be there," I said. "Do you want me to bring anything?"

He shook his head. "We don't need much, not with the power of nature at our fingertips. What we do need, I'll bring."

"So? How did it go with Florinda Daniels yesterday? I thought I'd hear from you before now," Detective Quinn asked when I answered my phone a little after two.

When I'd seen who was calling, I almost hadn't picked up at all. However, it wasn't Quinn's fault I'd tried a clairvoyance spell that had backfired beyond my wildest dreams. Or if not that, had at least made me vulnerable to a hex. It was, however, his fault that I'd become involved in Kensington Bosworth's murder investigation in the first place.

"You were right," I said. "Florinda doesn't like cops. Mostly because of her son, Dante. He was in a lot of trouble with the law when he was younger."

"He's got a record from his college days. Nothing that serious, though. What else did you find out?"

"Well, she and her brother weren't exactly close, but she wasn't happy that he didn't leave her any money. Said a nest egg would have been nice for her hardworking husband, but who knows? It sounds like she might have been expecting something from her brother—or her husband was. However, she already knew Dante got a chunk of change plus the paranormal collection from his uncle, so either the lawyer told her, or her son did. I'm betting on Dante. Did you check on what kind of car he drives?"

"It's a BMW, all right. The one you saw was definitely his. He confirmed it."

"Aha! Now you have a real suspect. One with a serious motive who's a lot more likely to have killed Bosworth than Randy Post." A whoosh of relief passed through me. I wasn't abandoning Randy after all. "Dante scored a huge inheritance and has a record with the police, plus he was jealous of—"

"Dante has an alibi."

The relief ebbed, and I just managed not to swear out loud. "His car was *right there*."

"It still is. He said he went to visit his uncle earlier in the day, around two thirty, but there was no answer when he rang the doorbell. When he went back to his car, it wouldn't start. He had to take an Uber to get back to work. We still have to confirm that, but he was at work during the time the medical examiner says the victim was killed."

"Work, huh. His grandmother implied Dante was kind of allergic to work."

"He works for Associated Lenders. It's a private mortgage lender. One of his colleagues claims he saw Dante around the office that afternoon."

Great.

"Now, did you find out anything about the Hermetic Order of the Silver Moon?" Quinn asked.

Skipping over my conversation with Steve, I said, "It was a magical organization in Savannah that supposedly died out in the 1950s. Maybe the foundation borrowed the name."

"You're kidding, right?"

"Listen, Quinn, I need to tell you something. I'm not sure I want to work on this case anymore. Randy Post didn't kill anyone, and I can only hope you'll do the right thing and find the real murderer."

There was a long silence, then, "Nice try, Katie. You really had me for a minute there."

"I'm serious."

This time the silence was shorter. "You are, aren't you? Why? What happened?"

What to tell him? That I lost my magic while casting a spell that would give me clairvoyance, so I could tell him the name of the killer? Quinn might know I was a witch, but he'd still have a hard time swallowing a story like that.

"I broke the rule," I said.

"Which rule? Wait, Katie, you don't mean—"

"The one where I don't get hurt."

"Where are you?" he demanded.

"At the bakery."

He exhaled. "Okay, you're at work, not the hospital, so you aren't hurt too badly. You had me worried."

I hesitated. "It's not physical. It's . . ." I sighed. "Well, actually it's magical."

"What are you talking about?" He sounded frustrated. "How can you get hurt magically?"

Thinking back to all the times I'd come very close to being hurt by magic, I simply said, "I'm sorry, Quinn. You wouldn't understand. I'd think you'd be happy to have me out of your life. Your professional life, that is. I do hope you'll continue to come into the bakery."

"Katie!"

"Bye, Quinn. I'll see you around." And I hung up.

The empty feeling in my stomach grew even bigger.

When I went back out front, Mimsey and Bianca were standing by the register talking to Lucy. I waved, and as soon as they saw me, they headed into the kitchen.

"Let's talk in the office." Mimsey's expression was grave.

"Um, okay." Yet I had a feeling whatever they wanted to talk about was anything but okay.

We crowded into the small space, and I closed the door. I indicated the older witch should take the desk chair, while I perched on the edge of the club chair with Mungo. Bianca remained standing by the file cabinet.

"How are you feeling, dear?" Mimsey asked in a sympathetic voice.

I opened my mouth to say *fine* or *okay*, then closed it. Finally, I said, "Not so great."

"Oh, honey." She reached over and put her hand on my knee. "I'm so sorry."

Bianca's eyes filled with tears. She nodded but didn't speak.

Mimsey said, "We've all been looking for a way to reverse what happened."

"I know. Thank you. I've been doing the same thing."

"Did you have any luck?" Bianca swiped at her eyes with the back of her hand.

I shook my head. "You?"

Mimsey pressed her lips together. "Not really. I

looked through my spell library late into the night, and the only thing I found that might apply to your situation was a reference to an anti-magic spell in one of my volumes on dark sorcery."

Bianca's eyes widened.

The other woman smiled. "Not to worry, my dear. I keep several such books, but only to expand my knowledge, not because I intend to practice any black magic."

"Anti-magic," I said. "Yes, that makes sense. That's what it *feels* like."

"I was afraid of that," Mimsey said.

That didn't sound good. I waited for her to continue.

Finally, she said, "You see, if that's the spell that was used, there isn't a counter spell for it."

Closing my eyes, I let that sink in. Then I had a thought. My eyes popped back open.

"Does the spell you're talking about have to be cast while the receiver is actually practicing magic?"

"It doesn't have to be." She sighed. "However, it's optimal. See, the larger the magic at the time of the spell, the stronger the effect of the anti-magic."

My shoulders slumped. "That's why Nonna said our magic was feeding the wrong spell. Dang it. How could anyone have known we were practicing magic right then and there?"

Mimsey gave a slow shrug. "I don't know. It's not exactly the kind of thing we broadcast."

"And why was I the only one affected? How does the spell you found actually work?"

A thoughtful expression settled across her features.

"It's a rather complicated spell, and the end result is a kind of vacuum that sucks away the magic of whatever or whoever it is directed toward. It can be quite specific, I'm afraid. Whoever cast it must have been aiming right for you. It's a strong spell, one that can cut through layers of magical protection, indeed using the protection magic itself as fuel."

I frowned. "Mimsey, how hard would it be to cast that dark magic spell? Could one person do it, or would it need a group? I've been assuming I was targeted because of my involvement in Mr. Bosworth's murder case, but could there be some other reason?"

"No, I have reason to think it was because you were asking questions about the murder. A witch working solitary could cast the anti-magic spell, and it calls for some rather unusual items."

"Like what?"

"Oh, some of the things you might expect. An upside-down pentagram, as opposed to the right-side-up version we use for our white magic spells. A feather plucked from a black rooster at midnight. Four iron nails left to rust for forty-four days. The dried heart of a rat. A sprinkle of dried bat wing. A piece of burial shroud and a handful of graveyard dust. That sort of thing. I was surprised a hand of glory wasn't part of the equation. It's an ancient spell, and that would be a good old-school addition."

I shuddered. A hand of glory was the hand of a hanged man that had been dried and pickled with a special blend of minerals. Bianca looked a little green just at the mention of it.

Mimsey continued. "But the reason I think there

is a connection to Kensington's murder is that the spell also requires the blood of a fearful man."

A fearful man. Like one who painted his whole house haint blue, then cast, or had someone else cast, a protection spell over it, and then installed a security system for good measure.

Bianca had grown even more pale than usual. "Are you saying that Kensington Bosworth was murdered so some nutjob could use his blood in an anti-magic spell?"

Mimsey pressed her lips together in answer.

I felt a little light-headed at the thought. "That's awfully dark."

The older witch nodded and stood up. "It most certainly is."

"No wonder Connell said there was something dangerous about the magic in this case," I said, then swallowed hard. "Do you think Mr. Bosworth was murdered because of me, then? Just to take my magic away?" It was bad enough to lose a large piece of myself like that, but to think that someone had died in order for that to happen was horrible.

However, Mimsey firmly shook her head. "No, I do not, Katie. I think you were, shall we say, collateral damage after the fact. Whoever wanted the blood of a fearful man to complete that spell wasn't gunning for you, at least not to start. It would take a long time to gather all those esoteric ingredients together—over a year to age the iron nails alone. But then you got in the way and . . ." She shrugged.

She was assuming no one would hate me enough to put that much time and effort into a spell just to use against me. And maybe she was right. On the other hand, I'd angered a few people in the course of my witchy investigations over the last two years. However, they were all firmly in prison, not running around breaking into houses and hitting people over the head with statuary.

Sighing, I rose to my feet.

Bianca stepped forward and gave me a hug. "I'm so sorry, Katie. I wish there was something we could do."

I ventured a smile. "My dad might be able to help." I told them about his plan to regain my spirit, which could be the same as my magic, that very evening. "He seems to think it could work."

My heart soared when Mimsey's head bobbed, and her eyes twinkled. "Oh, he's right, honey! A shamanic journey like that isn't at all like trying to undo a hex or reverse a spell. It's another kind of magic altogether— one that might just do the trick."

Chapter 17

Mimsey and Bianca left, and I got back to work. Iris had come in and was already mixing up the sourdough to slow-rise for the next morning's loaves. I tossed pine nuts, several handfuls of fresh basil, Parmesan cheese, garlic, olive oil, and lemon juice into the food processor and gave it all a whirl. The pesto would go into the scones that were slated to be the next day's special.

My phone vibrated, and I drew it out of my apron pocket. Steve Dawes had sent me a text.

And suddenly what Mimsey had said about the killer wanting the anti-magic spell for someone other than yours truly came to mind.

Of course. The Dragohs. The killer wanted the spell to use against them. It's a member of the Hermetic Order of the Silver Moon.

Thumbing the text open, I read:

King's Castle, 5pm. Be there.

I texted him back. *Why?*

Just come.

I sighed and began to text back that I had no interest in joining him at the King's Castle bar for a drink. Then I paused. I'd met Steve when I was still coming to grips with the fact that I was a witch. He'd been my friend—sometimes more and sometimes less, but mostly my friend—during that time and since. Also, the Dragoh clan he belonged to was less fussy about the type of magic they practiced. I felt hopeful that my dad would be able to help me, but it wouldn't hurt to have a chat with Steve and tell him what had happened. He might know something about the anti-magic spell. Whether he did or not, he needed to know someone might be planning to use it against the Dragohs.

I texted back that I'd meet him after the bakery had closed. He sent a smiley face in return. I put my phone back in my apron pocket and went to inventory the contents of the pantry.

Lucy agreed to take Mungo home with her, then I'd pick him up before going to meet Dad at the carriage house. My aunt and uncle took off, and Iris and I closed things down in the Honeybee. It didn't take us long, and I figured I'd get to the bar about 5:20.

Out on the sidewalk, I twisted the key in the lock and turned to Iris. She surprised me by throwing her arms around me in a big, squeezy hug.

"Whoa," I said. "What was that for?"

"I don't know," she said. "Something's up. I can tell. Are you okay?"

I took a deep breath. "I will be." *I hope.*

"Good." She looked down at her toes, then back up at me. "Katie, I know I'm not in your spellbook

210

group, so if it has something to do with, you know, magic, you might not think I can help." I opened my mouth to speak, but she held up her hand. "And I might not. I mean, I'm still pretty new to all this spell stuff. But if you ever want to just vent, I'm a pretty good listener."

Tears pricked at the back of my eyelids. I took a step forward and returned her hug, just as big and squeezy. "Thanks. I might take you up on that sometime." Then I realized I'd been so caught up in my own drama that I hadn't really talked to her much that day.

Stepping back, I asked, "How was your date last night?"

A soft smile lit up her face. "Oh, Katie. It was *wonderful*. He's just *wonderful*."

I couldn't help grinning. "I take it you're going out with him again."

Her chin bobbed in the affirmative. "In about an hour." She gave me another quick hug and turned away. "See you tomorrow, Katie!"

Her good mood was infectious, and I walked to my car with a tad more bounce in my step.

Inside the King's Castle bar was dark and cool. The space was narrow, with a central aisle that reached from the front door to the rear wall. The only daylight came in through the windows on either side of the entrance. An impressive mahogany bar with red Naugahyde stools ran all along the right side. Behind it, under-shelf lighting illuminated the bottles of liquor, which were visually doubled by the mirrored wall behind them. On the left, booths with high-backed, scarred wooden benches offered patrons more private seating. Industrial-looking lights made from up-cycled washtubs cast focused spots of light onto each table.

Sophie King was mixing drinks behind the bar. She waved when she saw me come in, and I raised my hand in response as I scanned the customers. Several of the booths were occupied. As I stood there the door opened behind me, and two businessmen walked past me and slid onto a pair of the red stools.

I spied the back of Steve's head. He was sitting in a booth toward the back of the room. I started toward him, then noticed there was a man sitting across from him.

Dang it. I wanted to talk to Steve alone.

As I debated whether to slip out and text my apologies, Steve turned and saw me. His eyes lit up, and he gestured for me to join them.

Reluctantly, I made my way toward them.

"Katie! Fancy seeing you here. Can you sit for a moment?"

Suppressing my irritation, I half smiled. "Yeah, what a surprise! It's been such a long time since I've seen you."

He grinned at my sarcasm. Then suddenly his smile faltered, and something flickered behind his eyes. His gaze became assessing, and I realized that he could probably sense the power—or lack of power—in other people just as I'd always been able to do. His eyes flashed as he scooted over and patted the seat beside him.

"Right? Listen, I want you to meet my friend Dante Bundy. Dante, this is Katie Lightfoot. Her family owns the Honeybee Bakery over on Broughton."

The blood drained from my face, but I managed to paste what I hoped was a pleasant look onto my face as I numbly sat down.

What's Steve up to?

Then I got it. He thought he was doing me a favor. He might get a scoop on a murder story, but he was also trying to help me out by introducing me to Dante. He probably had no idea that Dante had an alibi for the time Mr. Bosworth was killed.

If he really did. A coworker had seen him go into his office? Could he have slipped out again without being seen? Because Quinn had seemed awfully vague.

"Pleased to meet you," Dante Bundy said. He sounded anything but pleased, though. Clearly, I was interrupting.

"Likewise," I murmured, and looked him over.

Dante was solidly built, meaty, one might even say, but tall enough to carry it. His hair was the white-blond of a California surfer dude, and he sported the deep tan to match. The orange tone of the tan made me think it had been sprayed on, though, and the hair color was a bit too flat to be natural. He was dressed in black jeans and a Hawaiian shirt. I wondered whether it was how he dressed for work or if he had the day off.

"Dante." Sophie King called out the name on the receipt in her hand, and our companion immediately slid out of the booth to retrieve his order from the bar.

Quickly, I whispered to Steve, "Hey, thanks for thinking of me, but I should go. He's never going to talk to you while I'm here."

He grimaced. "Actually, he probably won't talk to me anyway. Turns out he's still holding a grudge from our school days."

"You invited him here?"

A nod.

"Then why did he come if he's still upset with you?"

A shrug.

Dante came back with a tray loaded with two Guinness stouts and a basket of sweet potato fries. "Did you want something?" he asked me in a flat tone, still standing. He couldn't have been more unwelcoming.

Instinctively, I tried to reach out with my intuition to see what kind of hit I'd get off the guy. But of course, there was nothing.

I met his eyes. They were gray and cold.

Are you the one who did this to me? Did you kill your uncle and take my magic?

I stood up. "No, thanks." Looking back at Steve, I said, "We'll have to catch up sometime." Meaning: "Call me when you're done here."

He looked startled. "Oh, hey. Are you sure?"

Normally, I would have figured out a way to question Dante, bring up his mother, or make like I knew his uncle better than I did. But I didn't have the stomach for it right then. Maybe after I had my magic back, I would.

"Positive. If you gentlemen will excuse me, I'm just going to run back to the restroom and then pick up my order from Sophie over there." If I was lucky, I could slip out without Dante realizing I hadn't ordered any food.

I nodded to Dante and went past him toward the back of the bar. In the restroom, I splashed cold water on my face and dried it on a paper towel. Then I paused in front of the mirror. I looked like the same old Katie Lightfoot, at least on the outside. Dark auburn hair, green eyes, freckles. But the old Katie would still have been trying to find a murderer if the clairvoyance spell hadn't worked. The old Katie wouldn't have given up. Deep down, I knew that—warning or no warning from Connell.

I blinked and looked away. I wasn't the old Katie anymore.

For a second, I wondered whether Declan would still love the new-and-not-so-improved version.

Stop it. You can't afford to think things like that. Stay positive and wait to see what happens this evening.

I pushed the thought into a dark recess of my mind as best I could but still felt the weight of it there. Sighing, I turned and pushed through the door.

Steve and Dante were talking. My friend looked very earnest. Though I could see Dante only from the back, he was leaning forward, and there was an intensity to his body language. Steve's eyes flicked up at me for a split second, then returned to his companion.

I slowed, not wanting to interrupt them if Steve had finally managed to get his old college buddy to talk to him. The booth behind them was empty, so I silently slipped into the seat facing away from Dante.

The high back of the seat would hide me if he were to turn around, but even in the busy bar, I could hear him over the backdrop of conversation.

"No sirree," he was saying in a rough voice. "I don't give a rat's ass whether you Dragohs let outsiders into your clan. Couldn't care less."

"You know that wasn't my call," Steve said.

"Whatever. It doesn't matter. I have my own group now." He gave a little laugh. "And you druids might be hearing from us pretty soon."

There were a few seconds of heavy silence, then Steve's voice, low but harsh. "Are you actually threatening me, Bundy?"

Dante laughed, and I felt him get out of his seat. Not wanting to draw his attention, I ducked my head away and busied myself with my tote bag, which I'd crammed into the corner of the booth.

"Thanks for giving me a call, Steve. Real good to see you. Maybe we'll run into each other again soon. Oh, and thanks for the drink. I'd offer to pay, but we both know you're the rich one."

"Not the only one, not from what I've heard," Steve said. "Not since your uncle was murdered and you get the bulk of his estate."

"How did you know that?" Dante sounded angry.

"We know a lot of things," Steve said. "Like about the Hermetic Order of the Silver Moon."

Dante muttered an expletive, then there was the sound of rapid footsteps.

"You can show yourself now, Katie. He stormed out."

I popped my head over the top of the booth to see

Steve was sitting by himself. Sure enough, Dante had left the building. I got up and slid into the seat across from Steve.

"You heard?" he asked.

I nodded. "Quinn says he has an alibi. Someone saw him at work during the time window Bosworth was killed. I don't know if I believe it, but Quinn seems to."

Steve's lips pulled back in a wry grimace. "It might not matter if he has an alibi. He has friends now."

"You mean the Hermetic Order of the Silver Moon druids?"

He nodded. "I checked with Father, and there have been some quiet and unsubstantiated rumors that they've gotten the band back together, so to speak. Dante might not have killed his uncle, but I have to wonder if he knows who did."

"Maybe." I nodded, thinking it through. "Maybe Quinn can do something with that."

And maybe the old Katie Lightfoot wasn't gone altogether.

Steve sat back. "Hmm. Sure. Tell Detective Quinn all about the Dragohs, Katie. No problem."

"I think I can avoid going that far."

He sighed.

I noticed the dark circles under his eyes for the first time. "What's going on with you?"

A shrug.

Then I remembered his awkwardness in front of Mr. Bosworth's house when I asked about his girl-friend. "Are you and Angie doing okay?"

His lips twisted in a sardonic smile. "I'm doing

217

okay, and she's doing okay. We're just not doing okay together anymore."

"You broke up?"

A quick nod, and he cleared his throat. "It's for the best. What about you? I mean, that's quite the shielding spell you've got going there. I'd almost think you weren't a witch."

Stricken, I blinked away the tears that suddenly threatened.

The skin tightened across his face, and his eyes widened. "Katie-girl?" He leaned forward and scanned my face. "What's up?"

I looked away. Forced myself to look back.

He waited.

"I, uh, I tried a spell last night. Apparently at the same time that someone was casting a spell on me. Or *at* me, I guess I should say. Have you ever heard of an anti-magic hex?"

He stared at me. "You're kidding."

I held his gaze. "Nope. Not kidding."

Sympathy infused his eyes. Or was it pity? "Oh, honey. I'm so sorry."

"You know what I'm talking about, then?" I asked. "You've heard of that spell? Because I have to wonder whether it came from the Silver Moon druids. Mimsey says one of the ingredients is the blood of a fearful man. Given the protection spell around Mr. Bosworth's house, I'm thinking it was him."

His forehead wrinkled, and he stared toward the back of the bar as if his memories somehow lived over my left shoulder. "I seem to remember something about it. From way back, but now I'm wondering . . ."

"Wondering what?"

"Father said Anderson Lane called him this morning. He said his magic wasn't working."

"Oh, no," I breathed. I hadn't warned the Dragohs in time. "Did he say he was magically attacked?"

Steve shook his head. "I don't know. Honestly, I didn't take it terribly seriously. Anderson can be a little . . . you know."

"He still drinks?"

"Like a fish. And though it gives me no pleasure to say it, of all the Dragohs, he's the least powerful and the most unstable."

"Maybe that's why he was chosen for the next attack. Will you ask your dad?"

"Right away. He'll want to know if we need to take Anderson's claims seriously—and if the rest of us are in danger."

I stood. "Let me know what you find out. Like I said, I'm pretty sure whoever did this to me—and maybe Anderson—also killed Kensington Bosworth, and Quinn needs to know that. In the meantime, my dad is going to take me on a little trip to see if we can find my magic again."

"Trip? Where are you going?" Steve rose to his feet and tossed a couple of bills on the table.

"I'll let you know when I find out."

Chapter 18

That evening, I arrived at the carriage house before Dad. Unlocking the front door, I flipped on the bare bulb overhead, walked across to the French doors, and opened them to let Mungo into the backyard. All day, whenever I'd looked at him, I'd found him watching me. I couldn't know like I used to, but it seemed as if he were watching a car wreck more than offering the loving gaze he usually reserved for me.

Well, me and bacon.

He stopped at the threshold and didn't venture farther.

"No?" I asked. "Okeydoke."

Together, we explored the house with no one else there for the first time in months. Without furniture, the space reminded me of the first time I'd seen it, back when I'd been figuring out how to relocate to Savannah from Akron. I'd fallen in love with the small, tidy rooms immediately, imagining how it would feel to own my own home, to have it be mine, all mine.

Now it would be mine and Declan's, and as I walked from room to room with Mungo on my heels, I visualized us living in the updated and larger space together. Of course, we'd spent enough time there that it wasn't much of an imaginative stretch, but things like the expanded loft upstairs where Declan liked to watch baseball and football games, the big bathroom with two sinks, the walk-in closet and doubled kitchen area would make a big difference.

Never mind the tiny doubt flickering in the background of my thoughts, the one that wondered whether everything in my life was going to change from the happiness I'd found since moving to Savannah to . . . something else.

I was standing in the bathroom admiring the new tiles in the shower when I heard the front door open.

"Katie?"

"Back here, Dad," I called.

Moments later, he joined me in the doorway. He was carrying a small, scarred leather bag that looked like it had been through a war zone.

I smiled up at him. "The tile looks great. Thanks for stepping in and taking over."

"Sure," he said. "I enjoy it, actually. Feels kind of Zen. Tomorrow I'll start the grout." He reached out and removed a plastic spacer from between two of the tiles on the backsplash behind the sinks. "Are you ready for tonight?"

Taking a deep breath, I nodded. "More than ready."

"Let's go out back, then." He looked down at Mungo, who was gazing up at him with adoration.

"You come, too, little one. Never hurts to have a descendent of wolves nearby when you go on a spirit journey."

Yip!

Dad flipped the light off in the living room. We went outside, and across the cement patio. The moon was six days past full, waning but still bright enough to lend a silvery light. Two years before, Declan had helped me cut out and plant garden areas along the perimeter of the lawn, and now mature plants nudged against the back and side fences.

There were neighboring yards on each side, but the property backed up to a designated green space. One of my neighbors was an accountant, a nice man who never seemed to be home, but I was quite close to the Coopersmiths on the other side. Luckily, they were on vacation in Myrtle Beach. I adored Margie, mom to three munchkins and wife to a long-haul truck driver, but sometimes she wandered over to visit at the most inopportune times. This was one night I definitely didn't want to be interrupted.

One garden was devoted to magical plants, including white bryony, blackthorn, the witch hazel from which I'd made my wand, and a rowan sapling with a powerful talisman buried among its roots. Eventually that tree would grow up to become the centerpiece of that area. Cutting diagonally across the right angle formed by the fence corners, a small stream merrily chattered over small rocks. I'd loved the sound of it the first time I'd heard it but at the time had no idea that having live water running constantly across my property would be so important to practicing the Craft.

222

Another plot was devoted to herbs, many of which also had magical properties, and yet another was where I grew vegetables for our table and sometimes for the bakery. Even in the dim light, I could see the tomato plants were heavy with heirloom fruit, and the peppers needed to be harvested. I made a mental note to pick the cornucopia within the next couple of days and share it with Ben and Lucy.

Shortly after moving in, I'd had a small gazebo built in the middle of the yard. It was constructed of unfinished redwood and furnished with a small round table in the middle. A hodgepodge of chairs I'd rescued from the thrift store provided seating around the table. Next to the gazebo, an outdoor fireplace awaited the chill of coming months, but in the heat of summer, there wasn't yet any wood in the rack beside it.

Dad scanned the yard, nodded, then went up the steps of the gazebo. He grabbed a couple of chairs and brought them back out to the yard. "Let's clear everything out."

"Okay." I went to help him. Soon we had the chairs and table out by the fireplace. I quickly used the hand-stitched besom, a traditional witch's broom, to sweep the floor, then put it out by the fire ring as well.

Standing in the cleared gazebo, we gazed down at the ten-inch pentagram I'd painted in the center of the floor. The table usually disguised it, but now the white paint glowed in the moonlight against the darker purple background.

"Let's sit outside and chat a little," Dad said.

We went back down the steps and sat in two of the thrift store chairs.

I waited.

"What do you know about shamanic journeys?" he asked.

"Not much. That it's a journey of the spirit, and that one's spirit animal is usually involved." I sighed. "I guess I should know more, since you're a shaman and all."

He smiled with his eyes. "Oh, I think you can be forgiven. After all, we didn't practice in our household the whole time you were growing up. Well," he amended, "your grandmother did, but your mother did everything she could to keep our practices discreet."

"After the neighbors saw Nonna dancing naked in the backyard on Beltane. Mama told me." Nonna had been performing a fertility spell for the garden, but she had old-school notions, especially about what a witch was supposed to do on the first of May.

He laughed. "Right. Anyway, there are many kinds of shamanic systems. Since I have Shawnee blood, I practice a version from that tradition."

"Your talent is hereditary, just like Mama's, right? Lucy says my power comes—" I grimaced. "*Came* from the double whammy of your two traditions."

"Yes, that's probably true. I'm descended from a long line of shamans, but my bloodline has been diluted through several generations, and as you know, I wasn't trained by my father."

"Because he passed when you were only four," I said, repeating what I'd been told growing up. "Uncle Sosa trained you, right?" I vaguely remembered a cheerful man with kind eyes, but mostly I recalled how his long white braids had fascinated me as a toddler.

"Who's not really my uncle, of course, but was my father's best friend. Sosa was a Cree medicine man and shaman as well as an anthropologist. He studied not only shamanic rituals of different Native American tribes but also those of indigenous peoples of Australia, South America, Mexico, and the Celtic traditions of Britain. All of which are a little different in practice but aim toward the same result."

"What's the difference between a medicine man and a shaman?"

"Medicine men and women are healers that use more traditional techniques. Things like herbs and sweating. Shaman mediate between this world and the next. We're still healers, but on a different level."

"A supernatural level."

"Right. Usually, I go on the journey for someone else—though I have gone for myself, of course—and then I bring back what they need from the Otherworld."

"Otherworld?"

A brisk nod. "You've got the upper world, the middle world, and the lower world. The middle one is the here and now. The upper one is, well . . ." He pointed to the sky. "And the lower world is between here and the underworld."

"Upper, middle, lower, and under. All layers of the Otherworld, and the middle is where we are now. Gotcha."

"So, I go on a journey, usually to the lower world, and bring back the part of a person's soul that is missing."

My eyes widened. "Missing soul parts? This kind of thing happens to other people?"

"All the time. Not as, er, dramatic as what happened to you, but trauma or illness or any number of other things may break off a piece of a person's soul." He shrugged. "I go retrieve it and breathe it back into them."

I felt a rush of pride and love for my father. He was a healer on a whole different level from what I did with my herbs and spices. All this time I'd had only a vague notion of how amazing that was.

"This time, though, I want you to go on the journey as well. I might not recognize your magic in the same way you would, but you will know what you need to retrieve when you see it."

Excitement mixed with fear and hope. "You sure?"

"Absolutely. You're my daughter. I want to do this together."

"How does it work?"

"Enough talk. I'll show you."

Taking a deep breath, I licked my lips and stood up.

Back in the gazebo, Dad opened his leather bag and took out a woolen blanket. He spread it on the floor, over the pentagram. "You lay down on this on your back. I'll remain sitting, so I can drum you in."

Drum me in? But I just nodded.

He laughed. "You're going to have to relax. Ever do any meditation?"

"Off and on," I said. "Sometimes it seems to work,

and sometimes I just get twitchy and give it up until I feel guilty enough to try again."

"Mmm. You're a bit type A. Would probably do you a world of good to have a regular meditation practice, but never mind that for now." He retrieved a small drum and a handled rattle. "This is actually a miniature Celtic bodhran." He pronounced it *bow-rawn*. "Not a tribal drum. Sosa gave it to me, and I just like the sound of it. The rattle is Shawnee, though."

It was made from the shell of a turtle and made a soft clattering sound as my father shook it.

"Mr. Bosworth had something like that," I said.

"I'd sure like to see that whole collection," he said, removing a long, striped feather from the bag next. He held it up. "Pheasant." And finally, he took out a cup made from a hollow dried gourd.

"Be right back." He bounded down the steps and went to the stream at the edge of the property. Moments later, he was back, the gourd filled with water. He reached into the bag one last time and took out a vial, removed a small pill, and dropped it in the water.

"Is that peyote?" I asked in a tight voice.

"What?" He laughed. "No, honey. *That* is a water-purifying tablet I picked up at a sporting goods store this afternoon. When you come back from the Otherworld, you're going to be parched. Natural water will best quench your thirst, and while that stream seems pure as crystal, I'm not taking any risks."

"Ah." I felt better, not only because I wasn't expected to take some psychoactive drug, but because I knew Dad had my best interests at heart—on all levels.

Well, of course he does.

Suddenly impatient, I asked, "Can we start? Not having my magic is like having a deep itch that I can't begin to scratch."

He smiled and nodded. "No time like the present. Lie down."

I did and tried to relax. The hard wood of the floor felt like stone despite the blanket.

"Now set your intention clearly," he said.

"I *intend* to get my magic back," I grated out.

"Try to let go of your anger."

Deep breath in, then another deep breath out. "Doing the best I can on that, Dad."

He laughed. "Okay. Now, release expectations."

I sat up. "How do you have intention without expectation?"

He frowned. "Like you do with any spell. You trust the elements, the energies of the universe that you're tapping into, you make your intention clear, but do not force it. Right?"

"I never really thought about it like that, but I guess you're right." I lay back down.

"Maybe it would be best if you simply think of this as another kind of spell, plus a little visualization—especially at the beginning." He took his boots off and settled in next to me, cross-legged.

"What am I visualizing?" I asked.

"A tunnel of some sort. It can look like anything you want, but I want you to construct an entrance into the earth in your mind."

"Then what?"

"Wait. Listen to the drum. If it feels right to walk

down into the entrance, do that. Watch for your dragonflies. Watch for other animals as well. Be patient. See what comes next."

That all sounded very different from any of the work I'd done with the spellbook club, but I tried to keep an open mind and trust my dad. Still, I couldn't keep the worry out of my voice when I asked, "Where will you be?"

"I'll be there. As will Mungo. Right, boy?"

Yip! My dog nestled in next to me.

Dad smiled and leaned over me. "There's nothing to be afraid of. You can come back from this journey anytime you want. All you have to do is open your eyes. It's literally that easy."

I looked into his kind brown gaze and let out a breath. "Okay." I ran my hand down Mungo's back, then closed my eyes.

The drumbeat that started was low and slow. Gradually, the tempo increased, and I found myself relaxing into it.

Losing myself in it.

Drifting on it.

Tunnel. Imagine a tunnel, I told myself.

Problem was, I was just a tad claustrophobic. Not weird about it or anything, but the idea of going down a tunnel to the lower world felt a little scary.

The image of a staircase popped into my mind. It led down in a gentle spiral. A dragonfly drifted in lazy circles above it. In my imagination, I gripped the sturdy railing and began going down the steps. Mungo brushed by my leg and ran ahead, leading the way. I was aware of the hard floor against my back, a breeze drifting through the gazebo, a hint of moonlight behind my eyelids. At the same time, I kept stepping down, down, down in my mind's eye.

Suddenly, I didn't know if I was just imagining the cold metal of the railing against my hand and the sound of my footfalls, or if I'd begun the journey proper.

It doesn't matter. Just go with it.

The sound of the drum became my heartbeat. Or perhaps it was the other way around. After a while, I lost count of the steps but was drawn forward by the hint of illumination below my feet. It grew brighter and brighter, until Mungo and I reached the bottom of the staircase. The dragonfly swooping and bobbing ahead, we stepped into a short hallway. It was made of stone and had no windows, but the bright daylight that came from the open door at the end of it beckoned welcomingly. Mungo raced toward it, looking over his shoulder at me as if to tell me to hurry up.

However, I felt no urgency, only wonder. I trailed my hand along the fitted stones. My fingertips came away wet, and I realized I could smell the water running over the rock, bright and crisp and clean. Once I noticed that, I could hear it, too. The sound of my father's drum was there in the background, too, a little faster than the beating of my heart now.

At the end of the stone hallway I stopped, laughing with delight at the scene in front of me. I stepped into the room. On my right was a door open to the outside. Beyond, stepping-stones led through a lush garden to an opening in a low stone wall and a dirt path. Beyond that, I could see . . . forever. High mountains pushed up from vast plains bordered by crashing seas. Cityscapes mingled with plowed fields, and the spaces between and above were filled with all manner of bird and beast.

The dragonfly zoomed back inside, bringing my attention with it. Shelves and cubbies covered the other two walls of the room. They were crammed with jars, bottles, and carved boxes in all shapes, sizes, and colors. I knew the containers were filled with herbs and spices, dried fruit and mysterious powders. In the middle of the room, a well-worn wooden table held a basket of rising dough, its sour fragrance mixing with the plethora of herbal scents in the air. A spinning wheel sat in the corner, in front of a hearth that held no fire.

I'd walked into a hedgewitch's kitchen. *My* kitchen, I realized.

Yip!

Mungo ran to the door to the outside and stopped at the threshold, again looking over his shoulder at me. However, I turned toward the spinning wheel and the hearth.

There's no fire on the grate. It's missing. The fire is missing.

A movement at the corner of my vision made me whirl and peer into the shadows. A scratching sound set my teeth on edge and sent a shiver between my shoulder blades. Nonetheless, I took a step forward.

"Mungo," I called in a hoarse voice. "Dad, where are you?"

A streak of blackness shot across the room. I screamed. A rat, almost as large as my terrier, scurried by. Mungo snarled as it flashed past him and into the garden, then took off after it.

I was fast on his heels, terrified, but determined.

Because that rat had been carrying something that looked an awful lot like a glowing ember in its mouth.

My missing fire. My missing *magic*.

We ran out the door, through the garden, and out to the path. The path led us to a copse of trees, and then beyond, to a meadow. In the middle, a single enormous tree reached branches down to the ground and up to the sky.

The rat paused at the bottom of the tree trunk and looked back at me. Then it turned, and I saw my fire flashing in its jaws as it scurried up the trunk and into the branches above. I ran to the base of the tree and looked up. All I saw was a tangle of branches and leaves that seemed to reach into eternity.

"The blasted thing's gone, lass."

I whirled and saw a small man crouching among a scattering of wildflowers about twenty feet away. He was wearing riding breeches, coat, and high boots that went over his knees. His face was as wrinkled as a dried apple, but his blue eyes were bright. I recognized him from an old photo in Declan's family album.

Still, I gaped. "*Connell?*"

"One and the same, Katie, m'lass. 'Tis lovely to see you, indeed. These circumstances, though." He shook his head sorrowfully, then met my eyes again. "Not so lovely. I'm afraid the rat is gone."

I stared at him, then up at the tree, then at him again. "With my magic? No." I reached up to see if I could reach the lowest branch, but I wasn't nearly tall enough. "No. I won't let him. I'll find a way to go after him, to get it back. I *have* to."

Connell stood. "You can't, lass."

"Yes, I can!" I shouted.

"He's right, Katie," my dad said, stepping out from behind the tree. He still held the bodhran and was gently tapping it in the same rhythm I'd been aware of ever since descending the staircase. "You can't follow someone else's path back to the middle world. You have to go back the way you came."

"But—"

He shook his head.

"Yer da is right," Connell said, nodding to him. "'Tis a lovely drum you have there, sir."

Dad nodded back, his face puzzled. "Um, thanks."

"I don't care, Connell!" I said, still peering into the dark of the leaves above. Then, in almost a whisper, "I have to try."

"No, Katie," Dad said. "We have to go."

The drumming increased in tempo, then in volume. The rhythmic sound of the turtle rattle joined it, and I found myself no longer in the meadow, but in my witch's kitchen. Then I was in the hallway, then on the spiral stairs . . .

My eyes snapped open, and I sat up on the floor of the gazebo, gasping for breath.

Dad handed me the gourd of water, and I sucked it down as if I hadn't had anything to drink for days. When it was gone, I handed it back and let my hand drop. I felt utterly defeated.

"It didn't work."

Tentatively, Mungo crawled into my lap, and I wrapped my arms around him. He licked my chin once, then leaned against my shoulder.

"It partially worked. You discovered your fire. Maybe we can try again," Dad said, but there was something in his voice. "I'm encouraged that your dragonfly was there."

"Why?" I couldn't keep the defeat out of my voice.

"Because that's part of your magic, too. And because . . ." He trailed off.

"Because . . . ?" I prompted.

"Because your totem is all about resilience and metamorphosis." His tone was quiet.

It took me a moment to understand what he was getting at. "You mean you think I'm going to have to get used to feeling like this. That I'm going to have to make the best of living the rest of my life without magic." Tears filled my eyes.

Sighing, he stood. "I don't know, honey."

I felt my nostrils flare, and I swiped at my eyes with the back of my hand as I put Mungo down and struggled to my feet. "No."

Dad had begun to return the items he'd brought with him back into the worn leather bag. His hands stilled, and he gave me a questioning look.

"No," I repeated. "I don't accept that. What was that rat?"

"It was a metaphor—" he began.

I interrupted. "I get that. For whoever took my magic in the first place? Or for something else?"

He hesitated, then slowly nodded. "I think the former."

234

"Then also the same person who took Kensington Bosworth's life. Who cast a spell using his blood." My lips set in a grim line. "And I'll bet it's a druid. In fact, I bet he's a member of the Hermetic Order of the Silver Moon."

My father was studying me. "Perhaps. But it might not be a 'he' at all. If the Silver Moon group is like the Golden Dawn group, they admit women as well as men."

I handed him the blanket. "I don't know who that rat was, but they have a part of me, and somehow, someway, I'm getting it *back*."

Dad nodded soberly, then suddenly his lips twitched in a grin. "Good. You obviously have plenty of fire left, honey."

Chapter 19

Wanting to be alone, I stayed at the apartment that night instead of going back to Lucy and Ben's with Dad. I slept hard and long, and since I'd never had to set an alarm clock to wake up on time before, I overslept the next morning. My fiancé came home from the firehouse a little after eight to find me sitting on the couch, still in my pajamas. Mungo was curled beside me, watching me as I stared out the window at the birds pecking at the feeder I'd put out when I moved to Declan's.

He stopped in the doorway. "Uh-oh."

I glanced over at him.

"A day off, huh. Well, honey, you deserve it after all you've been through. I'm glad Lucy convinced you to stay home. We can hang out and—"

"She didn't."

He stripped off his T-shirt, tossed it in the general direction of the washing machine, and dropped into the red rocking chair across from where I sat. "Didn't what?"

My eyes cut to his well-defined torso. It normally would have given me untoward thoughts, but not this morning. "Didn't convince me. I overslept, then texted her this morning that I wouldn't be in at all, and she's left me alone. Which is good. I have some thinking to do."

Actually, it felt pretty crappy that she hadn't even called.

"Are you sure she got the text?"

"Of course she got the text," I snapped. "And Iris was coming in early. I'm sure they can handle everything just fine."

"And if they can't?"

I shrugged.

He crossed his arms over his chest. "Katie, this isn't like you."

I lifted a hand, then let it drop back to the cushion. "I don't know what's like me anymore."

"The shaman thing didn't work, huh?"

"No kidding. How'd you figure that out, Sherlock?" I knew I was snapping at him and didn't like myself for it one bit.

His lips thinned. "I'm clever that way." He stood. "First off, Connell hinted that you and he had some kind of encounter, plus your dad called me last night. It would have been nice if you had, too, or at least returned my texts." He turned toward the bathroom. "I need to take a shower. You need to check in with your aunt. They might be just fine without you, but I doubt it. You're the soul of that bakery, darlin'. And it's part of your soul, too."

"You don't understand," I mumbled.

"Maybe not exactly. Not about losing your magic. But you seem determined to lose yourself entirely. Your dad told me last night that you seemed bent on figuring out who did this to you. What happened since then?"

"Nothing! I'm just trying to figure out my next step. Did you ever think of that?"

It was true. The problem was that I didn't know where to start, and the longer I sat looking out the window, the more powerless I felt.

A deep tenderness entered Declan's gaze, and it was in his voice as well when he said, "I'm on your side, darlin'. I'll do anything I can to help you figure this out." He suddenly rubbed his eyes.

Were those tears?

"I wish I'd listened to Connell when he tried to warn you the first time, back when he was being subtle and working through me, back when it would have made a difference," he said.

I stood and padded over to him. Putting my arms around him and pulling him close, I whispered into his ear, "It's not your fault. Warning me wouldn't have made any difference. I'm just that stubborn. You know that."

He gave a little laugh. "You are that."

A little smile strayed onto my face, but then I saw the sadness in his eyes before he turned away to go into the bedroom.

It gave me pause. Maybe I was still being stubborn— only about the wrong things.

Sighing, I grabbed my phone from where I'd left it on the end table and realized I'd inadvertently muted it. The screen lit up with eight messages from Lucy, mostly texts, but also a voice mail.

"Oh, no!" I exclaimed.

"See?" Declan said from the bedroom doorway. "Lucy's been trying to get ahold of you all morning. She called me, so I left work early to make sure you were okay."

"Well, you didn't need to. . . . You shouldn't have. . . . But . . ." I headed into the bedroom. "Can I use the shower first? I need to get to work."

"Sure, hon."

"Stop grinning like that," I said as I passed him.

However, it did feel better to be needed.

Driving seemed to jump-start my mental juices, and on the way to the Honeybee I ran through the suspects in Mr. Bosworth's murder again, talking out loud to Mungo, as was my habit when figuring things out. We might not have the witch-familiar connection at the moment, but he still made a good sounding board.

"Like I told Quinn, Dante Bundy is my favorite suspect. He inherited a pile of money, a valuable collection of magical items . . . hey, I wonder who got the house? That's got to be worth some dough."

Mungo blinked at me from where he was buckled into the passenger seat.

"I hate to ask Quinn anything else about the will, especially after I brushed him off during our last conversation. Maybe Jaida can find out. Anyway, it sounds like Dante is also a member of the newly reformed Hermetic Order of the Silver Moon. A chunk of his uncle's money goes to them, too. And since the Silver Moon folks are supposedly a foundation, they might not even have to pay taxes on it."

Then I remembered something. "Wait a second. Mrs. Standish said Kensington Bosworth had cut back on his donations to her organizations a couple of years ago and was instead giving money to a different one. In practically her next breath, she mentioned some vague rumor that he was hanging out with some shady characters. If he'd started directing his philanthropy toward the Order, then those druids have been back together for at least two years—and very much under the radar, or else the Dragohs would know. On the other hand, Steve made it sound like Heinrich Dawes and the other Dragohs might have indeed had an inkling that the Order was re-forming."

I slowed the car as a traffic light ahead turned red.

"So, if Mr. Bosworth was giving money to the Order for that long plus left them more in his will, he must have been a member, too. Which is weird, because no one seems to think Mr. Bosworth had much of a gift for magic. But if he was, and . . ." I trailed off, not liking the thought that had sprung unbidden to mind. Taking a deep breath, I forced myself to say it. "And if the Dragohs did know, would they have threatened him?"

Mungo sneezed.

"What's that supposed to mean?" I asked.

Then again, maybe he just had a tickle in his nose.

I sighed. "Steve was pretty clear that even with the rivalry between the Silver Moon druids and the Dragoh clan, there wasn't any actual violence. I think they'd do a lot, but they wouldn't go so far as to kill Mr. Bosworth. But if they 'discouraged' people from joining the Silver Moon group to the degree that it died off from attrition, then maybe they did try to scare him. Or not. Because they supposedly didn't know anything more than rumors. Unless, of course, someone is lying. Dang it!" I exclaimed.

Mungo jumped.

"Of course, someone is lying. For Pete's sake."

The light turned green. I pressed on the accelerator, my mind racing.

"But you know, it was pretty weird how magically dead it felt in Caesar Speckman's shop. Given the age of that building and the fact that it was once a real magic shop, along with his sideline dealing in items that are used in real spells and ceremonial magic, I should have sensed *some* kind of power in his store, whether he believes in what he traffics in or not."

I might not have my magic to guide me, but I still had logic, empathy, and native intelligence. I pictured the dorky souvenir shop owner, with his thinning hair and printed T-shirt. Not only was the atmosphere in How's Tricks devoid of power, but Caesar himself was as bland as could be. Suspiciously so? Maybe. Caesar warranted another look. Maybe I could get him to chat with me a bit more about Bosworth that afternoon when I went in to pick up the bridesmaid lockets.

Bringing my thoughts back to my favorite suspect, I said, "Despite all that, Dante supposedly has an alibi. I wonder if a visit to his workplace is warranted? Just to double-check what his coworker has to say." I

241

shook my head. "Okay, moving along, what about Florinda? She said she didn't want any money, but that's kind of hard to believe. Even if it is true, she would have liked it for her husband, and probably for her son as well. Perhaps she felt guilty for gambling away the money her father had left her and wanted to make up for it. Or . . ." I fell silent. The more I thought about the possibilities, the more confusing it seemed.

But I wasn't about to give up.

Think, Katie, think.

What about Florinda's husband? I didn't know a thing about him other than his last name was Daniels, and his wife said he was hardworking.

I glanced over at Mungo, who was watching me with interest even though I'd stopped talking. "I'm going to have to call Quinn and tell him I changed my mind about helping." I rolled my eyes. "That should go over well. Okay, who else? Well, Malcolm Cardwell said his great-aunt was a witch of sorts, so perhaps there's a magical connection there. But he doesn't benefit from Mr. Bosworth's death. In fact, he's out of a job now."

Pulling into a parking spot, I shut off the engine and turned to Mungo. "You know who else is out of a job? The housekeeper, Olivia Gleason. The one person on my list that I haven't had a chance to follow up with." I unbuckled my seat belt and reached for the door handle. "Now, how do I go about approaching her?"

My eyes widened when I stepped inside the bakery from the alley. The place was a madhouse. People packed the tables and reading area, while lines had formed at both the register and the coffee counter. Iris turned as I entered, a frantic look—and a smear of flour—on her face.

"Where have you been?" she hissed.

"I—let me drop my stuff," I hedged, and hurried into the office with Mungo in my tote bag. Back in the kitchen, I quickly donned a half apron embroidered with clusters of red cherries. "What is going on?"

"Busload of tourists." Iris slid a trayful of hot cookies onto a rack and began to fill a tray with already cooled pastries. "They dropped them off on Broughton to shop and explore the historic district, but apparently every last one of them needs a pastry and a drink first."

"Gotcha," I said. "What can I do?"

She shoved the tray at me. "Display case."

I took the tray and trotted out to refill the diminishing contents of the case. As I bent to arrange the rows of scones and muffins, Lucy turned toward me from where she was ringing up a purchase at the register.

"How are you?" she murmured.

A brisk nod. "I'm okay."

"Really?"

"Yup. Really." One way or another, I had to be.

A smile blossomed on her face. "Welcome back, honey." Despite the line of people reaching to the door, she appeared as Zen as ever.

I straightened and nodded toward the crowd. "Good thing we got rid of that bell over the door."

She laughed and turned to the next customer.

*　　*　　*

Two hours later there was a lull between the tourist traffic and the lunch rush. I helped police the seating areas, collecting dishes and wiping down surfaces. When things were a bit more under control, I excused myself to the office to make some phone calls.

First, I called Detective Quinn. He answered with an abrupt, "Yeah?"

"Hey," I said. "Sorry to bug you, but I have a question." Actually, a couple of them, but I'd ease into that.

"I thought you were done with the questions." There were voices in the background, and I heard a rustle of clothing as he covered the microphone on his cell. His voice then, but I couldn't really make out what he was saying. Then he came back on. "Listen, Katie. I've got to go. We have a break on another case."

"Can you just tell me really quickly if you learned anything when you talked further with Olivia Gleason?"

"She found Bosworth, but couldn't really add anything to that. Seriously, I need to go. And you can stop playing Nancy Drew, or whatever your version of her is. We got the forensics back on the Bosworth case, and like it or not, Randy Post's fingerprints are the only ones on the murder weapon. He doesn't have an alibi, he has motive, and there's a witness to that fact. I've got a call in for an arrest warrant."

"But, Quinn—"

"Talk to you later," he said, and hung up.

I stared at the phone for a few seconds before looking up at my dog. "Mungo, they're actually going to pin this on Randy if I don't do something." A part of me had believed that since he was innocent, that couldn't happen.

Boy, was I ever wrong.

Mungo made a sound in the back of his throat and cocked his head at me.

I sighed, then called Jaida to let her know what Quinn had just told me. She said she'd take it from there, and I left her to contact Randy and Bianca and whoever else might need to know.

Before I could decide what to do next, the phone rang in my hand. It was my mother.

After a quick debate with myself about whether I could possibly duck her calls for the rest of my life, I decided I probably couldn't and answered.

"Hello, honey," she said after I'd greeted her.

Her voice was low, her tone quiet. That was not how my mother operated. Her usual mode was full steam ahead, and even at her mellowest she faced the world with firm confidence.

"Dad told you," I said.

"He did. Honey, I'm so sorry. I know he did the best he could."

"Oh, gosh. Of course he did." In my wallow of self-pity, it hadn't even occurred to me that my dad might be feeling guilty about the failure of the night before. "It wasn't his fault that I didn't get my magic back last night. He knows that, right?"

"I think he does, deep down. But we're both so worried about you."

"Well, don't be," I said. "I'm going to be just fine. After all, I lived most of my life without knowing anything about magic or spell work or hedgewitchery, so I've had lots of practice, you know . . . not practicing . . ." I trailed off, the words hanging there in the air between us. I'd tried to sound light and airy, but as soon as I heard myself, I realized how passive-aggressive I sounded.

"Hmm," I said. "That came out wrong. Just know that I'm not giving up. If there's a way for me to get my magic back, I'll find it."

There was a long silence. Then she said, "I'm sorry."

"Mama—"

"No, I really am. I thought I was doing a good thing by hiding your gifts from you, but it wasn't my right to do that." Her voice had grown stronger, and I imagined her perching on the overstuffed armchair by the phone stand in the living room. My parents hadn't had a landline for years, but Mama still kept her cell phone in the same place where my grandparents' phone sat for decades. Doing so was orderly and traditional, just like she was. Her professionally colored hair would be perfectly arranged, and more likely than not she was wearing a modest sundress with a light cardigan draped over her shoulders.

She continued, "However, I can't change the past. I would if I could, but I can't. So, we're simply going to have to do the best with what's happened. I spoke with Lucy, and she said your spellbook club is on the job."

"They are," I assured her, unwilling to share what Mimsey had told me about the anti-magic spell. "I'll have my magic back in no time."

"That's my girl," she said. "Now, I might have a solution to your wedding cake quandary."

And she was off and running. My mother was nothing if not resilient, and I had learned a long time ago that it was easier to let her believe what she wanted to than to try to dissuade her. And if she was willing to let the question of my magic drop, so was I. Her wedding cake idea wasn't so bad, either.

After we hung up, my mind immediately went back to what Quinn had said about Olivia Gleason. She hadn't added anything else to his investigation? Really? She saw Mr. Bosworth almost every day, in his home, when his guard was down. She must have known him pretty well. She did his laundry, cleaned his house, cooked his . . .

Of course. That was it.

I knew how to approach the woman who had found the body.

Chapter 20

"Of course I want to help!" Mrs. Standish exclaimed when I told her what I had in mind. "I'll call her right away and ask her to meet me at the Honeybee. Then I'll call you back and let you know when to expect us."

"The sooner, the better," I said. "I'm afraid I don't have her number, though."

"I'm on it, chief," she boomed. "We met once at Kensington's, and I'm sure I can track her down. Skipper! We need to find the number for Olivia Gleason tout de suite." She was still talking when the connection was severed.

What else? Maybe go to see Dante Bundy's coworker?

I felt a rush of frustration. I'd promised to do what I could for Randy, and I'd failed. I'd lost my magic in the bargain, and now it felt like I didn't know much more than when I'd first heard Mr. Bosworth had been killed.

But I do know more. Lots more. Pieces of the puzzle.

I just didn't know how they fit together.

Heck, I don't even know exactly which ones belong in the puzzle and which ones don't.

I was putting my cell back into my apron pocket when it rang.

"Mrs. Standish! That was quick."

"Told you I was on it," she brayed. "We're meeting there at one o'clock."

"This afternoon? How did you manage to get Mrs. Gleason to meet you with only two hours' notice?" I asked.

"Well," she said. "I might have laid it on a *bit* thick. Sounded downright desperate for a new housekeeper, ha ha ha."

"Oh, dear. What if she thinks you're serious?"

"Now, don't you worry, honey. I *am* serious, serious as sin. We're utterly and completely frantic for a new housekeeper since dear Alda left. And if Olivia Gleason fits the bill, I'll hire her in a heartbeat. Full-time, too. With benefits. I can't believe I didn't think of it myself."

"But she could be a murder suspect," I protested.

"For heaven's sake, Katie. I think it goes without saying that I won't hire her if it turns out she killed Kensington. Not only would she be in prison, but murdering one's employer is terrible precedent for acquiring a new position."

Still shaking my head over Mrs. Standish's logic, I gave Mungo a scratch behind the ears and went out to help with lunch.

Skipper Dean was having lunch with a friend and didn't come with Mrs. Standish to interview their

249

potential new housekeeper. She showed up early and ensconced herself in the reading area with a tall glass of sweet tea and the half-dozen assorted pastries I'd selected—on the house. I slipped the RESERVED sign onto its hook, so no one would bother them while they were talking.

Except me, of course. The idea was for Mrs. Standish to start the interview, then she'd invite me to join them.

Mr. Bosworth's housekeeper walked through the door at exactly one o'clock. Unlike the woman with red-rimmed eyes and unkempt hair that I'd seen sitting at Mr. Bosworth's dining table when I'd gone to meet Quinn the night of the murder, this Olivia Gleason was quite striking and put together. She carried a soft leather briefcase and wore a beige pencil skirt with a white blouse and stadium pumps. Her blond hair was in a smooth French twist, and her gray eyes scanned the people sitting at the tables.

She and Mrs. Standish saw each other at the same time. She hurried over to the reading area, sparing a brief glance at the RESERVED sign, and with an eager smile shook Mrs. Standish's hand. They sat down, and Olivia opened her leather bag and removed some papers, which she handed to Mrs. Standish.

I went over to them. "Hello. Can I get you anything?" Never mind that we didn't typically offer table service at the Honeybee.

Olivia looked up at me, then down at the pile of pastries on the table.

"Oh, those are for both of us, dear," Mrs. Standish said. "What would you like to drink?"

"Do you have any peppermint tea?" Olivia asked me.

"Absolutely."

"Iced?"

"Coming right up." As I left to make her tea, I heard Mrs. Standish exclaim over her references.

"You worked for Mrs. Dwightshire-Smith? Oh, that's excellent. Excellent, indeed."

I impatiently made the tea, practically tapping my foot as it brewed, then poured the double-strength concoction over a tumbler of ice. Trying not to look like I was hurrying, I took the tea over to Olivia Gleason.

"Well, you certainly won't need to moonlight at that caterer if you come work for me. I adore that you are willing to cook for the skipper and me as well," Mrs. Standish was saying. "Katie, come meet Olivia. Olivia, this is the woman who suggested that I contact you."

I looked at Mrs. Standish with alarm but saw her eyes were twinkling and realized where she must be going.

Olivia looked interested. "I'm so sorry. You look familiar, but . . . ?"

Perching on the edge of one of the wingbacks, I inclined my head. "I knew your former boss, and when Mrs. Standish mentioned she was looking for some help, I thought of you."

Her expression cleared. "That's where I've seen you before. You were helping the police after Mr. Bosworth—" The muscles in her throat worked. "After he died." Her distress appeared quite genuine. "Poor Mr. Bosworth."

"Yes. It must have been awful, finding him like that."

Wide-eyed, she nodded.

"Detective Quinn said the security system was turned off when you got there?"

She looked over at Mrs. Standish. "I wouldn't want to gossip about my employer."

Mrs. Standish leaned forward. "Of course not, dear. I certainly wouldn't want you to go around gossiping about me, should we come to an agreement. But this isn't gossip. Katie is helping the police. You saw her there, didn't you?"

Olivia's head bobbed.

"I knew Kensington, my dear," Mrs. Standish said. "And I admire your loyalty, especially as I doubt he was the easiest man to work for—nor the most generous."

"He was, well . . . different." She trailed off. Licked her lips. "But I really liked him."

I sat back and tried to sound casual. "He was a regular customer here. I agree. He was different, but nice."

"He loved the bread from this place. Always insisted on buying it and bringing it home himself." She swallowed audibly.

Regretting her obvious pain, I nonetheless soldiered on. "That collection of his was pretty interesting. It must have been a pain to clean all those knick-knacks."

"Oh, I had nothing to do with that." She gave a little shudder. "Which was fine with me. Some of those things were really weird."

Great. So no way would she have cleaned off the Ginegosh statue after Randy touched it. No wonder his prints were still on it.

The question was, why hadn't the murderer's been, too?

Gloves, of course.

"Did you like working with Malcolm Cardwell?" I asked. "He seems like an okay guy."

"Oh, he was. Is, I mean. I hope he finds another job soon."

"Right. He has a large family, doesn't he? Mr. Bosworth must have paid him well."

She smiled thinly.

"Were there any problems between them that you knew of?"

"Oh, gosh, no. They were very, um, professional." She leaned forward and looked between us. "I think Mr. Bosworth was a music lover, you know? That by employing Malcolm he felt as if he was acting like an old-school patron."

Given that Mr. Bosworth had been old-school in so many other ways, that made sense.

Mrs. Standish had fallen silent as Olivia and I chatted, but now she asked, "Olivia, dear? How on earth did you come to work for Kensington in the first place?"

It was a good question. If Olivia's references were as good as Mrs. Standish had made it sound, working for Mr. Bosworth for so few hours that she had to moonlight must have been a step down.

Her answer was straightforward. "I was between jobs and needed the work."

I changed tack. "Did you know his nephew, Dante Bundy?"

Mrs. Standish sat a little straighter.

"Sure. He was at the house all the time," Olivia said.

"They got along?"

She shrugged. "To the best of my knowledge."

"And his sister?"

"Dante's?"

"No, Mr. Bosworth's sister. Florinda. Did she or her husband ever come to the house?"

"Never."

Apparently, brother and sister had been estranged for a very long time, indeed. But I had a hard time seeing that as a real motive for murder after so long.

"You were there when the security system went in, right?"

She nodded. "Detective Quinn asked me about that, too."

"Yes, of course," I said, allowing her to continue to believe that I was asking all these questions because I was working with Quinn.

Then I almost asked whether she'd witnessed any problems between Randy and Mr. Bosworth, but decided that might be leading the witness, so to speak. So I changed my question to, "What were your impressions of the man who installed the security system?"

"Randy? Oh, I liked him. Nice guy. I can't believe they think he killed Mr. Bosworth."

I forced a smile. "Where did you hear that?"

Her eyes widened. "Oh. Um, from Mr. Cardwell."

"I see. So, do you have any ideas about who might have done it?" I asked, still smiling encouragingly.

Mrs. Standish shifted in her seat, her curiosity almost palpable.

"Did he have any enemies that you know of? Anyone he was fearful of?"

Olivia slowly shook her head, but her expression had become speculative. "No, nothing like that. No threats or anything. There was that time, though . . ."

I waited. Miracle of miracles, Mrs. Standish kept quiet, too.

After a few seconds of hesitation, Olivia said, "I did see him badly frightened one time."

"Recently?"

She nodded. "A car pulled up in front of the house. I couldn't see who was inside of it."

"Was it a BMW?" I couldn't help asking.

"No, it was a red car, actually darker than that. Wine-colored. It had a funny front grille like a smile between the headlights. A convertible."

There had been a wine-colored convertible outside the murder victim's home when Declan and I had answered Quinn's summons. Declan had pointed it out, which was why I'd noticed Dante's BMW and Steve's Audi—after it had pulled away. What had he said about it?

A Thunderbird. 2005. Last year they made them. Hard to believe it's the same car as Lucy's old '64 model.

And suddenly, I could hear the sound the engine made as it pulled away from the curb and slowly drove away. The rumble of a big V-8. Declan would have been proud that I knew that.

The same rumble I'd heard in the alley before the spellbook club had begun the clairvoyance spell?

Yes. I'd bet my life on it. Or at least my magic.

Quickly, I pulled my phone out of my pocket and did an Internet search for 2005 Thunderbird convertibles. When I had the image on the small screen, I showed it to Olivia.

She nodded. "That looks right. Like I said, it was dark red, but yeah. See the front grille?"

Feeling energized, I returned the phone to my apron. "What did Mr. Bosworth do when he saw the car on the street?"

"He got really pale, and then he started sweating. I asked if he was okay, and he said he was. That he'd suddenly felt faint, but now he was okay. But I'd seen how he looked at that car, and I could tell it scared him." She looked at Mrs. Standish. "I hope it's okay to talk about these things. I mean, I wouldn't want to speak out of school."

The older woman patted her on the hand. "Don't you worry a bit about that. Now, let's discuss numbers."

I took that as my opportunity to leave. In the office, I texted Quinn. He might be wrapping up another case and sure that he had his man in the Bosworth murder, but he still needed to know about the dark red convertible.

Because I needed to know who owned it.

Chapter 21

Dante Bundy was looking less and less like Mr. Bosworth's killer, but I was determined to cover all the bases, just in case. I looked up the phone number and address of Associated Lenders. It was in Southside. I entered the information into my phone, then called the number from the Honeybee's landline.

A woman answered, sounding bored.

"Um, hi. Is Dante Bundy available?"

"Nope. Already left for the day. Take a message?"

Bingo. The coast was clear for me to stop by and chat with Dante's coworkers. "No, thanks. I'll try again tomorrow." I hung up and turned to Mungo, lounging on his club chair.

"You want to come on a ride with me?"

Instead of popping to his feet like usual, he put his head down on his paws and regarded me unenthusiastically.

I sighed and nodded. Despite my trying to discuss the murder case with him on our way to work that

morning, things were anything but normal between us.

"Okay. I understand."

He closed his eyes, though I suspected he was pre-
tending to be asleep.

I gathered my tote bag and went out to let Lucy
and Ben know I was taking off for about an hour.

"Okay, honey." Lucy's voice was calm, but her eyes
were worried. "Do you want one of us to come with
you?"

I frowned. "I'm going to an office that's probably
full of people. I think I'll be okay."

She smiled gently. "I only wondered if you wanted
some company."

"Thanks, Lucy. I hate to take you away, though.
It's bad enough that I've been asking you to cover for
me so much lately."

She patted my arm. "Anything I can do to help.
You know that. Ben, too."

He nodded his agreement from behind the coffee
counter.

I felt tears threaten and forced them back. What
was wrong with me?

"Thanks." I swallowed, hard, and went over to Ben.
"Caesar Speckman has a special order ready for me,
so I'm going to pop by and pick it up."

"Oh?" He didn't say more, but curiosity sparkled
behind his brown eyes.

For the wedding, I mouthed silently while flicking
my eyes toward Lucy. She didn't notice because she
was helping a customer now.

"Ah," he said.

"What do you think of him?"

"Speckman?" Ben shrugged. "Seems like a nice enough guy."

"He seems to like you."

"Yeah. He's okay."

"Hardly a ringing endorsement," I said.

Ben came around the counter. "Now, Katie. Don't make trouble where there isn't any. Caesar and I would probably be great friends if we only had something in common. Every time I've seen him, he's wearing a shirt with a sports team on it, but it turns out he doesn't like sports, not even watching them on television. The guy doesn't even play golf."

I grinned.

He held up his hand. "I know, I know. There are other things."

"No, I get it. No connection."

He nodded.

"Do you know if he's married?" I asked.

"I don't think so," my uncle said.

"Relationship?"

He rolled his eyes. "How should I know? Ask him yourself." Then he paused. "Unless you think he's a murder suspect. Do you?"

I hesitated. "Not really. I mean, he lost a good client in Mr. Bosworth, and he doesn't seem the, er, magical type."

You never know, though. I sure wouldn't have pegged most of the spellbook club members as witches.

At my car, I threw my tote into the passenger seat and started the engine. The tiny bud vase the Bug featured sat empty and sad. Since learning I was a hedgewitch, I'd always made a point of filling it with fresh herbs and flowers with magical significance to whatever was going on in my life but had completely forgotten to put anything in it the last few days.

So, what would I select? Basil for protection and clarity. Lavender for peace. Maybe a sprig of rosemary for feminine power.

At least I still knew how to use the natural magic inherent in plants, even if I couldn't augment it with my own power. I vowed to fill the vase as soon as I had the chance.

A few blocks away, I found a prime spot to park on Bay Street and made my way to the stairs that led down to River Street and the alley where How's Tricks was located. The alley was just as abandoned as when Cookie and I had visited, but when I pushed into the shop, Caesar Speckman was ringing a couple out at the register. He saw me come in and raised his chin in acknowledgment before turning back to count out his customers' change.

I browsed for a few minutes while he finished up. Keeping an eye out for anything unusual or suspicious, I moved from display to display. Nothing looked out of place or unexpected for a souvenir shop. I swept my gaze over the brick interior, wondering what tales the old brick walls might tell. I'd done the same in the carriage house right after I'd bought it. It had seen its share of joy and tragedy through the years, and Lucy had helped me to smudge it with burning sage to clear the energy held there, to create a new beginning. It was a common thing to do, a ritual of renewal employed by many, whether you be-

lieved in the actual magic behind it or not. Perhaps
Caesar Speckman had done the same thing. It might
account for the lack of power I'd felt before.

The couple departed. I smiled and nodded to them
as I stepped up to the counter. There was a book
tucked next to the register, with a dollar bill serving
as a bookmark. The tan leather binding was faded
and blotched with water stains, but I could make out
the image of a sun embossed in flaking gold. Below it
was a title that made me catch my breath.

Grimoire of the Golden Dawn.

I craned my neck to see if there was an author
when Caesar's hands suddenly whisked the volume
behind the counter.

"Katie! Great to see you!" Caesar wore a Macon
Bacons team shirt today, again with Dockers and
white sneakers. If he didn't like sports, as Ben had
said, he must have been amused by the names of
some of the local sports teams. I eyed the display of
shirts on the wall. Or else he simply wore the T-shirts
as a way to advertise his wares.

"Hi, Caesar. What was that book? It looked like
something I might be interested in buying." I had a
feeling I could never afford such a thing, but I itched to
take a look inside. From what Dad had said about the
Hermetic Order of the Golden Dawn, the organization
had spawned much of modern Wiccan practices. There
might just be something in that book that would help
me, and Anderson Lane, get our magic back.

"Oh, dear. I'm so sorry, but I already have a pur-
chaser. Special request, you see. Took me forever to
find it."

My heart was pounding, but I managed to keep my voice calm. "Can you tell me who asked you to track it down?"

"Sorry, darlin'. He likes to play things close to the vest."

He. That was a start.

"Would you tell him I'd like to talk to him?"

"I can try. Can't guarantee anything, though."

"Maybe I could just take a look at it?"

He peered at me, and when he spoke his tone was less friendly. "It's already sold. Why are you so interested in some old spellbook?"

I managed a thin smile. "Just an interest of mine."

"Ah! Well, then. I'll be sure to let you know when I run into anything I think you might like." He suddenly beamed at me and reached below the counter to retrieve a half-dozen jewelry boxes. "But today, you have perfect timing. UPS just delivered your lockets an hour ago. I unpacked them right away."

Still feeling the pull of the Golden Dawn grimoire, I reached into my tote for my wallet. "Thanks for getting them for me so quickly."

One by one, he opened the boxes and pushed them toward me to inspect.

I fingered them and turned them over, looking for scratches or flaws, but found none.

"Six silver lockets," he said. "I assume they're not all for you. May I ask . . . ?" He peered at me.

"Actually, they're bridesmaid gifts."

"And you're the bride?"

I nodded.

"Well! Congratulations!" He began putting the lids back on the boxes.

"Thank you."

"I imagine you'll need them engraved, then?"

The idea had occurred to me, but because I'd intended them to contain individualized spells, I had decided it would be better if they were completely unadorned on the outside. Simple silver pockets of magic. Now I wasn't sure what to do about the spells. Should I have Lucy cast them? She was my maid of honor, and I'd wanted to surprise her, too. But perhaps I should just go ahead and engrave them and let each witch create her own spell to carry.

Torn, I asked, "Can you do that?"

"Nope, not here." He winked. "But I know a guy. He does good work."

I smiled weakly. "I'll keep that in mind. Right now, I'll just take the lockets."

"Okeydoke." He put them in a bag and rang them up.

I handed him my credit card.

"Excellent, excellent." Then he bent, retrieved another box out from under the counter, and shoved it at me.

Perplexed, I opened it. Inside was a silver pentagram studded with blue sapphires and tiny diamonds.

"Um, it's lovely," I said.

"Are you interested?"

"Oh, gosh. Thanks for thinking of me, but I don't think I can afford this right now."

"I can give you a really good deal." He named a price.

I blanched. "Sorry."

He sighed and put it away. "No, no. I understand. I got this for Kensington's collection, but he never had a chance to see it." Another sigh. "Or pay for it." His gaze rose to mine. "If any of your friends are in the market for this kind of thing, could you let them know? I'm looking for other clients now."

I would have felt sorrier for him if he hadn't been so stingy about letting me look at the grimoire, but I nodded. "Sure. Say, how well did you know Kensington Bosworth?"

He shrugged. "Mmm, well enough, I guess."

Caesar's name had been in the margin of Mr. Bosworth's datebook, but not on a particular day. "Had you seen him recently?"

"Not for a month or so. I sold him a knife. An athame. Celtic, you know. It was quite old. Beaten pewter, and the handle was inscribed with all sorts of knots and spirals. Beautiful."

"Really. Where did you come across a specimen like that?"

His smile tightened. "Oh, now. A man can't give away his secrets, now, can he? Not if he wants to stay in business."

Well, well. My magical intuition might be gone, but I could still read between the lines. Mr. Bosworth's magic dealer had acquired the ceremonial knife illegally.

He handed me the bag. "And another big congrats on your big day coming up. You let me know about the engraving, okay?"

"Okay."

Outside, I headed down the alley and toward my car. Time to check on Dante Bundy's alibi. Thoughts ping-ponged through my brain as I walked.

Caesar Speckman dealt in illegal goods. And Mr. Bosworth bought them.

However, that didn't fit with the causes Mr. Bosworth had supported. Native American cultural preservation did not involve stealing tribal relics. Quite the opposite. And Skipper Dean had said another of his charities had returned stolen antiquities to the Middle East.

Maybe I was wrong about Caesar. He hadn't come right out and said he'd stolen the athame he'd sold Mr. Bosworth. He hadn't given me any kind of obvious *wink wink* when he'd said it.

But that look on his face. He's hiding something.
He's hiding the Golden Dawn grimoire.

Yes, I realized, that was exactly what he had been doing. What if there wasn't a secretive buyer at all? What if the book had been sitting by the register because Caesar had been reading it between customers? There had been a bookmark in it, after all.

And what if the Golden Dawn grimoire contained the spell that had stolen my magic? However, Dad said the Golden Dawn group didn't practice dark magic per se, and that spell was pretty darn dark.

So maybe Caesar just liked to read spellbooks.

Even though he didn't believe in magic. He'd made that pretty obvious when Cookie and I had been in the shop.

He'd made it obvious.

And we'd believed him. Not only that, but he'd

recovered from Cookie's Voice awfully fast. The Golden Dawn grimoire had to be more than a coincidence.

My steps had slowed, and I realized I'd stopped at the bottom of the staircase that led from River Street up to Bay Street. I turned to ascend toward where my car was parked when I heard it.

The deep rumble of a V-8 engine.

My heartbeat doubled to a heavy hammering in my chest, and I whirled toward the sound. The front end of a wine-colored car was edging out of the How's Tricks alley. Its distinct grille was a spot-on match to the one Olivia Gleason described. I hadn't seen the Thunderbird there, but there were a couple of garage-type doors built into the brick walls of the alley. It must have been behind one of those.

The car turned toward me, and I ducked behind a post as it slowly rumbled by. Sure enough, Caesar Speckman was driving. For a split second, it was as if I were looking at the rat I'd seen on my shamanic journey, and then the notion was gone.

A dragonfly drifted lazily behind the car, then suddenly buzzed up toward Bay Street.

That man has my magic.

I spun and raced up the stone stairs, two at a time.

And I'm getting it back.

Quickly calculating where Speckman was likely to turn away from the river and toward town, I ran to my car, jumped in, and started the engine. The Bug roared to life, and I pulled away from the curb and made a U-turn. A car behind me honked. I waved my apology out the window and pressed the accelerator.

The Thunderbird didn't materialize as I'd hoped. Frustrated, I pounded the wheel and swore. Then I looked up at my rearview mirror and saw him two cars behind me.

I'd calculated correctly but I'd moved more quickly than he had. I turned onto a side street to let him go by, but he turned onto the same street. Wondering if he knew my car, I swung into a parking lot. Were we going to have a confrontation right there in public?

However, the car drove by and continued down the street.

I turned my car around, waiting for another car to go by, then pulled out and followed the dark red convertible. Fumbling in my tote bag while keeping my eyes glued to the street ahead, I finally located my smartphone.

"Call Declan," I demanded of the phone's personal assistant, not sure if it would work because I rarely used it. Soon I heard the sound of ringing and breathed a sigh of relief.

Speckman slowed for a stop sign, then accelerated through it. The car in front of me turned. I came to a full stop at the sign to give Speckman time to get ahead of me.

"Hey, darlin'," Declan answered.

"Deck, I need you to call Quinn. I know who murdered Kensington Bosworth, and I'm following him."

"*What?* Katie, don't—"

I cut him off. "Listen, I really need you to do this. It's Caesar Speckman, the guy who owns that souvenir shop. He was Mr. Bosworth's magic dealer, and I think he's a druid in the Hermetic Order of the Silver

Moon. He drives that Thunderbird we saw outside of Mr. Bosworth's house the night of the murder." I took a deep breath. "He took my magic, Declan. He killed Mr. Bosworth, and he took my magic."

"Do not, I repeat, do *not* approach this guy," Declan said.

"Don't worry. I'm not going to. I just want to know where he is so Quinn can come arrest him."

And then what? How do I get my magic back?

"Katie." Declan's voice held warning.

"I have to go now," I said. "I need to concentrate on driving and not letting him see me. Oh, God."

"Oh, God, what? Katie, did he see you?"

"No. Nothing like that. I just realized where he's going."

"Where?"

"To Kensington Bosworth's house."

Chapter 22

"Stay right there," Declan said. "Do not do anything. I'm calling Quinn now."

"Tell him to be quiet when he comes," I said, and hung up as Speckman parked across the street and down the block from Mr. Bosworth's house.

Quickly, I turned left onto the cross street, and then into the alley that ran behind the haint blue Victorian. I thought I'd be unobserved back there, but it turned out I wasn't the only one who had the idea of hiding in the alley. I recognized the vehicle parked right behind the house and hit the brakes.

It was a Ford Expedition with a stick-figure family of six on the back window.

Malcolm Cardwell had joined the party.

What the heck?

My heart sank as I thought of his lovely wife and passel of laughing children. Was he really involved in his employer's murder?

I wedged the Bug between a garbage can and a small shed on the side of the alley. After debating for about three-point-five seconds, I grabbed my phone, silenced it, and got out. Quietly, I clicked the driver's door closed, then shut it all the way with a hip bump. My eyes on the Expedition, I crept down the alley. Finally, I was close enough that I could see there was no one in the vehicle.

Breathing a sigh of relief, I straightened my shoulders and strode more purposefully toward Bosworth's home. I arrived at the gate from the alley into the backyard, paused, then swung open the gate and went inside as if I were more than supposed to be there. If anyone had been watching, they would have thought I was the homeowner herself.

The second I got inside, I latched the gate behind me and bent double to slink through the jungle of twisted wisteria and overgrown azaleas that populated Mr. Bosworth's back garden. It would be a delightful riot of color and fragrance in the spring, but now was a mass of glossy evergreen leaves and gnarled trunks.

Hard to navigate. Good for hiding.

Randy hadn't mentioned any cameras were attached to the security system. Then again, I hadn't asked. But Quinn would have mentioned if there had been camera footage, at least in the back garden, because it would have captured the images of the killer.

Ergo, there weren't any cameras.

Good ol' old-fashioned Kensington Bosworth. Typewriter. Datebook. Dictionary. Atlas—and security system sans cameras that send images right to your smartphone.

Which he also probably hadn't had.

I crept forward, low and slow. The branches scraped against my bare legs and caught at my skirt. My sneakered feet sunk into the soft ground beneath the bushes. The glass door into Mr. Bosworth's office came into view first. I sidled up to it and looked around the edge.

His inner office was smaller than the outer office. There weren't any display tables, merely a return behind his large desk that held a few items. I could see an empty stand with a label on it there. Even though I was too far away to see, I had no doubt the label read GINEGOSH.

A single glass-fronted bookshelf dominated the wall next to the door into the outer office, which I could see was open. Movement on the other side drew my attention. Trying to be quiet, I fought my way through the bushes to that window and peered inside.

Caesar Speckman and Malcolm Cardwell were standing in the middle of the room, beside one of the display cases. The top of the case was open, and Speckman reached in and removed one of the ceremonial knives. I shuddered at the sight but kept watching as Cardwell shook his head. Speckman's face turned angry, and he waved the knife. Cardwell took a step backward, looking afraid. Speckman said something and advanced toward the other man.

Come on, Quinn. This isn't looking good.

My phone buzzed in my pocket. Ducking out of view, I took it out and answered it.

"Where are you?" Declan asked.

"Where's Quinn?" I hissed back.

"He didn't answer. I left him a message. We're at

Bosworth's, but I don't see you. Speckman's car is here, though."

"I'm around back," I barely breathed into the phone.

"What?"

"I'm around back," I repeated a fraction louder. "Who is 'we'?"

"Your dad and I were at the carriage house. When I told him what was going on, he insisted on coming with me."

"Okay. I need you to call 911. Speckman and Cardwell are inside, and it doesn't look so great for Cardwell."

"Got it. And we're coming around to the alley."

"I'm not in the alley. I'm in the back garden. Stay out front and direct the police in. I'll come to you."

"The garden! Katie, be careful."

"I will." Hanging up, I turned back to the window to see what was going on inside.

Speckman was standing on the other side, looking right at me. His eyes narrowed, and he darted toward the inner office—and the door that led to the back garden.

I stumbled backward, right into a snarl of wisteria. My foot twisted as I went down, and I cried out. Lurching to my feet again, I tested my weight on my ankle. It hurt, but it wasn't broken. I turned to run.

Speckman was already outside and moving toward me faster than a dumpy guy who didn't like sports should have been able to. He was by my side before I could take more than a few steps. The knife he'd threatened Malcolm Cardwell with was still in his hand, and he grabbed my arm roughly with the other one.

"You interfering little witch," he said. "I thought I taught you a lesson, but you seem to be a slow learner."

"A lesson?" I asked in a loud voice, hoping Declan and my dad would hear me. "That's what you call taking my magic away?"

He smirked and waved the knife in his hand. Fear stabbed through my solar plexus. "Yeah, how 'bout that? That spell worked way better than I could have hoped. It was a great practice run. It worked pretty well the second time around, too." His tone was downright gleeful.

His words triggered the simmering anger I'd been carrying around ever since I'd learned I'd been the victim of dark magic. It surfaced through my fear, a hot and powerful rage.

"Come along." He jerked hard on my arm. "Join me."

I stumbled as he pulled me through the door of Mr. Bosworth's office, then again as he pushed me farther inside the room. I caught myself on the edge of the bookshelf and turned back to see him leaning one hip against the desk, the knife dangling from the fingertips of one hand. "I know you killed Kensington Bosworth. I know about the Hermetic Order of the Silver Moon and your stupid druid gang war."

Speckman's head jerked up in surprise. "Really. You're more of a problem than I'd realized."

"I know how your dark magic spell works and that you're such a sicko that you killed Mr. Bosworth just to get his blood for it."

He blinked, then frowned as he considered me. "Well, and because he was going to change his will."

I squinted at him. "But he didn't leave you any money in his will."

"No?"

Then I got it. "He left money to the Hermetic Order of the Silver Moon. So you get money as a member of the group."

His lips drew back in a smile that showed his teeth. I could have sworn his nose twitched. How had I not noticed how much the man looked like a rat? "Not just *a* member," he said. "The founding member. Of the new, updated Order. I came across references to the original one while researching magical items and learned all the members had died off. So, I hatched the idea of a new Order of Silver Moon druids. Kensington loved the idea.

"Well," he amended. "He loved it at first."

I gaped. "He was a druid?"

"He didn't belong to a clan, if that's what you mean. He was a powerful guy, though. His father had passed on not only his paranormal collection, but also the magical gift that runs in the males of the Bosworth family. Problem was, Kensington didn't like the idea of defeating the Dragohs. He wanted to be a good druid, just like I bet you're a good little witch. He especially didn't like the idea of casting a spell that stole another's magic." He made a face, then went on, almost as if he were talking to himself.

"And killing? Completely off-limits for him." A shrug. "So he changed his mind, and he was going to change his will and leave that money, *my* money, to some animal charity."

Well, Mrs. Standish will be happy to hear that.

If I ever got the chance to tell her, that was. Caesar had killed once, and he was being awfully chatty in a self-incriminating kind of way. It was as if he didn't think I'd have a chance to use the information against him.

But I knew help was on the way, and as long as he was talking, I wasn't above prompting him.

"So you have a full contingent of new druids, ready to go to war, and Mr. Bosworth backs out. Now he's scared of you, and he puts a strong protection spell on his house."

He pointed at me. "Close. He did get scared. I made sure of that, since I wanted his blood in my spell and his money in my bank account. And he did protect his house. But I got in anyway. Slipped in while the housekeeper left the door open while she unloaded groceries earlier in the day, then waited for Kensington in his office until he came home. I only intended to deepen his fright. I mean, I did want his blood, but for the spell to work the blood doesn't have to come from a dead man, just a fearful one."

I stared at him. That hadn't occurred to me. "But then, why . . . ?"

"Kill him? I saw the notes for his new will on his desk. I knew if I didn't stop him, I'd lose that money. So I grabbed the first thing that came to hand and, well, you know the rest."

"Do the other Silver Moon druids know?"

He shrugged. "Meh. It turns out I don't need a bunch of other druids cluttering up my plans. I mean, sure, there were the three of us for a while, but then Kensington defected and Dante kind of dropped out of sight. He might still come around. We'll see. He hates the Dragohs, that's for sure."

"Does he know you killed his uncle?"

"Not yet."

"Not until you need his blood, too?"

"I'd rather have yours," he said in the same light tone he might use to order pizza.

I glared at him. "There are two problems with that. One, I'm not a man, and two, I'm not frightened of you." It was true. I was just spitting mad. "There's a third problem as well. The police are on their way, and you are so going to prison."

He paused, then leaned forward and searched my eyes. Then he shook his head. "I don't believe you. You're too cocky. Here all by your little lonesome, sneaking around and peeking in windows." A slow smile curved his lips. "I think you followed me."

"Well, duh."

"And I think you did it because you want your magic back."

My world went still, and I hardly dared to breathe. "Can you do that?" I asked.

"Come into the other room, and we'll talk about it."

He's lying. You know he's lying.

Yet I couldn't help feeling a feather of hope. "Just tell me how that would work."

"In there."

I tried to pull away from him. "I'm not going any-where with you. Where's Mr. Bosworth's secretary? I saw him through the window. Have you killed him, too?"

He smiled. It was not a nice smile. "Of course not. Come along and see for yourself."

The police will be here any minute. Keep stalling.

Speckman must have sensed something, even if he didn't believe that I'd called the authorities, because his head jerked up, and he looked wildly around the room. He gave my arm a wrench and hauled me to-ward the outer office.

"Get in there," he grated. "Now."

Stumbling on my bad foot, I cried out.

"Stop yowling," he said, and suddenly the knife was within inches of my throat.

Heart thudding against my ribs, I swallowed and limped into the other room As I did so, I slid my hand into the pocket where my phone was.

When we were beside the Hepplewhite desk, he gave my arm another jerk. "Oh, no, you don't, you clever witchy girl," Speckman said, and held out his hand. "Give me that."

Frowning, I handed him the phone. Quickly, he thumbed the screen. "What's your passcode?"

I didn't say anything.

The knife, which had fallen to his side, came up again, almost casually. "Passcode!"

Sighing, I told him.

He tapped on the screen a few times, nodded, then grinned. "Just as I thought. You didn't call 911 at all, you little liar. That gives us more time together. Lovely."

He moved aside, and I saw Malcolm Cardwell lying on the floor beside one of the long display tables. He was unconscious, but I didn't see any blood.

"Why's he here?" I asked.

"He's out of a job and needed a little cash, so he agreed to sell me a few of Kenny's pieces that he conveniently left off the insurance list. Unfortunately for him, I never intended to pay him, so . . ." He waved his hand toward the unconscious man. "He won't say anything after he comes to, though. Can't tell the police what he was up to, can he?"

"My fiancé and father are outside," I said. "They called the police."

He laughed. "Boyfriend *and* daddy? Goodness. That's laying it on a bit thick, don't you think?"

I licked my lips and considered. "Okay," I said. "It's you and me. And you obviously have the upper hand. Will you tell me why you took my magic?"

He shrugged. "Because you had it, honey. Because I needed to see if the spell would work before I tried it on a Dragoh. After you and your friend came to see me, and she tried to use her Voice on me, I knew you had real power. I was watching your bakery, waiting for you to leave, when I saw her walk in. Soon enough some other ladies came along, too. It was after hours, so I guessed it was a coven meeting. And where there's a coven, there's probably some magic going on, which was supposed to feed my anti-magic spell." He whistled. "Boy howdy. I had no idea."

My lip curled. "What kind of a powerful sorcerer needs an anti-magic spell? It's like crippling an athletic opponent. Bad sportsmanship."

He gave a little laugh. "There's no sportsmanship in magic. And I'm not very powerful. Oh, you look surprised. Well, I know it, and I don't like it, but with the ability to take away my competitors' magic, I can level the playing field. Finally, the Order is fully funded, and I can really go to war with the Dragohs."

"Why?" I asked. "What's your problem with them, anyway?"

Something flared in his eyes. "They wouldn't let me join. Not enough power, I suppose."

I almost laughed. "They wouldn't let Dante in, either. What is the deal with everyone wanting to be a Dragoh druid? They aren't all that and a bag of chips. Besides, one does not join the Dragohs," I said, mimicking Steve's serious tone. "One is born into the Dragohs."

Caesar wasn't laughing, though. In fact, for the first time since he'd caught me in the garden, he looked truly angry.

I'd been scanning the room for options. Now I spun away from him and managed to put one of the tables between us.

"You're stark raving mad," I said.

"No. I just know what I want, and for once in my life, I'm going to get it."

Gritting my teeth, I flipped open the glass top of the case. It turned out to be the display of ceremonial athames.

Great.

But I steeled myself and grabbed one of them. It was the one Caesar had described to me in his shop—beaten pewter with Celtic designs on the handle. He slammed the lid back down from his side. The glass cracked with a sharp report.

But I had a weapon of my own now. It wasn't the least bit sharp, but it was heavy.

"Katie!"

Caesar whirled.

Declan stood in the doorway of the inner office. Dad was right behind him.

A string of expletives erupted from Caesar.

"Told you my fiancé and dad were outside," I said.

My smugness was short-lived, though. Fast as a snake, he came around the table toward me, knife thrust toward me. I twisted and brought the butt of my athame's handle down on his wrist. He shrieked and dropped the knife, then grabbed me with his other hand.

Declan ran toward us. Halfway across the room, he suddenly stopped and grabbed his head with both hands. Then he bent forward with an *oomph*. The sound came out on a whoosh of air, as if he'd been hit in the stomach.

Caesar bent to retrieve his knife from the floor, so I stomped on his instep.

He growled and tried again, so I stomped on his other foot. His breath sucked in, and he gave me a hard shake.

Declan straightened and looked right at me.

And I was pretty sure it wasn't Declan behind those baby blues. My suspicion was confirmed a split second later.

"Ah, naw yer don't, y' black rat. Let the lass go!"

Caesar ignored Connell, and we continued to struggle.

"We need th' man's blood, lass! Stab him with the wee knife!"

"What are you talking about!" I shouted.

"To trigger yer magic. Blood for blood," Connell called.

The thought would normally have made me feel faint, but my adrenaline was working overtime—and he seemed to be talking about getting my magic back.

Finally, I managed to turn toward Caesar enough that I could jab at him with the athame. He arched away, but not before the pewter blade made contact with his arm.

"Ouch!" he roared, and followed it with a string of expletives, most of which were directed at me and my gender.

It was only a scratch, but the wound welled. A drop of blood fell through the air, and I watched it as if it were in slow motion. I reached out and caught it on the back of my hand at the same time Caesar howled.

"Let go! No! You can't take it! No!"

Suddenly there was a bright flash of light. Time seemed to slow to a crawl, and my senses were filled with the roar and light of raw power. I felt it flooding over me, flooding *into* me.

My magic! It was back!

Without thinking, almost without effort, I reached out to the power that coursed through so many of the objects in the room, drawing it together into myself.

My wrist, held in Caesar's painful grip, took on an eerie iridescence. His mouth dropped open as my skin glowed brighter, and he let go as if I'd burned him.

I unleashed the power I'd gathered, and his knife flew across the floor, out of his reach, and embedded deeply into the wall.

Caesar staggered backward, then stood panting. "You . . . what did you do? Who was that, that *creature* that returned your magic . . ." He trailed off, then muttered a word under his breath. It sounded an awful lot like *begorrah*.

"Don't know what you're talking about, and don't care," I said, advancing toward him. "I've got my magic back, and you're going to prison for a long, long time."

"Well, you seem to have recovered from whatever happened to you," Detective Quinn said from the doorway. He sounded wry, but he looked shaken by what he'd just witnessed.

My smile was so wide it almost hurt. "I guess you could say that!" I crowed. Then I sobered. "Are there paramedics outside? Malcolm Cardwell is hurt. Declan . . . ?" I looked around.

And finally saw Dad leaning over my fiancé, who was prone in the middle of the floor.

"Declan?"

I rushed past Quinn and fell to my knees next to my dad. "What's wrong?"

"I don't know. There was that crazy flash, and then he just slumped to the ground."

"He fainted?"

"That's what it looked like."

Other people were coming in now, from the front of the house. A paramedic beelined to Cardwell, and another came over to Declan just as he opened his eyes. He waved him away and sat up.

"Are you okay, honey?" I asked. "What happened?"

He took a deep breath and looked around with a bewildered expression. "He's gone."

"Who's gone?"

"Connell."

"Well, I'm glad he showed up for a while there, though. I'm pretty sure he helped me get my magic back."

"He wrestled it away from Speckman. Once Speckman lost his hold on your fire, it found its way back to you through the catalyst of his blood."

"Connell did that for me." I felt my throat tighten, and gratitude flooded into every cell of my body. "Please thank him for me," I said.

Declan shook his head. "I can't. There was a backlash, and it pushed him far away. Connell's gone. Really gone. I don't know where." Tears filled his eyes. "I can't feel him at all."

Chapter 23

Declan refused to go to the hospital, even though he'd briefly lost consciousness.

"It's not physical," he said. "Katie knows."

I did know or thought I did. Losing Connell must have felt like it did when I'd lost my magic. Different but the same.

Quinn had questioned Declan, Dad, and me in turn, then told us we could go. We all went back to Ben and Lucy's. Now we were gathered around the table on their rooftop with a box of wine and five jelly jars.

"Now, tell me again what happened," Lucy said.

We did, for the second time, filling in our own perspectives as we went. When we were done, she turned to Dad. "So, you knew about Connell already."

He nodded. "But I hadn't known for long. I met the gentleman, as it were, during Katie's shamanic journey. However, I didn't know who he was until Declan told me on the way to help her this afternoon. Apparently, this Connell character was urging him to hurry. I've never seen anyone drive so quickly." He grinned at my fiancé and shrugged. "Or so well at the same time."

"Thanks," Declan said.

He was being awfully quiet. It worried me, but I understood.

"And thank goodness for the little guy," Dad said. "Connell, I mean. He saved the day and recovered Katie's magic for her. Then she was able to defeat that Speckman character without any trouble."

"The athame helped with that," I said wryly. "I never thought I'd willingly wield a knife against another person."

Lucy wasn't done. She poured a jelly jar of wine and handed it to Declan. "How are you, dear?"

In some ways Lucy was a kind of surrogate mother, though Ben more surely filled the role of surrogate father. But they'd known Declan a lot longer than I had.

"Connell sacrificed himself," he said, and suddenly grasped my hand. "He told me he was going to do something I wouldn't like, then the next thing I know, I have the sense that he's in some epic battle on another . . . plane?"

Dad nodded. "He met the rat—Speckman—who had Katie's magic in the lower world. He might have returned there to get it back for her. There would need to be a portal, though."

"That one drop of Caesar's blood?"

Dad nodded. "Apparently."

Declan frowned. "I'm sorry. I don't understand any of that."

"That's okay," I said. "I'm not sure I do, either." I glanced at Dad. "Not entirely."

He smiled.

Declan let go of my hand and sat back. Looked around the table at all of us. "I don't know if he's coming back."

Tentatively, I said, "I think I know how you feel. At least partly. Connell was *your* magic, and now he's gone."

He slowly nodded. "I guess it is kind of like that."

"And it's my fault."

There were murmurs of disagreement around the table, but I still knew the truth. I had my magic back, but at the cost of Declan's.

And Declan's was a sentient being.

A week later, Iris, Lucy, and I stood around the stainless-steel countertop in the Honeybee kitchen. It was covered with cupcakes. There were carrot and German chocolate, red velvet, strawberry, and devil's food. Lemon-soaked orange cupcakes were frosted with chocolate ganache, whirls of caramel buttercream topped the bourbon-pecan version, and whipped-cream clouds nestled on top of the pineapple-and-banana goodness of the hummingbird cupcakes.

"Is that enough?" Lucy asked. "No holds barred, Katie."

Nodding, I said, "I think so. For now, at least. I can always add more."

Iris did a little two-step, her grin almost too big for her face. "This is such an awesome idea, Katie! A wedding cake made of cupcakes!"

"Well, four tiers of cupcakes. I can still decorate with gerbera daisies, and this way we don't have to cut the cake. Everyone just takes whatever kind they want. We'll make it easy to know what they're getting. A slice of strawberry on top of the strawberry ones, a twist of candied orange peel on the orange cupcakes—like that."

"Genius," Lucy said.

"Not mine. Mama's."

Her eyes widened. "Really?"

"Credit given where credit is due. She came up with this idea."

"Well, that sister of mine is full of surprises."

"And ideas. Lots of ideas. Not all of which I love or even like. But this one? This one I snapped up without a second thought."

Iris giggled.

I shook my head and set her to filling the display case with our morning's experiments—the Honeybee customers might as well benefit from the baking samples for my wedding "cake"—and went to check in with Dad and Randy.

They were sitting at a table in the corner of the bakery, plates scattered with crumbs and coffee mugs drained to the dregs. I refilled both mugs, then settled into the third chair at their table and peered at the statue that sat in front of Randy.

"Golly, I see why that Ginegosh statue fascinated you so much. That looks awfully similar." It was about the same size, a little over a foot high, and carved from a dark hardwood. The head of the fox was very similar to the fox in the Ginegosh statue, but instead of a snake, Randy's figurine had the tail of a beaver.

Dad nodded. "I think it might be from the same

artist, or at least in her carving tradition. Maybe an apprentice or someone in her family. I couldn't tell much from the picture of the statue in a plastic bag, of course, so I hope to be able to see the actual Ginegosh after the trial."

Because, of course, the statue would be evidence in the trial against Caesar Speckman. After his arrest, he'd given a full confession but still claimed he wasn't guilty. That he was under the influence of magic. Which had set him up for a nice insanity defense, but one that Jaida felt wouldn't hold up in the end. It would help that Malcolm Cardwell had made a deal with the district attorney to testify against Speckman.

Dante Bundy had decided to sell the family collection and donate the money to the other charities Bosworth supported. However, he was of course going to keep the money his uncle had left him, and I had a feeling he was going to keep at least a few of the paranormal pieces from the collection. The most powerful ones. Why did I think that? Because he'd agreed to meet with Steve again. This time Steve reported that Dante had been a lot more friendly, but when Steve had come right out and asked about the status of the Hermetic Order of the Silver Moon, he'd suddenly become dodgy.

So. There was that.

Bringing my thoughts back to the discussion at hand, I said, "I'm not sure the Ginegosh statue will be available even after the trial. Don't they keep that stuff around afterward? You know, just in case?"

Dad and Randy shrugged at the same time.

"Maybe," my dad said. "Anyway, at least I was able to tell Randy a little about his family totem. As you already know, fox represents cleverness and strength, and beaver is all about creativity, cooperation, and motivation. It's a heck of a combination."

I looked at Randy, who hadn't said a word. He'd seemed quiet, almost sheepish, ever since the incident at Mr. Bosworth's house.

"That's great, Randy. You must be proud to have that as part of your family tradition."

He nodded. "Oh, I am. Yes."

"What's wrong with you?" I asked. "You should be happy as a clam now that the police don't consider you a murder suspect." Then a horrible thought occurred to me. "Oh, gosh. Tell me this whole thing hasn't messed up your relationship with Bianca. She hasn't said anything, but—"

He held up his hand. "No, no. It's nothing like that."

I waited. Dad looked on with interest.

"It's just that I feel bad, you know? Bianca told me you lost your ability to cast spells or something? I don't really get your Wiccan stuff—sorry, I know I should, but it's just not my . . ." He trailed off. Then, "All I know is that something bad happened to you because you were trying to clear my name, and—"

"Okay, stop," I interrupted. "Stop feeling bad. Whatever happened was my choice. And it's all good now. You're out of jail, I'm in a good place, you found out about your totem, Olivia Gleason has a new job with Mrs. Standish and Skipper Dean—all positive things."

He hesitated.

I gave him a fake glare.

Finally, he smiled. "Yeah. Okay. And, Katie?"

"Yeah?"

"Thank you."

"You are most certainly welcome."

It was almost eleven. Declan had gone to bed, but my old sleeping habits had returned, so I was still up. I sat on the firehouse-rescued sofa wearing my usual nightwear of soft yoga shorts and a spaghetti tank. The door to the balcony was open, and a warm breeze carried in the heady scent of the jasmine tobacco that grew in the courtyard below. It mixed with the aromas of peppermint and chamomile that drifted from the cup of herbal tea on the table by my elbow. The light was low, cast by the single reading lamp next to the teacup. Someone tinkled the keys of a piano in another apartment, barely audible beneath the sound of my own breath.

A paperback was on the arm of the sofa, one I'd been waiting to read once things settled down a bit, but it was still unopened. Soon I would crack the story, but for the moment I just wanted to sit and appreciate how it felt to be whole again. I looked down with affection at my familiar, stilling my urge to sweep him up into my arms. Mungo was conked out beside me, eyes squeezed shut and the tiniest doggy smile curling his black lips as he dreamed. Feeling a little sleepy myself, I found my eyelids drifting closed in contentment.

Suddenly, the scent of frying chicken filled the

room, and my eyes popped open again. Surprised that anyone would be cooking so late, I found my mouth watering as if I hadn't eaten for days even though I still felt full after the pulled pork and peppery slaw Declan had rustled up for our supper. I took a sip of tea to quell the reaction, and the scent faded as quickly as it had come.

My leg twitched. Now instead of desperately wanting a chicken drumstick, I felt an almost irresistible urge to run.

Maybe I should. It would help me sleep.

I was about to abandon my relaxing evening for my trail runners, when I saw Mungo's little legs churning as he slept. I smiled and wondered what he was chasing. His legs stopped moving then, and at the same time I no longer felt like going for a run.

For no reason whatsoever, the image of a chattering squirrel filled my mental movie screen.

Weird!

Shaking it off, I reached for my tea and drained it to the bottom. Mungo's eyes popped open when I stood up.

"Come on, buddy. I'm obviously more tired than I thought."

I shut the slider, checked the front door lock, turned off the light, and Mungo and I padded into the bedroom. Soon I was snuggled in next to Declan. As I began to doze, I knew I'd be up even earlier in the morning as a result.

I can start my book then . . .

. . . Smoke!

In an instant, I was out of bed and moving toward the kitchen. Nothing looked amiss. I quickly prowled the whole apartment, then returned to the bedroom.

"Declan," I hissed. "Wake up."

He jerked. "Wha . . . ?" Sitting up, he reached out and grabbed my arm. "What's wrong?"

"I smell smoke."

He threw off the covers and swung his feet to the floor. "Where?"

"Don't know. I looked around the apartment but didn't find anything wrong. Do you think there could be something on fire in one of the other apartments?"

Barefoot, he went out and opened the sliding glass door. Out on the balcony, he inhaled deeply a few times, then turned back to where I was standing in the doorway. "I don't smell anything."

Joining him, I sniffed the air, too. "That's strange. I don't smell it now."

Sighing, he went back inside.

I followed and closed the door behind me. "Sorry, hon. I really did think I smelled smoke."

He reached for me and wrapped his arms around me. "No worries. You can always wake me if you think something is wrong. Tonight, I'm actually grateful you did."

Pulling back, I met his eyes in the dim light coming in through the glass door. "Why's that?"

"Bad dream."

I waited.

"Sometimes I dream about the warehouse fire that Arnie Dawes died in. The smoke was terrible, choking."

"More than a dream, then. A nightmare."

He nodded. "Yeah."

I kissed him. "Let's go back to bed."

Hand in hand we did just that. Ten minutes later, Declan was snoring gently. I, on the other hand, was wide, wide awake.

And thinking.

I sniffed the air. No smoke. No chicken.

Mungo had been running in his sleep. At the same time, I'd felt the urge to run.

Declan had been dreaming of a smoky fire, and I'd *actually smelled smoke.*

Fried chicken is Mungo's favorite food after bacon. Could he have been dreaming of it?

Nah.

But I couldn't stop what I was thinking. Could it be? I mean, I'd often witnessed how teasing squirrels drove Mungo bananas when we visited the park.

How he ran after them.

No, that's impossible.

But what if? What if when Connell had retrieved my magic for me, he'd given back more than my normal gift? I mean, my gift was already more than normal, at least according to the spellbook club.

What if?

Beside me, Declan muttered something in his sleep, and my ears perked up. Was that an Irish accent? I turned my head to look at him in the blue light of his alarm clock.

Faintly, oh-so faintly, I heard a voice. Not out loud, but in my mind, not even really *heard*, but the hints of words, the suggestion of meaning.

"*Yes . . . I took the anti-magic far away, and now I'm lost. I don't know where I am, and I can't get back to Declan except like this. How can you hear me, lass?*"

I don't know, I thought.

But if I really could, if this was really happening, maybe there was a way that I could get Connell back.

For Declan, and for Connell himself.

The voice faded away, but two words continued to haunt me.

"*I'm lost.*"

Recipes

Magical Chocolate Peppermint Cookies

½ cup softened butter
¾ cup sugar
1 egg
½ teaspoon peppermint extract
1¼ cups all-purpose flour
¼ teaspoon salt
½ cup cocoa powder
½ teaspoon baking soda
¼ teaspoon baking powder
⅓ cup semisweet chocolate chips or cocoa nibs
⅓ cup crushed peppermint candies

Preheat oven to 350 degrees F.

Cream the butter and sugar together until light and fluffy. Add the egg and peppermint extract and beat another minute, scraping down the sides of the bowl. In another bowl, sift together the flour, salt, cocoa powder, baking soda, and baking powder. Add the flour mixture ½ cup at a time to wet ingredients, mixing thoroughly between each addition. Fold in chocolate chips, then place dough in freezer for ten minutes to chill.

Using a tablespoon, form dough into small balls and arrange 1½ inches apart on a parchment-lined baking sheet. Flatten the tops with the tines of a fork.

Bake for 10–12 minutes until the edges begin to dry. The tops will still look soft. Sprinkle the crushed peppermint candies on immediately but allow cookies to cool on baking sheet for 3–4 minutes before removing to a rack to cool further.

When completely cooled, store in an airtight container for up to five days or freeze for several weeks.

Yield: 1 dozen cookies

Honeybee Spice Cookies

½ cup softened butter
¾ cup dark brown sugar
¼ cup molasses
1 egg
1 cup all-purpose flour
½ teaspoon salt
½ teaspoon baking soda
½ teaspoon each: powdered ginger, ground cloves,
    allspice, cinnamon, and grated nutmeg

Preheat oven to 375 degrees F.

Cream together butter and brown sugar until smooth. Add molasses and egg and mix until thoroughly combined. In another bowl, mix together the flour, salt, baking soda, and spices. Add to the first mixture all at once and blend thoroughly.

Drop cookies by the teaspoonful on a parchment-lined baking sheet, leaving about an inch between each cookie. Bake for 7–10 minutes or until crisp and lightly browned.

Yield: about 30 small cookies

If you love Bailey Cates's *New York Times* bestselling Magical Bakery Mysteries, read on for an excerpt from the first book in Bailey Cattrell's Enchanted Garden Mystery series,

Daisies for Innocence

Available now wherever books are sold.

The sweet, slightly astringent aroma of *Lavandula stoechas* teased my nose. I couldn't help closing my eyes for a moment to appreciate its layered fragrance drifting on the light morning breeze. Spanish lavender, or "topped" lavender—according to my gamma, it had been one of my mother's favorites. It was a flower that had instilled calm and soothed the skin for time eternal, a humble herb still used to ease headache and heartache alike. I remembered Gamma murmuring to me in her garden when I was five years old:

Breathe deeply, Elliana. Notice how you can actually taste the scent when you inhale it? Pliny the Elder brewed this into his spiced wine, and Romans used it to flavor their ancient sauces. In the language of flowers, it signifies the acknowledgment of love.

Not that I'd be using it in that capacity anytime soon.

But Gamma had been gone for over twenty years, and my mother had died when I was only four. Shaking my head, I returned my attention to the tiny mosaic pathway next to where I knelt. Carefully, I added a piece of foggy sea glass to the design. The path was three feet long and four inches wide, and led from beneath a tumble of forget-me-nots to a violet-colored fairy door set into the base of the east fence. Some people referred to them as "gnome doors," but whatever you called them, the decorative miniature garden phenomena were gaining popularity with adults and children alike. The soft green and blue of the water-polished, glass-nugget path seemed to morph directly from the clusters of azure flowers, curving around a lichen-covered rock to the ten-inch round door. I wondered how long it would take one of my customers to notice this new addition to the verdant garden behind my perfume and aromatherapy shop, Scents & Nonsense.

The rattle of the latch on the gate to my left interrupted my thoughts. Surprised, I looked up and saw Dash trotting toward me on his short corgi legs. His lips pulled back in a grin as he reached my side, and I smoothed the thick ruff of fur around his foxy face. Astrid Moneypenny—my best friend in Poppyville, or anywhere else, for that matter—strode behind him at a more sedate pace. Her latest foster dog, Tally, a Newfoundland mix with a graying muzzle, lumbered beside her.

"Hey, Ellie! There was a customer waiting on the boardwalk out front," Astrid said. "I let her in to look around. Tally, sit."

I bolted to my feet, the fairy path forgotten. "Oh, no. I totally lost track of time. Is it already ten o'clock?"

The skin around Astrid's willow-green eyes crinkled in a smile. They were a startling contrast to her auburn hair and freckled nose. "Relax. I'll watch the shop while you get cleaned up." She jammed her hand into the pocket of her hemp dress and pulled out a cookie wrapped in a napkin. "Snickerdoodles today."

I took it and inhaled the buttery cinnamon goodness. "You're the best."

Astrid grinned. "I have a couple of hours before my next gig. Tally can hang out here with Dash." She was a part-time technician at the veterinary clinic and a self-proclaimed petrepreneur—dog walker and pet sitter specializing in animals with medical needs. "But isn't Josie supposed to be working today?"

"She should be here soon," I said. "She called last night and left a message that she might be late. Something about a morning hike to take pictures of the wildflowers." I began gathering pruners and trowel, kneeling pad and weed digger into a handled basket. "They say things are blooming like crazy in the foothills right now."

Astrid turned to go, then stopped. Her eyes caught mine. "Ellie . . ."

"What?"

She shook her head. "It's just that you look so happy working out here."

I took in the leafy greenery, the scarlet roses climbing the north fence, tiered beds that overflowed with herbs and scented blooms, and the miniature gardens and doors tucked into surprising nooks and alcoves. A downy woodpecker rapped against the trunk of the oak at the rear of the lot, and two hummingbirds whizzed by on their way to drink from the handblown glass feeder near the back patio of Scents & Nonsense. An asymmetrical boulder hunkered in the middle of the yard, the words ENCHANTED GARDEN etched into it by a local stone carver. He'd also carved words into river rocks I'd placed in snug crannies throughout the half-acre space. The one next to where Dash had flopped down read BELIEVE. Mismatched rocking chairs on the patio, along with the porch swing hanging from the pergola, offered opportunities for customers to sit back, relax, sip a cup of tea or coffee, and nibble on the cookies Astrid baked up each morning.

"I am happy," I said quietly. More than that. *Grateful.* A sense of contentment settled deep into my bones, and my smile broadened.

"I'm glad things have worked out so well for you." Her smile held affection that warmed me in spite of the cool morning.

"It hasn't been easy, but it's true that time smooths a lot of rough edges." I rolled my eyes. "Of course, it's taken me nearly a year."

A year of letting my heart heal from the bruises of infidelity, of divorce, of everyone in town knowing my—and my ex's—business. In fact, perfect cliché that it was, everyone except me seemed to know Harris had been having an affair with Wanda Simmons, the owner of one of Poppyville's ubiquitous souvenir shops. Once I was out of the picture, though, he'd turned the full spectrum of his demanding personality on her. She'd bolted within weeks, going so far as to move back to her hometown in Texas. I still couldn't decide whether that was funny or sad.

I'd held my ground, however. Poppyville, California, nestled near the foothills of the Sierra Nevada Mountains, was *my* hometown, and I wasn't about to leave. The town's history reached back to the gold rush, and tourists flocked to its Old West style; its easy access to outdoor activities like hiking, biking, and fly fishing; and to the small hot spring a few miles to the south.

After the divorce, I'd purchased a storefront with the money Harris paid to buy me out of our restaurant, the Roux Grill. The property was perfect for what I wanted: a retail store to cater to townspeople and tourists alike and a business that would allow me to pursue my passion for all things scentual. Add in the unexpected—and largely free—living space included in the deal, and I couldn't turn it down.

Sense & Nonsense was in a much sought after location at the end of Corona Street's parade of bric-a-brac dens. The kite shop was next door to the north, but to the south, Raven Creek Park marked the edge of town with a rambling green space punctuated with playground equipment, picnic tables, and a fitness trail. The facade of my store had an inviting, cottagelike feel, with painted shutters above bright window boxes and a rooster weathervane twirling on the peaked roof. The acre lot extended in a rectangle behind the business to the front door of my small-scale home, which snugged up against the back property line.

With a lot of work and plenty of advice from local

307

nurserywoman Thea Nelson, I'd transformed what had started as a barren, empty lot between the two structures into an elaborate garden open to my customers, friends, and the occasional catered event. As I'd added more and more whimsical details, word of the Enchanted Garden had spread. I loved sharing it with others, and it was good for business, too.

"Well, it's nice to have you back, sweetie. Now we just have to find a man for you." Astrid reached down to stroke Tally's neck. The big dog gazed up at her with adoration, while I struggled to keep a look of horror off my face.

"Man?" I heard myself squeak. That was the last thing on my mind. Well, almost. I cleared my throat. "What about your love life?" I managed in a more normal tone.

She snorted. "I have plenty of men, Ellie. Don't you worry about me."

It was true. Astrid attracted men like milkweed attracted monarch butterflies. At thirty-seven, she'd never been married, and seemed determined to keep it that way.

"Astrid," I began, but she'd already turned on her heel so fast that her copper-colored locks whirled like tassels on a lampshade. Her hips swung ever so slightly beneath the skirt of her dress, the hem of which skimmed her bicycle-strong calves as she returned to the back door of Scents & Nonsense to look after things. Tally followed her and settled down on the patio flagstones as my friend went inside. I saw Nabokov, the Russian blue shorthair who made it his business to guard the store day and night, watching the big dog through the window with undisguised feline disdain.

Basket in hand, I hurried down the winding stone pathway to my living quarters. "God, I hope she doesn't get it into her head to set me up with someone," I muttered around a bite of still-warm snickerdoodle.

Dash, trotting by my left heel, glanced up at me with skeptical brown eyes. He'd been one of Astrid's foster dogs about six months earlier. She'd told me he was probably purebred, but there was no way of knowing, as he'd been found at a highway rest stop and brought, a bit dehydrated but otherwise fine, to the vet's office where she worked. Of course, Astrid agreed to take care of him until a home could be found—which was about ten seconds after she brought him into Scents & Nonsense. I'd fallen hard for him, and he'd been my near constant companion ever since.

"Okay. It's possible, just possible, that it would be nice to finally go on an actual date," I said to him now. Leery of my bad judgment in the past, I'd sworn off the opposite sex since my marriage ended. But now that Scents & Nonsense wasn't demanding all my energy and time, I had to admit that a sense of loneliness had begun to seep into my evenings.

"But you know what they say about the men in Poppyville, Dash. The odds here are good, but the goods are pretty odd."

A hawk screeched from the heights of a pine in the open meadow behind my house. Ignoring it, Dash darted away to nose the diminutive gazebo and ferns beneath the ancient gnarled trunk of the apple tree. He made a small noise in the back of his throat and sat back on his haunches beside the little door I'd made from a weathered cedar shake and set into a notch in the bark. Absently, I called him back, distracted by how sun-warmed mint combined so nicely with the musk of incense cedar, a bright but earthy fragrance that followed us to my front door.

Granted, my home had started as a glorified shed, but it worked for a Pembroke Welsh corgi and a woman who sometimes had to shop in the boys' section to find jeans that fit. The "tiny house" movement was about living simply in small spaces. I hadn't known anything about it until my half brother, Colby, mentioned it in one of his phone calls from wherever he'd stopped his Westfalia van for the week. The idea had immediately appealed to my inner child, who had always wanted a playhouse of her very own, while my environmental side appreciated the smaller, greener footprint. I'd hired a contractor from a nearby town who specialized in tiny-house renovations. He'd made a ramshackle three-hundred-twenty-square-foot shed into a super-efficient living space.

There were loads of built-in niches, an alcove in the main living area for a television and stereo, extra foldout seating, a drop-down dining table, and even a desk that tucked away into the wall until needed. A circular staircase led to the sleeping loft above, which boasted a queen bed surrounded by cupboards for linens and clothing and a skylight set into the angled roof. The staircase partially separated the living area from the galley kitchen, and the practical placement of shelves under the spiraling steps made it not only visually stunning, but a terrific place to house my considerable library of horticulture and aromatherapy books.

Most of the year, the back porch, which ran the seventeen-foot width of the house, was my favorite place to hang out when not in the garden or Scents & Nonsense. It looked out on an expanse of meadow running up to the craggy foothills of Kestrel Peak. Our resident mule deer herd often congregated there near sunset.

After a quick sluice in the shower, I slipped into a blue cotton sundress that matched my eyes, ran fingers through my dark shoulder-length curls in a feeble attempt to tame them, skipped the makeup, and slid my feet into soft leather sandals. Dash at my heel, I hurried down the path to the shop. I inhaled bee balm, a hint of basil, lemon verbena, and . . . what was *that*?

My steps paused, and I felt my forehead wrinkle. I knew every flower, every leaf in this garden, and every scent they gave off. I again thought of my gamma, who had taught me about plants and aromatherapy—though she never would have used that word. She would have known immediately what created this intoxicating fragrance.

Check her garden journal. Though without more information it would be difficult to search the tattered, dog-eared volume in which she'd recorded her botanical observations, sketches, flower recipes, and lore.

A flutter in my peripheral vision made me turn my

head, but where I'd expected to see a bird winging into one of the many feeders, there was nothing. At the same time, a sudden breeze grabbed away the mysterious fragrance and tickled the wind chimes.

Glancing down, I noticed the engraved river rock by the fairy path I'd been forming earlier appeared to have shifted.

For a second, I thought it read BEWARE.

My head whipped up as I wildly searched the garden. When I looked down again, the word BELIEVE cheerfully beckoned again.

Just a trick of the light, Ellie.

Still, I stared at the smooth stone for what felt like a long time. Then I shook my head and continued to the patio. After giving Tally a quick pat on the head, I wended my way between two rocking chairs and opened the sliding door to Scents & Nonsense.

Nabby slipped outside, rubbing his gray velvety self against my bare leg before he touched noses with Dash, threw Tally a warning look, and padded out to bask in the sunshine. A brilliant blue butterfly settled near the cat and opened its iridescent wings to the warming day. As I turned away, two more floated in to join the first. As the cat moved toward his preferred perch on the retaining wall, the butterflies wafted behind him like balloons on a string. It was funny—they seemed to seek him out, and once I'd seen two or three find him in the garden, I knew more blue wings would soon follow.

ABOUT THE AUTHOR

Bailey Cates believes magic is all around us if we only look for it. She is the *New York Times* bestselling author of the Magical Bakery Mysteries, including *Potions and Pastries*, *Spells and Scones*, and *Magic and Macaroons*. Writing as Bailey Cattrell, she is also the author of the Enchanted Garden Mysteries, which began with *Daisies for Innocence*.

CONNECT ONLINE

baileycates.com

Ready to find
your next great read?

Let us help.

Visit prh.com/nextread

Penguin
Random
House